Mothballs
&
Coconut

Sabera Ahsan

Original title: Mothballs and Coconut

Author: Sabera Ahsan

Email: info@azahrabooks.co.uk

England 1st edition

ISBN: 978-1987401141

ISBN 978-1-9874-0114-1

9 781987 401141 >

Synopsis

Laila, Salma, and Aliya navigate their way through parental expectations and matters of the heart. Set in 1990s London, Mothballs and Coconut is a story of love, friendship and betrayal that crosses two generations.

DEDICATION

To all the single ladies who still believe in love.

Mothballs & Coconut

Sabera Ahsan

CONTENTS

Mothballs

&

Coconut

ACKNOWLEDGMENTS

Thanks to everyone who inspired me to write this book for over five decades. Special thanks to Homara, Sara and Sofia my sisters, and friends Melanie and Henna for reading the book cover to cover and providing me with valuable feedback. Had I not met my group of amazing Spanish friends at the Cervantes Institute, London in 2012 and formed our literary group *A Letra Viva*, I might never have had the courage to pick this manuscript back up and finally finish it. A final thanks to all those amazing mothers, grandmothers, and daughters who, despite all the barriers and challenges they face, do their best to be amazing inspirational women.

Chapter One

The Childhood – Salma

Our earliest childhood memories are perhaps the happiest and purest. The older we become, the more like a dream they seem. What was once so real and true, is now a hazy past life gradually swallowed and killed by a tough reality we call adult life. I know I lived that life; I know I did. Now and then, that warm feeling we call nostalgia creeps into my stomach and makes me hungry and ache for a life that has now forever disappeared— but it will always remind me of who I am, who I was, what I am no longer, and what I will never be.

It's one of those recurring dreams you have when you enter that other mystical world called deep, deep sleep, where your darkest fears and your wildest hopes emerge along monochrome corridors and saffron deserts. It's always summer in this particular dream—a hazy, late Sunday afternoon; fresh-cut green grass lightly brazen from the unrelenting summer sun. I remember cool summer breezes and coloured chiffon sarees swaying in the breeze. The inaudible mumbling of many voices, so warm and secure, when my life's journey was still etched in chalk. Guests stuff their ravenous mouths with fists full of fragrant, yoghurt chicken curry, peas, and potato. That's what we do when we get together—eat. Chopped salad with fresh hot chillies, buttery pilau, and yoghurty chicken with sprinklings of freshly chopped coriander. My mouth waters just thinking of it; my belly aches and yearns for the moment I can join them. After the men, after the boys, then the babies; finally, the mothers feed their children. The aroma wafts over the fence; I know our English

2

neighbours can smell the food, although they pretend not to as they barbeque their sausages and toast their white rolls. I don't care if they love or hate the smell, because this is our little world—one not to be touched, not to be interfered with at any cost. Back in the homeland, we marched in the streets and universities to save our poems, our books, our music, our legacy. Although we left our loved ones behind, we are still young, new arrivals full of hope, and we intend to rebuild this land with our wombs and blood.

I remember running in frantic circles around the garden until I could breathe no more. I recall the laughing, the calling, and the shouting. I am wearing my purple smock dress with cream and lilac checks. I feel I am falling a thousand times; I believe it was my 4th or 5th birthday. I recollect a scruffy, wild boy slightly older than myself, 7 or 8 years old. His wide innocent eyes pierce my heart and soul even at that early age, and I feel that genuine ache of true love; I am forever his. He is etched into my very essence in blood and sweat. He is my love, my soul mate, my playmate, my only future. We frantically escape from a crazed woman; she is unusually lanky compared to the other young mothers, skinny like a teenager, with jet-black bouffant hair and a powerful but high-pitched voice.

"Kal, Kal, where are you? If you don't stop hiding, I will smack your bottom until it's purple like an aubergine. Come out now!"

We can hear her voice screech through the summer breeze like a whistling kettle about to explode, but we don't care about her. She will not invade our world, so we keep on running to the world's end where she will never find us. The other mothers stand gently at one end of the lawn, giggling like new teen brides at today's childish gossip, sharing stories of another life, another world fossilised in memories of their loved ones they left behind. The array of burnished silk and cotton shimmers in the afternoon sun; their sarees hug their bodies tightly to reveal their hourglass-like figures. We flutter our small bodies through a multitude of brilliantly-coloured saree fabric; the soft silk, cotton, and chiffon brush against our faces like gentle butterfly wings. We hide under a table, trembling, until the woman's screeching stops.

I hear the gentle, sweet voice of a man from afar calling us to eat. His voice is soft and kind. There's always a melodic chant when he calls for me, his child. My name first, followed by a rhyming, alliterated list of other children's names. Just the sound of his voice brings a lump in my throat and an ache in my belly. That voice is my father's; he died when I was young. I will never forget him. He, too, is burnished in my very heart; a heart that partially died when he departed this life. When his earthly journey ended so promptly, I realised even as a child that the pieces of my existence would no longer ever fit together without my father in my life. Maybe the dream I have so often is of him visiting me or his way of watching over me as I lay down to sleep.

As the heat of the day fades and a saffron sky befalls a cool summer's evening, a little girl exhausted from the day's heat and endless play lies half-awake, half-asleep in the back seat of a car. She cannot see, but from the motions of the car, she knows she is nearing home. As the wheels pull into the drive, she waits for her father to lift her tired, now

4

fatigued petite body in his loving arms and deliver her to the safety and warmth of her room. But in this dream, time passes by and her father never appears, and she is left waiting, sleeping, worn out and motionless.

I detest it when the dream changes; I don't like leaving my garden or the calm sound of my father's voice. I do not understand this part of the dream. I approach the door as someone knocks persistently. I am barefoot; I open the door, but no one's there. At the end of the driveway, there's a silver estate car. In the driver's seat, a lady dressed in a blue burka sits up and looks straight ahead out of the car window, a motionless shell of a woman. The passenger door opens, and out steps another lady dressed in a blue burka. I can't see her face—just the loose outer shape of her heavy silhouette. Then another covered blue lady emerges from the car, and another and another. They stream out of the vehicle over and over; I watch them, beckoning them to enter, but they never reach the door. Why I'm not sure, and then I wake.

Every morning, I rise to the sound of a bird pecking against the wall at the top of my attic room window. It is early September; the leaves are now brown and soggy, and horse chestnuts line the pavements. I thought all the birds had already flown far away to warmer, more welcoming lands. Maybe, for the birds, autumn would arrive late this year; it's still mild, and the sun manages to break through the imminent autumnal sky. I fear the bird will peck through the entire wall and burrow into my bedroom one morning, filling me with sheer Hitchcock horror. The terror of waking one morning and finding a trapped bird flying frenziedly around my bedroom terrifies me to my very core.

My head and eyes feel weird and heavy, my body fixed in slumber, but the pecking doesn't cease. Now I'm not quite sure if it is the crazy bird or someone knocking at the door; they seem to have merged into one annoying sound. It takes me some time to register, but someone's now banging frantically at the front door. Who could be calling so early in the morning? Barefoot and dizzy, I slip out of bed and peer out of the attic window. I will tell you this; it is a scenario that every Asian girl who is living away from home fears above all things, both human and the supernatural. That is, being caught doing something you're not supposed to. An impromptu, inopportune visit from the parents is the most dreaded thing that can ever happen. Trepidation, alarm, horror, gripped at my throat and my belly muscles. In times of panic, a strategic plan always flashes through my brain, and I go into automatic pilot. I run down the stairs as lightly as I can and bang furiously on Laila's door.

"Laila, your parents! Your parents are here; get up."

I can hear her parents pounding on the door and calling her name. "Don't be lazy because it's Sunday morning." They cry.

Laila's father has a habit of chanting weird rhymes infused with a hint of wisdom like "Money doesn't grow on trees", or in this case, "Hello, Laila, this is Daddy; open the door when you are ready." Today's wisdom consisted of: "Early to bed and early to rise, makes a man healthy, wealthy and wise." He just continued repeating the same ludicrous rhyme.

The consequences of being caught are way too dreadful. Suddenly, Laila appeared at the door, clutching her dressing gown tight around her slim young body. Her face tired but startled. She still wore last

6

night's lipstick smeared all over her face; her kohl made dark circles under her eyes. Her body was stiff with fear and alarm. This usually calm, serene professional woman was like a child trapped in a tiny bird's cage, flapping the arms of her dressing gown as if they were wings.

"What am I going to do? What are they doing here at this godforsaken hour? Oh, my Lord! Help!" she whispered nervously.

I'm always good in a crisis. My eyes shot immediately past her shoulder and to a sleepy Raj also dressed in a pink womanly gown; lipstick also smeared across his face; spiky over gelled hair in peaks and troughs, so much so that he looked like a circus clown.

"Grab your things and just go through the back door—as fast as you can and jump that fence."

We both giggled nervously; I was now an accomplice in her crime of passion. She grabbed hold of my hand, holding it to her chest, as Raj scampered across the kitchen, ran out through the patio door and high-jumped the fence, but Laila knew full well the implications for him had he been caught in flagrante with her by her parents. Just before he left, he grabbed Laila urgently but gently by the shoulders and said, "Maybe this would be a good time to introduce myself?" She pushed him out of the back door with all her might.

"Go, just get out quick," she cried. And with that, Raj was gone. "He must have been joking. Please tell me he was being facetious," mumbled a traumatised Laila.

Deep down, I didn't approve of Laila and Raj's behaviour. I was naïve and prudish, inexperienced, but in spite of my beliefs, Laila was the kindest, most beautiful and nicest person I knew. Who was I to judge anyone? I led her mother and father into the hallway. While Laila frantically threw some clothes on to her body and wiped the evidence off her face, I entertained her parents. Laila's father was convinced we indulged ourselves with too many lie-ins. Her parents were fresh and awake and had arrived with the usual huge supply of gastronomic treats for a daughter who had picked up very few of her mother's culinary skills. Blinded by a father's love for his only daughter and oblivious to all that was going on in front of his very eyes, Laila's father was still banging out his early morning rhyme over and over, chuckling to himself now and then.

"She is still not sleeping, is she?" asked her father.

"She was probably in the hospital all night tending patients. She hasn't even had time to wipe the makeup off her face." Her mother began to cleanse her face with a dodgy looking hanky. Laila managed to prise herself away from her mother.

"Wait in the front room, and I'll be ready in 10 minutes." She must have felt wretched with guilt.

Laila was 26 years old. Her family was wealthy; her father was a well-known consultant gynaecologist, and he had come to Britain in the early 1970s. Her mother had decided to follow her own career path and had trained as a bilingual social worker; she now had time on her hands, and her only brilliant and beautiful daughter had graduated as a doctor too.

Laila's mother tried hard to do good deeds within the community. Aunty Shayla was forced to lead a double life—that of an intelligent, determined working woman and that of a typical Asian doctor's wife—when the occasion arose.

Laila's life had been happy and trouble-free. She had been brought up in a well-to-do south London suburb and had never known anything ugly in her life. She had attended Roedean; a renowned girls' school in Sussex on a hill looking over the sea and had achieved excellent grades. A brilliant student of Arts and Sciences, she could have been anything she wanted to be, but she chose a path that had been planned for her way before her birth. Laila had been groomed to follow in her father's footsteps. She was tall, fair and wore a perfect set of teeth and an American film actress style smile. And yet despite all this, unlike many of her peers, she was not at all arrogant, but was surprisingly kind and caring.

Despite Laila's remorse, she bravely faced her parents in the living room of the townhouse they had bought her in West London (before the prices had rocketed).

"Laila Baba, there is a family who is interested in meeting you," her mother explained. Laila turned towards me and screwed up her face in dismay. As her parents gazed at her full of hope, she managed to force a smile signalling her reluctant consent for them to engineer her life into an image of their own.

"They are here for the wedding in Wembley, and with your permission, we will all pass by before the wedding to pay you a visit and then you can meet the family," her father explained. Her mother gave him a gentle nudge on the arm so that he would stop before he gave the game away. She knew her daughter well; if Laila cottoned on to the preplanned, blind introduction, then she guessed Laila might suddenly be called to the hospital on some emergency or nightshift duty.

Laila would never let her parents know how much she loathed and despised meeting suitors and their families. When her parents first started presenting potential suitors, she would smile sweetly, listen very carefully to what the groom desired and hoped for in his ideal wife. Afterwards, Laila would retire to her room and sob for about an hour. Then she'd invent work-related excuses and extra responsibilities to get out of any future meetings. When there was nowhere else to hide, and the inevitable was about to happen, Laila decided for the sake of all concerned to master the art of an interested and enthusiastic bride. She played the perfect dutiful daughter flawlessly, but it wasn't a farce; it was because Laila loved and respected her family. They were growing older, and Laila knew she could never change them. But then, why should she? She was who she was because of the traditions and values her parents had brought her up to believe, despite the misdemeanours, and in spite of her clandestine relationship. Her parents were moral, respectful and hardworking; Laila wanted to be just like them one day. To force them to accept her way of life would be to kill the very essence of what made them her loving, dearest parents. As dangerous as it could be, she was happy to live her parallel lives for now. She had to be careful that the two worlds she existed in never happen to cross paths.

Laila decided to wear her lilac and silver saree that her mother had bought her last Eid. She had to look presentable for the mystery family who was coming to see her. Sometimes she toyed with the idea of wearing something scandalous like a short skirt or turning up in her jogging bottoms and a curry-stained T-shirt, unwashed hair and no makeup. She would sit down in front of the boy and say in a mock cockney accent,

"Look, mate! I've got a moustache growing on my upper lip; my breath smells like hell in the mornings. I can't cook, I've got a vile temper, and I'm sure all my hair is falling out. So, if you still want me, I'm all yours. Shall we set a date then?"

When she emerged from her bedroom, she looked stunning and perfectly groomed. She was fresh-faced and natural, which was a huge contrast to some of the other girls in our community who had been taught that beauty equalled thick white cake-like foundation plastered like builder's cement onto their face in a bid to make themselves paler and more beautiful. I always thought they looked like Indian geisha girls in sarees.

I watched the two families approach the front door from my attic room window and I tried to decipher who the beau would be. There were two boys; one was tall, way above the acceptable 6ft mark, with a thick head of floppy black hair with no visible signs of balding anytime soon. He looked slightly overconfident and had an arrogant air about him. He wore jeans and a long cream silk Panjabi top, and from a distance, it was hard to tell whether he possessed the typical vain traits of handsome, tall Deshi boys. The other young man was more formally dressed and sported a dark blue Burton's suit. He was smaller and possessed an unusually large head with a receding hairline. That's all I could see from my attic window. *Um, I bet Laila is being introduced to the boy with the receding hairline and the suit, not the tall, better- looking one,* I thought. "Let it be the handsome one; let it be the handsome one," I whispered to myself.

I crept down one flight of stairs and peered at the guests from behind the bannister. It was easy to see which mother had given birth to which son. *The lady with the 1940s style black hair, powdered face, thick purple lipstick, solid black kohl eyeliner with the saree blouse cut to her shoulders; I bet she's the tall boy's mother*, I thought. She looked somehow familiar. She wore gold earrings, several chunky necklaces and dozens of bracelets that lay like burnished tubing along her arms. A strip of ginger henna ran across the top of the other lady's loosely tied bun. She looked tired and forlorn and was somewhat more modestly dressed in her plain green cotton saree.

Aliya, the other girl who lived in Laila's house, had just returned from one of her amazing lawyer weekends; she'd been skiing in the Sierra Nevada in Granada. She barged into my room. "Who's the melon head in the kitchen?"

"Laila's in the middle of one of those marriage things—meetings arranged by her parents," I replied.

Aliya rolled her eyes and sniggered. She departed the room with one of her usual thoughtless comments, "He's not really Laila's type, is he? Aren't you getting married anytime soon? Maybe you should consider him."

I was very intimidated by Aliya; she was pretty, smart and spikily opinionated. She had no qualms about hurting your feelings with her prickly, mean comments. Aliya knew what she was doing; it was part of her personality, her defence mechanism to let everyone know she would hurt them before they dared hurt her. Luckily, she was hardly ever about the house because she spent all her weekends on luxury holiday breaks. Her evenings were spent socialising in city bars and rooftops with panoramic views of London, and the rest of the day she spent working at her law firm at some Magic Circle address in London. I wasn't quite sure where this was or what she did all day. I know it had something to do with real estate in Dubai and a Saudi Prince looking for property in southern Spain. She didn't like me very much. However, I know she did like shopping, because every day new haute couture and fashionista bags were hanging from her wrist.

I was just about to begin the tiresome Sunday afternoon task of marking books when Laila's head popped around the door. "Please come and keep me company downstairs," she begged. "I'm just so sick of pouring tea, smiling and doing pirouettes in my saree, only to end up in a semi in North London cooking curry and impregnated with triplets. I'm at the point of freaking out in front of them all. I want to erupt into a gangster rap or start breakdancing or belt out the Sound of Music just to scandalise them all. If you don't come down and keep me company, I'll probably do it. I will; I'll do it," she teased.

We all sat down at the kitchen table. The melon boy's face said it all, but he remained dignified during the whole ordeal. There was very little conversation exchanged between any of us. Laila refused to initiate the conversation, so we all sat in awkward silence and stared at a plate of smelly fish and onion bhajis until Laila got up and summoned me into the hall.

"This is a disaster, get me out of here now. What am I going to do? I have nothing to say to that boy. Nothing! Did you see how mortified he looks?"

As we were chatting, the tall boy passed us in the hall. Laila grabbed hold of his shirt sleeve with strange familiarity and began conversing with him intimately in a quiet corner of the hall. I left them to their discussion and walked upstairs towards the living room.

The mother with the short-sleeved blouse, chunky lamb chop arms and heavy makeup, was a friend of Laila's mother and the savviest matchmaker in the community. Auntie Lamb Chop, as she was commonly known, had successfully put together about four lucky matches. Whether the couples had stuck it out, run away, or taken flights back to the homeland was to be contested, but the weddings had definitely taken place. Had I ever been a matchmaker, I would never have brought my own better-looking son along, knowing full well he would overshadow and eclipse the boy I was trying to market to some would be family. I assumed that the melon boy had brought the other young man along just for moral support. As a matchmaker, I would also make all the men I meet, fill out a questionnaire which would feature questions like:

Question 1. Your wife is about to give birth, your mother is having an anxiety attack, and your favourite team is playing in the Premiership finals. How do you spend the next 2 hours of your life?

14

A) Taking your wife to the hospital and staying by her side throughout the whole birth.

B) Attending to your mother.

C) Forget the wife, forget your mother; you want to watch the football.

Eventually, all three fathers, the mystery handsome boy and melon head had disappeared into the living room. The sports channel was on, and they were discussing any one of three subjects: politics, religion, or sport. It was at times like this I would notice an ache creep up into the pit of my gut. The type of pain you dread and just hope will eventually melt away as sneakily as it had appeared. I wished with all my soul I still had a father and wondered how much he would have enjoyed talking to the uncles, but it was just too painful to contemplate the impossible.

It was time for Laila to parade herself in front of the mothers but something had changed, because she now played the game with such calm serenity and elegance. What had she and the tall boy spoken about earlier? Laila never betrayed her true feelings in the company of others; to do so would be to let her parents down. Laila knew she could always refuse later, and her parents would respect her wishes. Like a good Asian daughter, she greeted the boys' parents and sat down on a sofa as the family asked her questions, while I played the part of an invisible servant girl and served spiced greasy tea and Bombay mix.

"Serve the mishti your auntie has brought you, Baba!" exclaimed

Laila's mother.

I offered to go to the kitchen and fetch it, but on returning, I noticed that the tall boy's mother was staring at me fiercely as I placed the mishti on the table. Curiously enough, when I had fetched the Indian sweets from the kitchen, the son had behaved in a very similar manner towards me. The strange look from mother and son was one of two things: either they recognised me from somewhere or had taken an instant disliking to me.

Laila realised from a young age that an arranged marriage was on the cards for her once she had graduated from university. Matrimony after university was the natural progression. Laila had attended an all-girls' public school, so there had been very few opportunities to meet boys and fall in love. If you met Laila for the first time, she would come across as aloof and distant, so those who sought her affection never really dared to confront her with their feelings. Furthermore, she was a gifted student of the arts and sciences, captain of her sports teams and president of the students' union, so she had very little time to notice boys.

Laila was everything an Asian mother-in-law sought in a bride. I don't think they cared about the woman she might be within, as long as she could ponce about in a saree for a couple of months in a variety of silk and chiffon and make a cup of tea for guests. Perhaps I was too harsh; maybe this is just tradition and to break out into song while wearing a red miniskirt and boob tube was taking things too far, even in the name of cultural rebellion. From as young as fifteen years old, families were enquiring after Laila's availability, as if she were one of the prized daughters of Isabel, the Catholic who betrothed all her daughters at an early age to secure the throne of Castile. Luckily, her parents were not Spanish royalty, nor did they possess kingdoms, they couldn't even entertain the thought of losing their most precious daughter without her having finished her Pre-Reg year. Careful consideration would have to be taken when choosing a partner for their beloved daughter, if at all.

Despite the magical matchmaking qualities of the auntie with the lamb chop arms, many marriages had taken some distasteful turns in the last few years. Five to ten years ago, no-one had even heard of matrimonial breakups or the dreaded D-word, but recently, there had been a spate of conjugal disasters. Some break-ups were due to straightforward infidelity or hidden mental health issues; others failed to survive due to perhaps a clash of personalities, with the bride and groom fighting like kindergarten children. Finally, mother-in-law problems was another high contender. Laila's parents had to be very careful that none of these categories would ever apply to their beloved princess. The community seemed far more forgiving as the new millennium approached, but better to be single than to suffer any kind of marital humiliation or failure. If Laila were to marry, then her parents would let her choose her own husband, but it would be under their supervision, on their terms and careful guidance, although she would always have the final decision.

Laila's parents' biggest fear was that there were a huge number of girls coming into their twenties who were considered of marriageable age, and many eligible men in their late twenties or early thirties were beginning to bypass girls of their own age for the more youthful contenders. It would break Laila's parents' heart if anyone began to bypass their daughter.

17

Spending years at university was not paying off for the older girls in our community, and they were being left on the shelf. All the parents who had prayed so hard for a son but were blessed with a daughter were now suffering a double blow; in short, there were not enough decent, educated young men available. The other problem was that the boys' mothers were the fussiest women ever to walk the earth. Even before the interview stage, there would be a barrage of questions between the aunties. The usual ones at first: "Phosha, lampa, lekahphora?" which meant she was tall, fair and had a first-class honours degree from whatever uni she studied at. However, the questions would then begin to degenerate from the practical, onto the planes of the ridiculous. Mothers had in the past rejected wonderful girls on the most outrageous grounds. The nature of the rejections ranged from "bad tea pourer", to "teeth too white or crooked". I wondered whether girls of my generation weren't gaining the most horrendous complexes about themselves and at the same time suffering from low self-esteem. Many aunties had assured Laila's mother that she need not worry. Laila was a doctor and fulfilled every imaginable and physical criterion that mothers sought for their dear sons; it was as if Laila would be doing the picking and the choosing.

Laila had never planned on falling in love with someone at university. She looked on the chance to study medicine as a gift and one she would not gamble away by wasting her precious time in Union bars, spending daddy's money and idly flirting with undergraduates—the majority of whom were smelly, drunk, timewasters anyway. This attitude helped her acquire a reputation for being a reserved, snobby girl and yet savvy enough to be president of the student union for a year—that is, until she fell in love. By the time she had left university, not only did she achieve her medical degree with the highest grade she could imagine, but she had also acquired a boyfriend. There had been neither time nor the right opportunity to tell her parents of this new twist in her life, so she played the game of dutiful daughter and agreed to meet all the boys that were introduced to her. She would often tell me about the meetings with the families and the would-be suitors. Some were handsome and arrogant, others were meek but weak, and no one made an impression on her or stole her heart. Her mind was closed because her heart, for now, belonged to another.

Chapter Two

The Wedding – Salma

I realised Laila's conversation with the melon boy had gone from bad to worse, but I was curious to know more detail. Laila was already dressed for the wedding. Her parents had kindly asked me if I wanted to join them. It was free gourmet curry, so I thought, *why not?* I wasn't used to being dressed in a saree and had no clue how to put one on, Laila however, was an expert. I felt like one of the Bennet sisters in Pride and Prejudice, ready for an evening society ball with suitors galore waiting to reject me and make endless marriage proposals to Laila—the eligible one. As Laila enveloped me in waves of sparkles, silk, and chiffon pastels, meticulously folding the saree around my fragile body, she revealed more detail of the meeting with melon head. He had struck her as bizarre; all he had talked about was Doctor Who, Daleks, Sci-fi, the Star Ship Enterprise, and a galaxy far away. He did genuinely believe in aliens and found the girls from the Desh didn't seem to understand him, so he was looking for a girl with similar interests. Come to think of it, he did have an unusually large head—he was probably an alien too. Laila wasn't in the least bit interested. She had, in fact, just felt sorry for him; she didn't think he would have much luck with any woman. He was too obsessed with outer space, so no wonder his mother had gone prematurely grey through her henna tint. He probably would have to end up marrying some naive girl from the homeland who spoke no English and painted her face with industrial strength white paint and visited the beauty parlour to have her eye 'bru' threaded with two bits of string. Laila's mother had told us both over samosas and fish pakoras one day that even city girls back home were getting fussy nowadays. Laila remembered one meeting with a man obsessed with guns, Afghanistan, and training camps, who had become radicalised after meeting lots of international students and converts at an infamous science university after some girl had broken his heart.

"If we were to be married, would you be willing to wear a hijab, no makeup and join the sisters in organising religious talks and camps?" He insisted with a sense of urgency that made Laila believe he might be part of a dodgy religious cult.

"I'm kind of busy right now training to be a doctor plus I do nights, so I don't think I'd have much time for religious camping with the sisters," Laila replied politely.

She wondered why most would-be extremists tended to be scientists and not artsy types who wrote, painted things, or strummed on electric guitars. I told her she was wrong; the arts could be political too and a powerful tool to challenge oppressive regimes—but perhaps, not with our generation. I told her about my dad who had been caught up in student riots at university and hidden from a police raid in his dorms when an occupying government had tried to impose another language on all educational establishments and universities. People would die for mere words, never mind religious beliefs.

I was curious about the other boy, Kamal, but I didn't need to probe; Laila told me all about him in great detail. She had known Kamal since he and his family had moved to London about 15 years ago. She was perhaps ten years old at the time. Years later, they had both studied medicine at the same university. However, Kamal had graduated three years ahead of Laila. Laila was in her Pre-Reg year, and Kamal was well on his way to becoming a chief consultant of something someday, but for now, he was a womanising, flirty registrar. However, his mother on the other hand, was a chief consultant for marriages and matchmaking, although not always ones made in heaven. There were on occasion matches made in hell or 'the hellfire', as she would say. She would drag Kamal along with her in case she happened to stumble across a would-be daughter-in-law for herself and a possible bride for Kamal, her only prized son. Up to now, no girl had fulfilled her requirements, and Kamal just went along to appease the hysterics of his mother and her fear of never becoming a grandmother before the millennium fell and all the computers and clocks crashed.

Laila did not want to tell her boyfriend Raj about the marital meetings because she knew it would upset him. He did not understand it was something she just had to do for her parents' sake to keep them happy. Raj and Laila had met at university. He had read sports science and education and had decided to join the police force when he had graduated. Sergeant Raj was a talented sportsman and had good strong morals. They were well suited, but for their relationship to succeed, Raj and Laila would have to overcome many obstacles. He was the son of an English man and an Asian mother. His mother had died soon after his birth, and so he had been brought up by his father. She had been a servant for a rich family with an export empire, and she was gentle, well-mannered and beautiful. Raj's father met her when he was abroad on business, where she was the servant of one of his clients. With no comprehension of social norms, he fell in love with her, stole her away and brought her back to England. His

22

behaviour was deemed to be so scandalous that he lost all his contacts abroad. His business suffered, and soon there was very little money left to live on.

Raj's mother Lily never adapted to England; it was too much of a culture shock for her. She suffered from clinical depression and died just after Raj was born. They lived in a gloomy tower block somewhere in London while Raj's father spent a lot of time abroad trying to revive his leather export/import business. After returning from one of his business trips, he found Lily hanging by her saree in the bedroom. Raj was discovered in his cot covered in snot and sticky wet tears rolling down his swollen face. Raj´s father was devastated and never recovered from this. The sad irony was that his business trip had been a success, and their lives were about to change drastically for the better.

Although somewhat isolated from his community and even though he had not been brought up as a traditional Asian boy, Raj did regard himself as more of his mother's heritage than English because his skin was dark. On three counts, Laila's parents would probably disapprove of Raj. Both Laila and Raj had decided from the outset not to make too many plans, but now as the dizzy, hedonistic twenties passed them by, Raj was beginning to become impatient. Laila was his world, and he wanted to settle down and be married.

Laila always had a positive outlook on life and a logical solution to everything. She was not an intellectual, but she was bright and never let trivial things concern her. Eventually, the time would be right, and Laila would tell her parents. History, culture, religion—yes, they mattered, but they belonged to yesteryear and not her life. When the time was right, she would tell her parents.

As meticulous as she was in draping sarees around others, Laila needed help pinning her saree in the right places around her waist and shoulder. I was a novice at the saree thing, but I enjoyed the feel of the silk against my hands and twisting the folds of saree fabric between my fingers while imagining I knew how to create the perfect 'atchol' or pleats. Laila always looked stunning in her saree, with her picture-perfect Bollywood breasts, hips, and wavy hair. Her saree was sea blue with a silver and red trim. Every proud mother of a Deshi son wanted her for a daughter-in-law. They yearned for the outer packaging but knew nothing of the woman within. In many ways, Laila would make a bad daughter-in-law. If there were to be a power struggle between her and her mother-in-law, Laila would win. She had a strong independent spirit and would never be bossed around or told what to do.

Many of the mothers had come from landowning families from the villages in the homeland and had married a young man from a neighbouring village. Soon after the marriage, the groom would go on to study in the city or even England. Many mothers would spend months, even years living with the in-laws while bringing up their first born. All the while, they were learning the skills they needed to be the perfect grateful daughter-in-law, taunted by the sisters-in-law and revered by the groom's brothers. The pregnant mothers with toddlers in tow would then join their husbands in England and live in one bedroom of a terrace house fully fitted with damp stains and peeling retro wallpaper, only to be joined soon

24

after by another newly arrived immigrant family. Our mothers were still young girls when they married; some in their late teens, and others barely in their early twenties. The rest of their lives were dedicated to mourning the life they had left behind them and accepting all the new possibilities of what life in England had to offer. Our mothers would then spend another twenty odd years bringing up their offspring. So, most of their lives had been dedicated to this: cooking, nurture, and entertaining. These women were just a generation away from the village. Despite a humble beginning, their husbands worked incessantly, some studying by day and earning as little as £1 in a restaurant by night. As things got better, they bought their first 1930 semi for the sum of £500. Even with their somewhat now privileged existence in England, life must have been difficult for mothers in the early years of marriage. Outwardly they were so vulnerable looking, and yet somehow, they survived twenty or so years in Britain without having experienced any feelings of isolation, apprehension, and fear.

When the civil war had broken out between East and West, the mothers and fathers held meetings, smuggled letters to family members whose loved ones were in jail and remained positive about the future. Back home was such a different society to the one our parents had left behind so many years ago. However, mothers had found the perfect solution to happiness, and that was rearing their perfect children. If it were a daughter, she would be beautiful, and if it were a son, he would be clever.

My parents were from neighbouring villages. The great river ran through both communities, and during the rainy season, it was impossible to access the villages by any vehicle as the roads were too muddy. The only way in was by rickshaw or by foot. I often thought about how my parents' union had always been a matter of destiny. Both sets of grandfathers worked for the railway; they were majority landowners in their respective villages, and their families had gained the love and respect from their fellow neighbours over several generations. My mother was the third of nine children and the oldest of five daughters. She had four brothers, two of whom were her senior. Coincidentally, my father had also been the third of nine children, the oldest of five brothers with four sisters, and two being his senior. The matrimonial deal that was to unite my mother and father had been struck on a train through a mutual friend that both grandfathers had in common. My parents' lives and personal circumstances were almost identical, and yet they had only met once before they married. My father had travelled over to my mother's village a year before they were wed. It was all arranged; a cousin and his younger brother accompanied him. The young men's excuse, if they were caught, would be that they were searching for a new place to fish. My grandfather invited the men to stay and eat that evening and saw this as an opportunity to interrogate my father. "What are you studying at university?" "What are your plans to find work?" "How will you support a family once you are married?" "What do you think of communism?" These were just some of the questions my father was required to answer that night.

Unusually, my mother's younger brothers and sisters, except my mother, ate at the dinner table that evening, and the more taxing questions came from them. They could normally be found at dinner time playing around the lake or climbing mango trees. My mother's siblings' questions to my nervous father consisted of the following: "Why do you want to go to a place called Bidesh?" "What do they eat there?" "Do they like school?" "Are the lemon and coconut trees as fruitful as ours?" My father must have passed the test because a year later, the two families were united by marriage.

The reception hall of the wedding in Wembley was bursting with colourful, gold and silver spangled sarees. There were white and pink balloons and an array of late summer flowers on every table. Laila was immediately swallowed up by a crowd of optimistic would-be mothers-in-law. They were already grabbing at her face and fawning over her gold necklaces.

"So posh ah, so sweet. Have you put on weight?" enquired a group of inquisitive aunties.

At this point, Laila let go of my hand, and with a last apologetic look, she was swept away by a wave of gold bangles and henna hands, and I was left alone. This was the first Deshi wedding I had been invited to since I was a little girl. I always fantasised about miraculously bumping into Kal; he would be all grown up, polite, kind even, a teacher or humanitarian worker. I would spy the back of a young man's head and think, *This is it! This is the moment I will see my Kal once again,* but I never did. It was never his face or the happy boy I remember.

I was drawn to a window that looked below onto the courtyard where the bride and groom would soon enter. As a thousand mumbling voices in the background continued their chatter, I heard a beautiful sound of music from afar. It reminded me of the melancholic resonance in one of those old black and white Indian movies. The films where the browbeaten heroine is forced to live a life of loss and deprivation. Her loved one is gone, and famine has swept over the land, then as if from nowhere, the monochrome movie in my mind's eyes was immersed in colour, and the courtyard was filled with people, music, and life. The wedding party for the groom had arrived and with him an assortment of vivacious, high spirited people. They brought with them the joyful groom dressed from head to toe in the finest silk and gold. Around the wedding party, a group of men played a joyous traditional tune on a variety of national instruments. I found myself lost amongst all the many sounds and sights I saw. My mind wanders to the land of my parents where miles and miles of paddy fields and wide, dark rivers connect a network of tiny villages. At night, when villagers and families huddle around the hurricane lamp, all that can be heard under the monsoon moon are the crickets and the howling dogs by the graveyards. A solitary man bears his day's labour in a jute basket on a head, he walks silently along the many fields of rice; his only thoughts are of a warm plate of milk, sweet rice and a cotton mattress where he will eventually rest his weary body.

The groom was tall and handsome and looked regal in his majestic silk turban and gold Panjabi. I imagined how the bride would seem in her red and gold saree. She must look very striking. I wondered whether the marriage had been arranged or they had fallen in love. I'm sure this was a love marriage. You could always tell by looking at the bride's facial expression. Her head wasn't bowed in sadness, and there were no tears; she was too miserable and bossy to have been forced into anything. "Don't take any pictures of me until I say so; I am tripping on my saree!" she screamed as a hundred aunties rushed towards her to adjust her saree folds and safety pins.

The food was the best part of any wedding—always a majestic banquet of spice, colour, and flavours. The guests happily devoured the feast. Women sat with women; men sat with men and the young with the young. In previous years, guests who had attended the wedding had looked at the bride, assessed the jewellery, ate the food, gossiped and then left. Now the new generation of weddings demanded something different, and entertainment was provided, such as an Indian style dancer or a musical group.

I didn't know anyone at the wedding. Since my father had died, we had lived in relative isolation. Home was a grim town up north, not that all the north was grim. I seemed to remember that as a child, we mixed with many other families, but after my father's death, things seem to have changed suddenly. My mother had never really recovered from our loss, and much of the responsibility of bringing up my two younger sisters had fallen onto my shoulders. Suddenly, Laila's mother's arms were tenderly wrapped around me.

"You look all alone." Laila's mother spied a tall young man from across the room and beckoned him over. "Kamal come here…" she was unable to finish her sentence, as an auntie whisked her away to talk to a crowd of other brightly coloured aunties.

I recognised the two boys from this morning's meeting. Neither of the boys seemed to acknowledge me, despite having heard Laila's mother call them over. Even when our eyes met momentarily across the room, they feigned any knowledge of ever having met me earlier that morning.

So, I pretended not to have noticed them either. I think the melon boy was perhaps feeling down and rejected from this morning's get-together that he failed to meet his future Mrs. Melon head; the other boy, however, seemed to be scouring the room with an air of self-importance. Our eyes met a couple of times, and I quickly looked away. His stare was vacant and hard, and then he would look down at this watch as if he had somewhere more important to be. Pride prevented me from taking another look.

Laila knew everyone at the wedding. She had lots of childhood girlfriends and spent most of the wedding smiling and chatting away. Now and then she had gazed over to see if I was OK, but she knew I was quite happy in my own company. I sat at the table with three very glamorous girls involved in an equally glamorous conversation. They were talking in what I suppose were pretend 'posh' Bollywood actress accents.

"I'm so bored here; there are no cute boys. Let's eat all the curry and then go to Tiger Tiger in Piccadilly; they do Bollywood and Latin dancing on different nights. No, I changed my mind, what about Planet Bollywood? They do the best puri and dhal," explained one of the girls.

"No, there is one cute boy, Kamal, you know? The one that doesn't like anyone, only English or European girls."

"Oh yes! With the bossy, Deshi tiger mother. Even if he liked you, she would eat you alive first; best to have an ugly yes man." The Bollywood girls continued eating and giggling throughout the entire wedding. They continued to make comments about prospective husbands and their shortcomings. British Deshis in London seemed so self-assured and confident; they seemed to have carved out a glamorous parallel world all of their own. Soon there would be beauty parlours with eyebrow and facial hair threading with bits of string, on every London street corner.

I realised the wedding was drawing to an end because everyone began to gather near the exit and continued to chat for a good half an hour or more. Men held each other's hands as they talked business and politics, and the women excitedly jangled their jewellery in each other's faces as they gossiped about things that made them elated and happy. Children were happily left to their own devices and existed in their own world. They ran up and down the reception hall, stealing flowers and causing general chaos while weaving in and out of the guests with not a care. I could see Kamal and Laila's mothers speaking passionately about something. Kamal's mother was waving her lamb chop arms in the air and did not look happy at all. Kamal was headed towards his mother; he spotted her fury and then took an about turn. Laila suddenly appeared from nowhere and Auntie Lamb Chop's demeanour softened. Laila gave her auntie a big hug. She complimented her on something and then departed with her mother. The crisis was over.

One of Laila's university friends, Reena, had offered to drive us home. There were five of us in the car. We were visibly Asian women and noticeably wearing sarees, so our glitz, sequins, and sparkle stuck out like sore thumbs on the anti-clockwise route of the M25 motorway. Every passer-by seemed to do a double take at our car brimming with silk and perfume. As we laughed and gossiped in the car, our driver Reena became somewhat agitated. Some men in a car driving parallel to us had started to make gestures and noises, and a rush of panic engulfed the pit of my stomach. The car was a typical old Ford style banger; our world was a small one, a safe one, and this felt intimidating. We all decided that they were mindless idiots, and we should ignore them.

"Check if those are real skinheads or are they just bald?" suggested one girl in the car.

"Even nice blokes wear their hair very short—and soldiers. It's fashionable now," replied another of our passengers.

Our pursuers were persistent. They followed us, they called us. Maybe it was harmless flirtation. Their faces were mean, and their hair or lack of it was what worried me. I was hoping above hope that British society had moved on from those depressing, dark, concrete, punk rock days of the '70s. Music, television, film—people travelled more, consumed food from all over the world, so society must be more tolerant. Long ago, if you lived out of your community, you suffered from prejudice, and if you lived in the community, you lived in a fossilised ghetto.

My mind had wandered, and our female chauffeur friend Reena turned out to be an officer for the London Metropolitan Police Force. Reena stopped and then cautioned the young men bent on entertaining us from their vehicle. At first, they did not believe her and laughed, but then she produced her badge.

"Can I see your licence and insurance, sir?"

"You have got to be kidding me. You're not a police officer."

"Do you want me to show you my warrant card, sir?"

"Anyway, you aren't on duty dressed like that," hollered his friend from the back seat.

"A police officer is always on duty. Do you want me to call for back up? My colleagues can be here in about 10 to 15 minutes and can detain you for causing intentional harassment, alarm, and distress, as stated in Sections 4A and 5 of the Public Order Act 1986." PC Reena Majid was a walking Blackstone's police manual wrapped up in six yards of jamdani silk.

The men had not meant to scare us; it had all been harmless fun. They weren't skinheads; they were just silly students trying to be funny and flirt. We were more shocked at the revelation that this woman in a saree was an officer of the law and had the power to kick ass at will. She was also capable of quoting numerous breaches of the law from the top of her head. We all spent the rest of the journey on our best behaviour.

"Are you really allowed to say or do that when you aren't on duty, Reena?" Laila probed.

"No. Of course not, but they aren't to know, are they?" We all gasped in horror. "But I bet you had fun though, didn't you, ladies?"

Chapter Three

The Restaurant – Salma

Later that Sunday evening at a restaurant in Brick Lane, Laila and I related the Asian policewoman story to Aliya. Laila knew Reena was a policewoman all along.

"I just wanted to see the look on the girls' faces when Reena pulled her law enforcement badge out on those boys. Ha! It was hilarious," she giggled.

"It's not called an enforcement badge, Laila; it's known as a warrant card. I deal with police officers all the time in the bar, and no one has ever referred to it as an enforcement badge; that's in the US," retorted Aliya.

"Sorry Aliya, I thought you were a property lawyer, you don't practice criminal law, do you?" But Laila was in no mood for arguing, so she pulled a face and politely beckoned the waiter.

How different we are from our mothers! We didn't possess even half of the tenacity our mothers had when they came to Britain. Our strength was of a different nature. Fashioned here in Britain, we manifested that drive through so-called clever words, fashionable clothes, and high-flying careers.

It was nice to end the weekend together. I always felt a little gloomy at the thought of another Monday and the weekly battle that lay ahead. London to an outsider seemed like a wonderful place to live; the city where all hopes, ambitions, and dreams were made true. The reality was a lot tougher. In a city this big and this competitive, a small northern girl like me could feel very lost.

"My father started his career in London," I explained. Aliya and Laila were no longer speaking. "He used to be a waiter for restaurants to pay his way through university; then my mother joined him a few years later, and I was born about a year after to the day." I beamed.

"I didn't know your dad went to uni. I thought you were poor, and your dad sold knickers in the market," replied Aliya.

"Seriously, Aliya, do you never give it a rest?" Laila jumped to my defence.

"It's all right, honestly. My dad studied English Literature and History, Aliya. He waited tables, but no, he didn't sell ladies' underwear in any markets." I replied.

As I looked around the restaurant, I noticed couples and groups of men, but not that many Deshis. Some vegetarian restaurants I had visited in the north of London were always full of Indian families, but this rarely happened in the north; our restaurant was full of beer drinking locals.

"I've been spending many weekends away recently, as you know. Well, last week, we were invited to a dinner party with this new lawyer, and I think he took a shine to me," beamed Aliya.

"How do you know that, Aliya? Is this based on any hard evidence?" replied Laila with a hint of sarcasm. Aliya was too involved in

35

her story to care.

"His name is Jonathan, and he is a junior associate and the nephew of one of the senior partners. I get this feeling he has singled me out," Aliya said with a smile.

Aliya would occasionally pretend she was a barrister, as she would often throw in the word 'the bar' and make references to all her other barrister friends. Aliya's main role at work was to deal with rich clients who wanted to buy property abroad. With the eternal boom in the property market in the south, many people were re-mortgaging their homes and buying abroad. Popular locations were Marbella, Mallorca, Dubai, or the south of France.

Aliya rarely came out with us. She had a hectic social life and the obligatory work parties. She must have earned a lot of money; Aliya always wore designer clothes and ate out because she hated cooking. I don't think I ever saw her boil an egg or make toast. She would ruffle her recently washed hair in the kitchen as if she were Bridget Bardot and Laila would spend every morning sweeping and picking up her strands of ginger/blonde bleached hair from the floor and kitchen worktops. Aliya was prohibited from smoking in the house but would drag her smoke-ridden clothes through the house and along every flight of stairs, and Laila would have a fit. Aliya seemed to be from a very well-to-do family. She had no boundaries; Aliya just said and did whatever she liked. I fantasised about how romantic her relationship with the future senior partner Jonathan would be. Aliya, the exotic wife of a toffee-nosed city lawyer.

Laila and Aliya had a lot in common; they both had strong

characters and successful careers, and yet they argued all the time. Laila felt that Aliya spent too much money on clothes, makeup, and holidays and only enjoyed the company of her friends because they were rich, not because they were nice. Laila had accompanied Aliya once to her annual Law Ball and found everyone to be false and shallow.

My eyes were suddenly drawn to an Asian man and a white woman in the corner of the restaurant. It was Kamal, Laila's friend from the wedding. Auntie Lamb Chop's son. It was Aliya who spotted him first.

"Isn't that Kamal, your flirty cousin?"

Laila turned her head but seemed disinterested; she casually returned to her menu. "He's on a date, leave him," Laila explained casually. "All the same, in five minutes, they will be too busy sucking face to notice us anyway."

It was the first time Laila and Aliya had laughed together since I had known them. They were usually at each other's throats. Laila was right; Kamal hadn't even noticed we were there and was indeed too busy staring into the eyes of his date to care for us. I clumsily stared at him, and he looked my way but didn't recognise me and continued chatting with his girlfriend. Aliya's thoughts turned to the waiter for our table who reminded her of a driver her rich aunt from back home had employed once.

"My aunt and uncle used to have a garment factory and were filthy rich. They had a house made of marble, gold phones, and monobloc taps. There were never any mosquito nets, and you never saw nasty cockroaches in their mansion."

Laila was convinced she was lying because Aliya always referred to everything as if it were in the past, like a bygone era, as if what was gone could no longer be disproved.

"My auntie's house was in one of the most exclusive parts of the city."

"Really!" exclaimed Laila in her usual tone of disbelief after one of Aliya's stories.

"If any cockroach or mosquito dares enter the house, my uncle had them assassinated."

"Which part of the city does your aunt live in then?" probed Laila.

"In best part, of course, by the British Embassy," replied Aliya. She knew she was under scrutiny. "Isn't that where all the super-rich people live?"

"Actually no," replied Laila. "Posh people tend to live by the lake and the Radisson Hotel." It was Laila's turn to tell a Deshi story.

One time at a family football match, Laila had felt tired and sticky, as the rainy season was about to start. The chauffeur had driven me home. As a mark of gratitude, Laila had held up her hand—a gesture of thanks and a polite farewell. She left him standing by his car and presumed he'd now return to the football match to pick up the rest of the family once the game had finished. As no one was in the house, and Laila had just wanted to make the most of a rare solitary moment, so she played the music very loudly and decided to take a shower to cool down. About 45 minutes later, she descended the stairs only to see her auntie screaming obscenities at the driver.

"Where have you been for such a long time?" screamed Laila's auntie.

It was then that it dawned on her that the driver must have been sitting in the car all the time and had not moved in the 45 minutes Laila had been happily singing ABBA and Blondie songs in the shower. Even though he had been expected back at the football match immediately, he had been waiting for her all this time. Laila felt wretched.

"People back home should stop abusing their help staff," Laila protested to us all.

"You mean servants?" replied Aliya

"No, help staff, Aliya. You can't call them servants anymore," declared Laila.

They were at it again when the waiter served our table. He was a small framed skinny man and he talked so fast with such a strong Asian accent, our brains could hardly process his words. He smiled way too much and was fidgety and nervous, which irritated Aliya. A tall, quieter waiter then spilt some water on Aliya's dress, and all hell broke loose. "You bloody buffoon!" she shouted. I was shocked and embarrassed at her rudeness. She called the manager, even though we tried to dissuade her.

"Are you not going to sack him for throwing water on me?"

"Well, madam, he is one of our hardest working staff members," the manager replied.

I wanted to disappear. Laila, who was always the queen of diplomacy and good manners, tried to speak in the gaps and explain that other than that incident, we were pleased with his service. What struck me was the reaction of the waiter. He apologised, but he wasn't humble nor was he rude in his manner; there was an air of dignity about him. His boss continued to make excuses and offer things to make up for the mishap.

"I apologise. What can we do to make you return?" This infuriated Aliya even further, as she felt the manager was milking the situation.

I thought about how they only earned £1.00 an hour. Who could live off that? £8 per day times five days a week would be just £40. How could one survive off so little money per week, only to be humiliated by some snobby upstart girl who worked in a magic circle for lawyers? Why did that make her superior? It reminded me of how my cousin Beauty treated the servants in the Desh. As a child, she would kick and hit them. As an adult, she would humiliate them and even still probably beat them. The servants lived off £5.00 a month, and a family driver earned no more than £16.00, even though he would have to work from 9 a.m. until 12 p.m with virtually no breaks. If Beauty didn't change her behaviour towards the servants, I'm sure one day her chief lady servant would quietly stick a knife into Beauty's body as she lay sleeping under the mosquito net.

The manager brought over our coats as we made our move to leave. Laila, on realising that Aliya was about to complain again, quickly cut in and began congratulating the manager on the quality of the food and the restaurant—adding that Aliya was so impressed she had promised to bring her parents next time. He asked us where we were from, Laila told him we were all from the Desh.

"Oh really? You are not typical Deshi girls; I thought you were maybe from the south. My family are originally from Calcutta before the partition."

As Laila began to tell the manager what we all did for a living and who our parents were, to show how Deshi girls did come from good wealthy families too, Aliya began pulling faces and kicking her persistently under the table. She rudely blurted out, "I am not from any Deshi country; I am from…" Before Aliya had a chance to blurt out where she was from the manager replied in a sardonic tone.

"Yes, I agree, madam. The women from my country are known for their beauty and manners," the manager declared smugly. Laila smirked while Aliya's face glowered with pure fury.

Then as we left the restaurant, I wanted to go back to the waiter and say how sorry I was, so I made my excuses and ran back into the restaurant. As I rushed to the bar, I slammed into Kamal who was carrying two glasses of something. One was wine, and the other drink looked like coke or beer. It soaked the front of my dress. He apologised abruptly and then for a moment I was sure he was searching for something on my face and staring at me. He was just about to wipe my dress with his handkerchief when the skinny waiter cut in and started brushing me down with a smelly cloth. Kamal suddenly disappeared—he returned to his date. I gently pushed the waiter away. I told him I was OK, then I pulled my coat around me and left the restaurant. I felt a strange sensation in my belly.

Laila argued furiously with Aliya in the taxi. "What problem do you have with admitting your heritage? And don't you ever dare kick me again with those nasty, come and have meaningless intercourse with me stilettos," cried Laila.

Aliya would reel with joy when people mistakenly thought she was South American or, even better, Italian and not Asian. If people asked where she was from, she would answer, "Where do you think I'm from?" Aliya shared her conspiracy theory about how waiters talked, and it would get back to her parents, and then, using lawyer type spiel, she explained how she was the customer who had certain expectations and requirements that should be observed. "You know, the Deshi restaurants are like a mafia network," Aliya declared.

"What's wrong with you, Salma?" probed Laila as she rummaged around in her bag to pay the taxi fare. "Hey has anyone seen my purse I can't find it? Salma you look like you have just seen a ghost."

Suddenly, all eyes were on me. I had hardly spoken a word all night, and the Kamal incident had left me with a strange feeling as if my body were melting into a chaotic abyss in which I no longer had control of my destiny.

Chapter Four

The Immigrants

Before arriving in London, Bilal and Afzar worked in the Middle East for about two years. However immigrant workers were maltreated and paid a pittance, so they decided to risk everything they had achieved in the Middle East and travel to the United Kingdom. It was a widespread belief that the United Kingdom and America were the nations of opportunity, and both men had heard stories of Deshis who were now successfully living comfortably in the respective countries. When the Deshis returned to their homeland for visits, they always wore fine clothes and had plenty of disposable income.

Bilal's father was a local village teacher who had once stood up against a village mob during partition and saved the life of his Hindu colleague.

"No man will even harm one hair of the man who has educated your children, taught them to read and write, given them the chance to be more than farm labourers. If you dare to choose this mindless violent path, you will do it over my dead body," bellowed Bilal's father.

Bilal's family was isolated and shunned after this incident and they eventually moved to the city. For Bilal, the early death of his father and scarce finances had prevented him from following in his father's footsteps. His mother had travelled back to the village where she was born, and Bilal had returned to the city to improve his chances at a decent education, but he was only able to find work in a clothing factory or selling tea on the streets. Suddenly, his luck changed, as due to his good manners and breeding, the factory owner promoted Bilal to be his driver. The hours were long, but he was able to earn £16 a month, and many of his boss's clients would bring him food as he waited wearily in the hot sweltering city afternoon sun. He spent what money he could on books and read incessantly during his long breaks, but the job was mind-numbingly tedious, and the days were long.

When foreigners visited the factory, they were kind and polite and always worried whether he had eaten or rested. They always took an interest in his welfare, and before returning to their native country, they would reward him with a tip for his patience and loyalty. Their kindness filled him with hope, but then they were gone. He dreamed of one day going abroad and studying so that at some point, he might return to his homeland and show the same respect and gratitude to a driver like himself or a factory worker. He remembers one such Deshi man now living in Bidesh. After nearly thirty years of hard work, he was now an established doctor and his daughter was also studying medicine at university. He was very proud of her.

"I would like her to eventually get married to a kind hearted, hardworking young man, but my daughter has a free spirit. Just like her mother," the Bideshi doctor explained with a slight look of worry.

"I am sure your daughter and wife are in the best of health and have good hearts. That's what matters at the end of the day," replied Bilal.

"If you are ever in London look me up!" but before Bilal could exchange any details with him, they had arrived at their destination and the doctor's relatives descended on the car and were showering him with garlands and kisses.

He was always intrigued by the Deshi girls who were brought up abroad. They were confident and demanding, but they lacked the arrogance and cruelty of some of the rich girls living in his homeland. In many ways, there was something more natural, even uncomplex about the girls from England. They lacked refinement, they wore less makeup, their lips weren't caked in bright red lipstick, and they refrained from smothering their faces in unnatural white powder or face lightening creams. The Bideshi girls were not afraid to let their skin turn dark and bask on the rooftops under the city's sweltering sun or dance unchaperoned in the monsoon rain. Bilal could appreciate how they struggled to fit in; they would scream at the sight of the cockroaches and then be chastised by their families for travelling in the rickshaws unaccompanied. They seemed to find some strange solace in eating aloo bhajis or often requested to be dropped off at the bathrooms at the Sheraton or Sonargaon hotels. The Bideshi girls would arrive at the airport hot and flustered by the crowds, wearing tight inappropriate clothes, but over time, a transformation would take place. The western clothes and the long, loose, unkempt tresses were replaced by coconut oiled hair and a loose cotton shalwar kameez from the shop Aarong. He enjoyed listening to their gentle memsahib English tones, so reminiscent of an uprooted jasmine flower - broken and now floating lost in unfamiliar waters. He smiled quietly when they conversed with him in their funny, broken accents, but above all things, he would never forget how these girls from Bidesh would treat him as if he were almost a human being.

Afzar was very different from Bilal; his dream was to move to America as soon as the opportunity arose. Britain was just a stopgap; he had plans to become a rich and famous businessman. Living abroad meant that you could borrow huge loans from the top banks or find a family member or firm to sponsor you, and then all your dreams could come true. He had heard that Britain was a cold, hard place and people were hostile toward those who came from the Indian subcontinent and the Deshis were at the bottom of the pile. However, the US had no such prejudices, and it was a land where dreams come true, so his sights were set on America. It was a nation where you could make huge amounts of money and be anything you wanted. He had heard rumours of the big lottery, where people could win a place to live in the US forever, but he had no time to wait for the lottery; he needed to go now and fulfil his dream, even if it meant living as an illegal alien for a while. He would keep his head down and live in Hispanic areas where he would blend in. He loved learning everything he could about America. He would watch all the popular shows through the wrought iron bars of a rich man's house by the lake. While working in the factory, he had discussed ways of leaving his homeland with other co-workers.

A Man Power agent visited the factory to recruit workers for a Saudi construction company. The flight and the agency fee cost at least £500, which amounted to years and years of wages. Afzar's friend Bilal had managed to save £200 from the tips and by living a very meagre life— free from gambling or wasting his money at the cinema. Bilal's mother had died some five years ago from old age and cholera. Bilal managed to raise money by selling the small plot of land his mother had left him in the village; it was the last of her legacy, but he knew the local landlord would only offer him half of what the land was worth. But what about Afzar? How could he leave him behind? A brotherly affection had grown between Bilal and Afzar. Bilal felt responsible for his friend, and he couldn't possibly leave Afzar alone. Bilal had saved enough money to travel to Saudi with an agent from Man Power Services, but he didn't have enough money for Afzar. Even if he were able to sell his mother's precious wedding necklace, it still wouldn't be enough. The necklace and tarnished black and white photo were the only memories he had left of her; he had treasured these as a child and planned to give them to his bride one day. With the sale of the land and the necklace, he had managed to raise £800. The agent wouldn't accept this amount, but after much bargaining and humbling himself for the sake of his friend Afzar, the agent accepted the £800 plus half of both Afzar and Bilal's wages for the first three months. Bilal could now dream of the day when he would be studying to be something and someone.

Life in Saudi was hard; they were treated with little regard or respect. They shared one small room with eight other men. The locals would beat them or humiliate them for bizarre reasons, and they were treated like herds of cattle, not human beings. The worst offenders were men from neighbouring countries and even on occasion, their Deshi countrymen, when given some position of responsibility, were inflexible and cruel towards the unskilled labourers. Bilal and Afzar's first job was sweeping the streets. There was a hierarchy of jobs, even in unskilled labour. After some months, Bilal found a job with a construction company and was soon promoted to a driver. The site manager took a shine to Bilal due to his polite, educated manner. However, while things steadily improved for Bilal, the same could not be said for Afzar; he was still sweeping and cleaning at the airport. Bilal suspected that Afzar was gambling away whatever little money they had both saved. If the authorities ever caught Afzar, a brutal punishment would await him and his associates—the punishment for gambling was flogging in Chop-Chop Square. Both men struggled on for over two years, and then one day, an opportunity arose to travel to Europe. Bilal wasn't so sure it was the best method to travel to Europe, as it involved handing over all his money to human traffickers, but Afzar had arranged it all.

Bilal only wanted to enter the UK legitimately with a student visa so that he could study at university. Bilal, being an intelligent man, had to use his time to practise his English whenever and wherever he could. In Saudi, there were lots of opportunities to speak English, as many American and European people had settled in the country and worked for big international companies. Sometimes they would talk to him while he was driving them to the airport or a meeting. The foreigners were polite, kind and interested in his welfare.

They could travel to Eastern Europe through Turkey, then to Greece or head north via Hungry. It would cost them thousands of pounds each. Bilal had just enough money saved, but it was for his studies. With more time in Saudi, he could have eventually saved enough for one year's undergraduate study at a university in Britain, but Afzar had become involved in some kind of trouble, and if he did not leave the country soon, he could find himself in danger of a severe beating from the Saudi authorities. Bilal could not abandon his friend, as he had become like a younger brother to him. Like so many others, they struggled their way across Eastern Europe. With the little money they had left, they found menial jobs. They came across good people, but also, many were ruthless and cruel.

Bilal often thought of the European businessmen and all the kindness they had shown him in his home city. During difficult times, he wondered where these people were. Knowing that there were people in the world with such humanity and kindness kept him from giving up his dream and the distant hope that one day, he would be in a position to go back to his home as a kind, generous man and make a difference. He missed his homeland so much; it seemed so far away now. The land where he had grown up, the village where he had played as a child, the favourite tree he had climbed outside his house as a young boy, and all the stories his father would tell him of far-off lands where there were great scholars and philosophers. As an adult, he had realised that knowledge was not unique to the west; many of the ancient and great philosophies had their roots in Eastern culture.

Nevertheless, he knew he had no opportunity of breaking the cycle of poverty he was now destined for unless he broke that cycle in his present life. Even in a country like his, educational opportunities were only available to the rich and privileged classes. Democracy and political change failed to open up opportunities for the poorer classes as promised. With increased international investment in the country, the gulf between rich and poor was growing wider and wider. On the streets of the wealthiest European towns, they used their money to sell goods to locals and wealthy tourists.

Bilal and Afzar travelled briefly to Spain and Italy and sold silk ties and perfume, from the Esplanade in Alicante to Las Ramblas in Barcelona and on the narrow-paved streets of Sol in Madrid. Finally, they found themselves in France at a hellish, apocalyptic-like encampment called Calais. The prospect of Britain was not far away, but crossing the English Channel was the hardest part. Had they managed to enter Britain directly from Saudi, it would have cost them both tens of thousands of pounds each. Had Bilal been in possession of that kind of money, he would have studied in the city or applied for a student visa for Britain, thus fulfilling his dream of studying legally. Nothing was straightforward, and nothing was for free.

Bilal and Afzar had been lucky in London; they lived in an area occupied mostly by Deshi people. They could buy Deshi fish, wonderful fruits, and other foods from a nearby store and speak to local people on the street. It was a strange sensation at first when they had arrived in London, but now they were growing accustomed to life here. It was easier to keep Afzar out of trouble in England. People seemed so much more genuine and more honest here than in countries they had lived in previously.

Once or twice, Bilal had travelled west and visited one of the universities; he had managed to walk on to the campus and watch the students from the campus gardens—no one asked who he was. He thought it was a wonderful place. The whole atmosphere was different to where they lived; it was a different world to the tower blocks of East London. It was cleaner, brighter, and there were smartly dressed students from every nation. Britain seemed a just and free country. Most of the money he had earned in Saudi had been spent on his visa. He was saving next to nothing working in the restaurant, and after months, he slowly began to realise that the hope of studying may be a far-off dream that would never come to pass.

Nevertheless, he would never stop hoping or praying for his dream to come true. He had come so far; how could he give up now? His biggest fear was that they would be discovered to be illegal and sent back, and then he would be left with nothing, as he had sold everything he had ever owned. He could not go directly to university; his English would have to be adequate, so he would have to study a pre-university access course. All this took money, and he had none. To study on the course, he had to be in Britain legally, and he was not, but Bilal never stopped praying or hoping.

As they walked home from the restaurant, they discussed whether it would have been a better idea to have handed in the purse to the owner and wait for the customer to ring the restaurant to claim the lost item.

"I found it, Bilal Bhai. I will take it to the house of the lady. The girls were rude and disrespectful to us, so I will leave it in their letterbox."

"Not all the girls were unkind; just one. But as you wish, Afzar; perhaps it would be better to give it to the boss." Bilal feared that if he gave the purse to the boss, the girls would never see their property again.

"Afzar, we need to keep a low profile; we have no papers."

Afzar wasn't listening; he was thinking of girls. "The girls here are different from the young, educated girls from our hometown. They are probably more westernised in their dress and speak more freely, but even back home, young student girls are substituting their traditional dress for western fashion."

"Yes, you are probably right, Afzar," replied Bilal, somewhat distracted.

Even though it was a summer evening, Bilal still felt cold; his mind wandered to whether his luck would ever change or whether he had made the right decision to come to England illegally. He knew they were lucky because the owner of the restaurant had organised accommodation for them. They shared a small room, kitchen, and bathroom with four other boys in a tower block in the East End of London. They were all from the Desh and all illegal. They ate at the restaurant, and the rent was taken out of their wages. They didn't all work in the same restaurant; it would be too risky. They were lucky; at least two of the boys in the house could cook. Life was cold and hard, and there was little greenery around, but at least here they weren't beaten or disrespected.

They were only a few blocks from home. It all happened very quickly. One second, they were walking home; the next they were being pursued by three men who seemed to appear from the shadows. They had not immediately sensed the imminent danger. Despite all the humiliations and beating they had suffered and witnessed in Saudi, nothing had prepared them for this. Bilal managed to run free, but Afzar was caught and lay curled up helplessly as he was kicked and beaten. Bilal stood terrified, breathless and in shock. The perpetrators shouted angrily and with a vile hatred that Bilal had never experienced. His heart beat so fast that he could no longer breathe; the fear was so great he could feel the vomit well up in his throat.

When the attackers had gone, Bilal cried as he ran to his friend who lay on the ground like a sacrificial lamb, a faceless mass of blood and skin. He crouched over his friend, sobbing as if like a child again when the school bullies had once beaten a dear friend close to unconsciousness. But this time, there was nothing and no one to protect them from life's horrors. Afzar lay in a pool of blood; his face was bruised like an aubergine, clots of blood oozed from his fat lip, his eyes were no longer visible—they were two pools of crimson red. Afzar was unrecognisable; he was barely breathing. Bilal ran to a nearby phone box and called for an ambulance. The operator asked for his name and without thinking, he gave it. There were no thoughts in his head but prayers to God that his friend might still be alive. The human body was so fragile, and then to be kicked and beaten in this manner, he reflected. As he vomited into a bush, he could, at last, hear the ambulance and its ominous wail in the distance.

Chapter Five

The Week at Work - Laila

Salma had moved to London in the summer of 1998. A mutual friend had introduced us, and Salma was renting the attic room in my house for the new school term. Salma was originally from a town in the north of Manchester. She had been nervous, as it was the first time she'd lived in any other city. She'd lived at home during teacher training for several reasons. Firstly, Salma's mother was unwell and secondly, her family didn't have the money or resources, so living in halls in an expensive city like London just wasn't an option. Our parents were from neighbouring villages. My father knew Salma's father briefly in the 1960s from college, but they had studied in very different faculties. Salma's father Harun studied literature, and my father studied medicine. Harun was a good man from a humble but landowning family. He was also a dreamer. There were very few prospects for literature graduates in the 1960s, apart from journalism, activism, or becoming a village teacher. When Salma's father had decided to take his chances in England, he had worked as a manager in a mutual friend's restaurant. Things had ended acrimoniously, so my mother had told me, as he'd been accused of taking a large quantity of money from the business and a gold necklace had gone missing. Not only was he sacked, but he was shamed within the community. Salma's family was ousted from social circles, and soon after, her father died from something—no one's quite sure of what. Salma's mother suffered a nervous breakdown and so Salma, as she was the oldest, took on full responsibility for her mother and sisters. My mother says no one knows what Salma's father did with such a large quantity of money or the necklace. There was never any evidence of how much was stolen or whether it was ever recovered. All we know was it was a lot of money; enough to buy a whole house in those days or build a palace in a village in the Desh. My mother, who has a good heart and thinks of the best in everyone, wasn't sure he did embezzle his friend's business and thinks the money had been taken by someone else and invested in something untraceable like a big house or piece of land by the lake in the Desh. My father also said it was very out of character, as he remembers that Salma's father Harun was painfully honest and generous at university; even when he had very little, he would share his tiffin box with the poorest of students.

Gossip is a daily ritual amongst the 'aunties'. It's their lifeline and an integral part of their existence; without it, they would have very little to say to one another. Salma's family lived relatively isolated from the 'inner circle' we called the community and so, since the incident, I never really saw her on any social occasions when I was growing up. A mutual friend from teacher training college invited her to a wedding, and we met there. We sat at the same table. Salma had tried to engage in conversation with a girl sat at our table. "I heard you were taking the tube back to central London. Do you mind if I follow any of you back after the wedding?"

Natasha, known for her prickly ways, had descended into new depths of bitchiness since she had become engaged to the second most eligible bachelor in the community after Kamal. "What is that?" enquired Natasha as she looked Salma up and down with an air of disdain.

"What's what? Salma replied, puzzled.

"That accent emanating from your mouth."

"It's from Manchester?"

"Ooh is that what it is?" she replied.

I decided to rescue poor Salma. "I'm not taking the underground, but I can take you to wherever you need to go in a car. I love the north; we used to visit friends there when I was a little girl, and on the way, we would have picnics on the side of the motorway and visit the lakes."

"Eww, how horrifying! I've never travelled further than the North Circular," replied Natasha.

I decided to interrupt Natasha as soon as I could. "Yes, we used to visit your fiancé a lot back in the day when he was a northerner too, you know? Before he adopted that faux southern accent and lied about his origins." I could be brusque too. Salma giggled, and Natasha walked off in a huff.

Aliya, who worked for the magic circle of prestigious law firms in the city was another prickly type. She was obsessed with her career and appearance. Aliya must have been paid a fortune because she constantly bought clothes, ate out, often shot off for weekend skiing in Andorra or Granada and surrounded herself with an obnoxious bunch of Hooray Henrys. When she did bother to buy food, it was all wrapped in plastic which she would leave rotting in the fridge for weeks. She never seemed to have enough money at the end of the month to pay her rent, so I spent days chasing her, which made me feel as if I was a greedy old landlady. We didn't see eye to eye on anything, and I'd often think I should have given her notice, but she redeemed herself through some good points. Aliya was ambitious, with a strong personality, hardworking, intelligent, and she had occasionally been there for me when I'd needed to talk about issues and relationships. No subject was taboo, although with many Deshi girls I know in my social circle, sex, drugs, and rock and roll were no-go areas.

As Salma didn't have a permanent teaching job, and the population was booming from immigrant children in London, supply teaching jobs were in abundance. Initially, Salma was asked to cover maternity leave at an all-girls' school in the East End of London. Like her father, she had studied English as her main subject, and RE as her minor. The girls at Salma's school were tough to handle and very demanding, but her biggest challenge had been crossing the city by underground. Salma found the daily journey to work daunting and exhausting—weaving through recently arrived lost tourists at Victoria Station or suffocating under someone's city suit or armpit on the London underground. We both curled up on the sofa equally exhausted after our challenging day at work.

"I am so exhausted weaving through that tube station. I just stood there lost at the bottom of the escalators. People didn't care; they just rushed past me. I nearly fell over twice," Salma confessed.

"People can be like that here on public transport. It's like they lose their sense of humanity," I replied.

"I was so tired I fell asleep and missed my stop," Salma explained, a little embarrassed.

"I know; Kamal told me. He saw you sleeping."

"Kamal?" she replied in astonishment. "Who is Kamal?"

"You know the guy that was here the other day? When Raj stayed over and had to escape from my parents?"

Kamal had been made arrogant by a ridiculous, vain mother, and yet all the nurses and even female doctors at the hospital would chase him, but as I had known him for such a long time, I never found him the least bit attractive. His mother was loca about finding him the perfect model of a bride. She would be mortified if she knew what a Don Juan her darling only son had developed into.

Why Kamal hadn't woken Salma up or spoken to her on the tube, I hadn't a clue. Despite my knowing him for many years, he was a hard man to understand, with a dark, secretive side. Or was it merely conceit?

Chapter Six

The House Party – Laila

It was the weekend, and we were invited to a 'house party' in north London. One of my old university friends had just bought a house. They were a group of friends I didn't have time to see on a regular basis, especially when the routine of real life kicks in. A&E takes its toll on you, and I hardly had time to sleep and eat between shifts, and then there was Raj and my parents to deal with, plus all their matchmaking to fit into the equation. My friend Sirena lived with a group of very liberal Asian boys, Rikki and Prakash. The other boys in the house were your typical mixture of lawyers, trainee dentists, and accountants. Aliya had surprisingly offered to go along to this party even though her social lawyer agenda was usually quite tight and complete. Despite her apparent strong and overconfident self, she found it hard to spend time on her own.

Salma, who was a recluse, seemed a novice at social occasions and sat on her own in the corner of the room. She looked shy and awkward, lost in her world of fairies and bygone eras. I had lent her a reasonably trendy dress and helped her with her makeup. The glasses had gone, and she emerged as an attractive, graceful woman. As my eyes glanced across the room, the disciples of chic and glamour that attended these parties always made me squirm. The queen of glamour for this evening was a tall, confident girl dressed in long white flared trousers; she wore very little else on top, except for a white buttoned vest. Unlike Salma in the corner, she showed herself off with an irritating degree of self-belief. It was a conceited self-assurance that she was the coolest, the most fashionable and the most desirable Asian girl in the whole of London as she swayed her hips to and fro to the music. Her sister had been talent spotted at school for a Bollywood movie; she was now so envious of her sister's success that she was bent on following on in her footsteps at any cost. If she walked around with the belief, she was a Bollywood actress, sooner or later, the universe would reward her, and someone would spot her, so she too would be a Deshi star. Well, not an actress perhaps; a presenter most probably. She had the added advantage of speaking English with a North London pronunciation.

The guests had found their comfortable groups to hang out in and were talking over an assortment of subjects from interest rates to job promotions. The hosts were very attentive, and I was soon engaged in a political debate about Middle East peace or lack of it. Working for an international organisation as a volunteer doctor was something many people in my profession were beginning to opt for after their Pre-Reg year, and I admired them. It's what I wanted to do with all my heart; however, a more comfort driven version of myself then talked me out of it. There would be no glamping or ensuite yurts in the Amazon rainforests or the foothill of the Andes. If I had wanted to do this, I had to rid myself of the city diva within.

"You can't do the Camino de Santiago and stay in Paradors along the way," Lola, a Spanish nurse, had explained to me in her dreamy Mediterranean accent. "You have to do it rough, like the original pilgrims."

I wasn't sure my police officer boyfriend Raj would be willing to follow me to all these far-off hostile lands or the foothills of the Andean mountains. He had his own hostile lands to deal with here on the streets of London and the constant rejections from the accelerated promotion scheme. Aliya was skulking in a smoky corner of the room, a glass of wine in hand, looking very self-assured and vying for first place with a white trouser Bollywood dancing girl. Aliya would wait for the first male victim she could cut down with her blunt, judicious comments: "Yes, I am a lawyer, and yes, I do work for one of the most prestigious law firms in the country. It's part of the Magic Circle. What else do you need to know? I can send you my CV," she would add in a sarcastic tone that would send any potential flirting man off to the hills to hide.

Aliya was a lot more Asian than she cared to recognise, although the realisation of such a thing would aggravate her. It was interesting how her eyes had immediately centred on the confident Bollywood girl. Aliya disliked other females with her levels of confidence, especially other Asian girls. She had no problem if the girl was white British or European, as their backgrounds and experiences were different. Aliya would use her 'Asianess' when it suited her. She set herself up as a dark, eastern temptress and played the role perfectly for her English male audience, but there could be no other competition to compete with the part she played.

"Aliya! That's an unusual name. Where is it from?"

"Oh! Can't you guess? Where do you think it's from?" She loved it when the man chatting her up would roll out a long list of nationalities. She hated it if they guessed she was Asian first time around. One of Kamal's Spanish friends had told her she was too dark skinned to be

Spanish. It wasn't meant as an insult; it was just an obvious and honest comment. She detested him. "At least I don't look like a bloody Spanish waiter," she mumbled under her breath.

As the evening wore on and the cliquey groups gravitated towards the dance area, the house suddenly began to fill with a larger variety of people. Small groups and exclusive couples blocked doorways and staircases. The politically correct types were always to be found debating and putting the world to rights in the kitchen. Why the kitchen? I don't know. Salma continued to cling to the security of the large sofa that engulfed her, lost in her world and not a care for those who mingled around her. I served Salma a coke and encouraged her to follow me into the kitchen, as I would introduce her to some of the guests. Once in the vicinity of the political debaters, I had introduced Salma to everyone, but she just wandered back to the solace and security of that large sofa.

Kamal turned up with his latest non-Deshi conquest from the hospital—the pretty blonde woman we had spied in the restaurant where I had lost my purse. She was a nurse that had worked in Saudi Arabia for a year. Living the high life amongst the expats had made her arrogant. While living in Saudi, she had rarely ventured out of the European complex, and yet she had managed to adopt some very extreme views about Arab culture and the local faith. I had argued with her once at a staff party about the United States and what constituted a US citizen.

"People of dark complexion can't be real US citizens; it doesn't make sense. I see so many dark looking people with these foreign accents who claim to be from the US, and they obviously are not, are they?" She declared superciliously.

I tried to point out the obvious to her: "You know that native Americans are the real indigenous people of the US? The USA is a society of immigrants who built their nation from the sweat and blood of slaves, plus, a large part if it is annexed from Mexico. That's why there are cities with Hispanic names like Los Angeles, Las Vegas, and San Francisco," I explained, proud at my historical knowledge and ability to think laterally.

The view that the US was principally made up of hillbillies was an antiquated view that had no place in modern North America today. I continued to argue with her. "So, your distant relative who had immigrated to the US twenty years ago from a different continent is a bona fide citizen because they were Caucasian and could fit in. But an Asian family, despite their children being born and brought up in the US, could never truly be regarded as an American?"

"True," she answered.

I laughed so hard it hurt when she had explained her theory to me. To her, west meant white. The discussion became very public, and a crowd of staff and colleagues were listening in on our heated debate.

"So then, according to your argument, what does that make me? What am I? English, British, or Asian? Go on, then. Answer! Let's hear the real truth about your feelings about immigrants in this country," I asked her. I understood my tone had become a little aggressive.

She refused to answer, which I interpreted as "No, you're not British at the end of the day."

I continued, "So you're British because you're of white Caucasian heritage, even though your family is originally from a different country, and I'm not because I'm …" At this point, one of my colleagues put his arm on my shoulder and told me to leave it and calm down. "No, I will not calm down," I answered as I pushed his arm away and repeated the question, but her hands were already covering her ears.

"I'm not listening; I'm not listening," she screeched. She stood up and then ran out of the room. Everyone fell silent.

"I didn't start that!" I objected, but I now looked like the baddie. How strange! I'd spent most of my life protesting that I was from my parents' country of origin and not British, and yet when someone tried to deny me my 'Britishness,' I was prepared to fight tooth and nail for it. However, my position as a doctor put me in situations where I would have to interact with her at some level, and so I always behaved professionally at the hospital.

"Hey, Kamal! You picked a great one there to introduce to your mum." I was determined to annoy Kamal at any cost.

"Give it a rest, Laila!" Kamal snapped back in reply.

"You're so into yourself you didn't even bother to greet me!" I complained.

"I said hello to Aliya, didn't I?" Kamal replied in his defence.

"Yes, but what about my new roommate Salma?" I probed.

"Didn't you see her on the tube the other day and not even bother to wake her up? She missed her stop."

"Who the heck is Salma?" he protested innocently.

"You know Salma; she was at my house when your mum came to match me with the melon boy. The girl you failed to wake up on the tube the other day."

Kamal looked over at her. "Never seen her in my life. Who is she? She looks depressed."

"Shut up, you! You are a snob," I replied.

I noticed him sneak a look back at Salma as she quietly sat still, engulfed in the monster leather sofa, lost in her thoughts and memories.

For most of the evening, two girls had been catching most of the guests' attention. They stood out from everyone else at the party because they were visibly intoxicated, loud and dressed rather garishly. They were dancing together without any shame and oblivious to the embarrassment they were causing to themselves and the rest of us. Furthermore, their accents were not southern; they seemed to be from the Midlands or somewhere north. Noticing my expression of utter shock and horror at these two aliens, one of the boys from the house decided to tell me of their astonishing story.

"Two years ago, those girls Rozi and Dolly had travelled from Birmingham to London on the pretext of studying something at a London university. However, in reality, they had never enrolled on a course at any

London university. It had been a pretext for escaping from home. In their defence, the girls had been dreaming and planning this for a long time. When the joys of studying away from home were devastated by horrible A Level results, they had refused to give up their plan and had concocted a fictitious course in London. They had planned to retake their A Levels at a college and make an application for a university place for the next academic year. Things had not gone according to plan, as the girls were tempted by the bright city lights and had wasted their time partying and spending money they did not have."

"How did they live?" I asked.

"Well, they had mastered the art of 'crashing' and living off the generosity of others. My friend and his fellow housemates were the current victims of the girls' swindling ways, but it had caused much antagonism among the housemates. The grace period and the generosity on the part of the house occupants were now running out for the girls. It was rumoured that the girls were spotted up to no good and news had travelled back to their brothers in the Midlands. The brothers belonged to some boy band type Asian street mafia. The brothers, backed up by some Deshi vigilante group, were on the hunt for the girls and had vowed to hunt the runaways down and take back home, kicking and screaming if necessary.

The evening had been somewhat tame, apart from the two runaway girls and their hysterical behaviour. Most of the guests were sitting in small groups, chatting and laughing, and the music provided a pleasant mood for the evening. No one was particularly too loud nor drunk. To be intoxicated where many of the guests wouldn't be drinking could cause offence and unease. Salma and I had overheard a conversation about two illegal

66

immigrants who had made headline news. One had been found virtually beaten to death in a side street near the East End and the other man had been spotted running away from the scene. He was now being sought out by the police and wanted for questioning. It was frightening what one human being could do to another in the name of colour, culture, or religion. At the hospital while working in A& E, I'd seen so many young men, even women, brutally beaten by strangers, drunken friends, or even partners.

The political group at the party huddled around the kitchen table and continued to debate the immigration policies in Britain and whether they were fair. Kamal's nurse was kept well away from any talk of politics.

"Did the West have some responsibility towards the refugees? Was the state able to withstand such a heavy influx? Was globalisation responsible for the increase of refugees in Europe? Which countries were doing the most, and in which European country did immigrants get the best deal?"

Salma—normally pretty quiet when in public—shocked us all and began to speak her mind about some of the hotly debated issues. She related some of her experiences of working with refugee children in school.

"We're an ageing society, so we are going to need to invite an immigrant workforce into the country because there won't be enough young people to sustain all the old people in the country."

Kamal's girlfriend who was once again within the vicinity of the political debate looked straight at Salma and concluded: "Yes, but immigrants are such a huge drain on our healthcare system. What happens if they have Aids or other diseases? We have to pay for them!"

I considered her comments and then was about to respond that the NHS was made up of an immigrant workforce when Aliya waded in to the argument. "Where are your ancestors from then?

Furious and defeated Kamal's girlfriend slid away. "Aliya that is not how we should teach people to be tolerant, our DNA is made up from all kinds of invaders and settlers. Not one of us is pure anything. That's the lie they invent to keep us all hating each other," I chastised. Fascism would never cast its shadowy cloak over Europe again and the daughters of 1960s immigrants would make sure it never did. Not on our watch.

And then I thought of Eduardo, a six-year-old Guatemalan child I sponsored through Earth Vision, a religious charity group. I think it was Salma who had asked me if I was interested in sparing 15 pounds a month, the price of half a yuppy meal. Eduardo had not attended school yet and could neither read nor write. He had sent me a picture he had drawn of some multicoloured sheep and trees. The project leader Milagros had written a letter on his behalf. It reads:

Dear Sponsor,

My family calls me Eduardo.

The geographical area where we live is mountainous, and the weather is hot, and the zone is dry. My house is made of wattle and daub walls, tile roof and a dirt floor. The health post is 3 km away. My family and I usually eat beans, rice, eggs, and corn tortillas. When I grow up, I wish to be a doctor.

With much love, your child,

Eduardo

I cried when I read it. I don't know why. Eduardo wasn't starving or anything. That was the moment I realised I wanted to work in a small village in South America and help all the boys like Eduardo who wanted to be doctors when they grew up. In his next letter, he told me he couldn't read and write, but my money would go towards his schooling. I asked Kamal's Spanish friend Dr. Francisco to buy me lots of picture dictionaries and early years writing material the next time he visited his parents in Spain. I felt an odd maternal affection for this little Latin American boy. His skin was dark and golden; his hair was black. He looked just like an Indian boy. I didn't want children, but I knew I wanted to sponsor more boys and girls from every continent and at least one from my own parental Desh. Since watching several films about Latin America, I developed some odd passion for the language and culture. Had I not studied medicine, Hispanic studies would have interested me greatly. Once in Retiro Park in Madrid (on a school exchange), I had heard a group of Peruvian musicians play some enchanting flute music. It made my heart sing; it was like listening to the purest spring water flood down from the Machu Picchu Mountains. The musicians asked my friend and me if we were from South America, as we looked like the girls from his village.

Many colleagues had travelled abroad and worked for charities as doctors. My life was comfortable here and I don't know if I'd be cut out for something like that. As a child, I had comforted a starving old woman as she ate rice on my grandmother's veranda. *She's just hungry; surely, I can make her feel better*, I thought. It was the first time I had ever witnessed such hunger and desperation. My father was so proud of this act he took a photo of it and kept it safe. I had vowed then and there I would be a doctor and look after sick, old and poor people. As grown-up, selfish, materialistic ways had got in the way, I felt I wasn't full filling that promise I had made to myself as a child. I wondered whether these experts in politics and social anthropology had at all realised or remembered that they were only one generation away from being immigrants themselves. What made us different anyway? We may not speak like migrants or even live like them, but despite all our education, fine talk, and money, we certainly looked like immigrants. Many of us lived a million miles away from a life of fear and racial hatred, but I couldn't stop thinking, *If any of us had been in the wrong place at the wrong time, could we have ended up like that poor boy in the hospital?* It didn't bear thinking about.

As the evening continued, Kamal made moves to leave the party with his date. I suggested that Salma—who looked thoroughly bored and about to fall asleep at any moment—follow Aliya.

"Sorry, I've got plans; I am sleeping over at my lawyer boyfriend's house. We're all going to play chess; I fancy joining them. Tonight's been a total waste of time," declared a smug Aliya.

"OK, don't rub it in, Aliya. See you Sunday night then, or Monday evening." I turned to Kamal. "Kamal, hey, before you leave, take Salma home, will you?"

"What?" he replied, shocked. "I've got a date!"

"Come on; she is about to pass out from boredom—obviously not from intoxication like the two lightweights." I gestured over to the two girls. The two runaway stick insect girls became increasingly annoying as the evening continued.

"Salma doesn't know anyone, and it's too dangerous at this time of night for her to travel home alone. There's a gang of crazy men on the loose beating up foreigners like us. Come on, Kamal, be a gentleman. You know you can be one when you try."

Kamal took a good long look at Salma who was indeed lying there, just like Sleeping Beauty with her head tilted to one side. His voice softened suddenly. "Yeah, sure, I'll take her home."

"To MY house, Kamal, not with you and that crazy bigot nurse of yours. I shudder to think." He tutted at me as if disapproving of my joke.

"I will be taking both ladies to their respective homes, Laila. What do you take me for?"

"I know you, Kamal Rehman. I've known you for a long time and probably better than your mother."

"Yeah, whatever, Lali Lu. I know you and all your dark secrets too."

I woke Salma gently from her slumber and sent her on her way with Kamal and his nurse.

The runaway stick girls Rozi and Dolly had advanced from the kitchen to other parts of the house and were trying to hold silly conversations with several groups of people at the party. The guests couldn't hide their embarrassment; it was like witnessing two girls gone astray from their hen night and who had accidentally gatecrashed our posh yuppie party. One guest politely asked the host to do something about Rozi and Dolly, as they were bothering his recently arrived Deshi wife. He was reluctant for her to be exposed to this behaviour.

Rikki decided to do the honourable thing and take personal care of the two girls. I suppose he felt somewhat responsible, as it was, he who had met Rozi and Dolly at a bar in Southbank and invited them to stay until they were financially sorted. One of the girls, Rozi, was now so intoxicated that she sat head slumped on the sofa like a ghastly paralysed rag doll. Dolly spent her time slobbering over Rikki. This unethical behaviour attracted the particular attention of one girl in the room.

Nabila was the unmarried cousin of Rikki. She had been a traditional kind of girl as a child, but as adulthood approached, she had realised that if she did not adapt her ways, she would be alienated by many of her peers and regarded as an old fuddy-duddy before her time. Right in front of her eyes, she had seen lots of girls marry or become engaged, but sadly, no offers seemed to come her way. She secretly loved her cousin Rikki, and to be accepted into Rikki's trendy elite inner circle, she had adopted the role of friend/confidante/agony aunt.

She constantly vetted potential suitors for her cousin, and where she found herself powerless to interfere, she would befriend the girlfriend, take her out shopping or for lunch. In this way, she always had a legitimate

72

reason for being around the boys' houses and very much in their lives. Nabila had made an effort in the early days with the too skinny girls from Birmingham, but they had on several occasions left her waiting outside in the cold on Oxford Street or not turned up, or even ran away from her in broad daylight like two naughty school girls.

From what I could make out, Rozi was the skinny runaway that was still very much standing despite all the free alcohol she had virtually snorted through her nose like a drug. She had come to regard Rikki as her knight in shining armour, or maybe Rozi just knew that her time was up. So, endearing herself to one of the housemates would guarantee her a few more days or weeks in the house. Rozi's arms were around his neck, and she seemed to have lost all power in her leg muscles. Everyone else's reaction to this appalling scene was to ignore it and carry on with their little conversations. At first, gentle and kind Rikki became ever increasingly embarrassed at the scene, as this could easily frighten away potential female suitors. When Rozi began verbalising her affection so vocally and so loud that no one could do anything else but stare, Rikki had finally had enough and carried her upstairs in his arms. Unfortunately, to a particular person, Nabila, this was also too much to handle. As soon as Rozi parted her rouge stained lips and attempted to land one on Rikki's terrified tightly pursed lips, Nabila rushed upstairs behind them as if the love of her life were about to be stolen away in the most humiliating circumstances possible.

Nabila burst into the room, and pushing past her cousin, she tried to grasp Rozi by the hair but just missed. She managed to grab on to Rozi's flimsy dress, and with the sheer force of Nabila's pull, she tore the dress into tissue-like shreds. Rozi was dragged down the stairs squealing like a wounded rabbit. Nabila opened the front door and threw her out into a cold November night. The noise from Rozi had been so inhuman that everyone had immediately dashed to the scene of the commotion. The poor girl was on her hands and knees, vomiting vilely onto the concrete drive.

Chapter Seven

The Scrabble Party - Laila

The parties attempted to imitate traditions of the past, mixed with a hint of trendy nouveau riche British-Asian. Our parents' safe curry and genuine, unpretentious parties always won the day for me. Eating curry with our hands, uncles talking politics in one room, the silk sarees and midriffs and crazy kids flying all over the house. As for the runaway girls, Rozi and Dolly, when one door shuts on you, another magically opens. Regrettably, the door that was to open was my unfortunate door. The girls had nowhere else to go. My North London friends saw me as some soft-hearted do-gooder and knew I would never say no to these two homeless freaks. What could I do? I had a bad feeling, but someone would have to house, feed, and clothe these girls until they sorted themselves out. Normally, Rozi and Dolly would find some naive Deshi boys to house them, but this time their luck had run out, and with no more gullible Deshi boys on the horizon, the only person left to help them was me.

Rikki and the boys from the house party promised me it would be a week at the most and that they were looking for a solution as we spoke. I asked my housemates if they would be comfortable playing host to the two runaways. Salma as her usual charitable self, had said yes immediately, but Aliya was a different matter. She flatly refused, but to her annoyance, I had to take an executive decision and just went over her head; after all, I was the landlady of the house.

"Why? Why should I have to house those two slaggy tarts? I am not paying for their amenities, you know? Never mind, I'll stay at Jonathan's city pad in Docklands." She insisted on always emphasising it was a city pad and in an up and coming location where no other person we knew could afford.

It wasn't an easy week with the two girls living virtually on top of us. Entertaining two entitled teenaged women and holding down my ever-changing shifts at the hospital at the same time was difficult. The girls never cooked, never cleaned; they spent a great deal of the day giggling and watching satellite TV and endless videos of Friends. The living room was covered in crisp packets and chocolate stains. As I was on nights and ate at the hospital, I had no time to cook, but Salma had on occasion shared her food with them. For two such giggly girls who were in constant conference with one another, they had very little to say to the rest of us.

Aliya had been so furious with the situation that she decided to stay out of the way, fearing she may do them some serious harm. Aliya decided to spend most of her time at Jonathan's until they were permanently gone. When she had returned to pick up some of her clothes, Aliya had accused the two girls of using her clothes, makeup, and food. She was determined I shouldn't charge her rent for the month as it was in breach of her tenancy contract. Just before Aliya had launched into a full-scale world war with the two girls, Salma had managed to calm Aliya and offered to buy her new makeup. It was an uncomfortable week, but somehow, we got through.

I was having my usual problems with Raj. Very soon after graduation, we had decided to become engaged secretly. Although very English in his outlook, he did feel some yearning toward the Indian subcontinental culture. He yearned to settle down and have a family although I did not. Other than that, I think we were well-suited, with similar temperaments. Raj had spied me across a union bar disco. Once we began chatting, he was pretty full on. He was sporty, played rugby and would often turn up on a Saturday afternoon with teeth missing or dislocated arms and legs. It became a Saturday routine that I would stick my boyfriend back together with tape and glue.

My intention was, in theory, to marry someone my parents would introduce me to, but then life doesn't always wait. There were several young men of my background and culture, but although they were polite, there was no intellectual or spiritual connection. With Raj, I think it was purely physical; he was handsome and strong and had soft silky olive skin.

Some of the Asian medics at the university had formed a large clique and over the five years of study, there had been many scandals, broken hearts, and swapping of partners. I couldn't be a part of that. There always seemed to be pressure to show off how much money your parents had. Most of the young Asian medics were from families where their parents were also doctors, so they came from privileged backgrounds. I was horrified at two fellow female medics who had proudly boasted about spending over three thousand pounds of their maintenance grant on clothes and partying in just one term. They declared poverty at the student union finance office, only to be given another three thousand pounds to spend on more parties and clothes.

Salma was having a hard time. She worked part-time at an all-girls' school in the East End of London and taught English Literature and

Religious Education. Supply teaching meant she could be sent anywhere. The kids could be hard work and often even potentially violent; it depended on which school she went to. Throwing chairs, tables, rulers, and scissors across the room at a teacher's face and being called a b-i-t-c-h was a typical day in supply teaching. Often young naïve supply teachers wouldn't last the day, and after some kind of incident or simply crying at the sheer frustration of the job, they would be politely shown the door and forced to hand over their security pass, never to return. The places where Salma worked were often run-down concrete blocks from the 1960s. She was small, gentle but tough as boots inside her Asian silk demeanour and had the ability to calm any hormone driven teenager into submission. It was the kind of strength and character only moral virgins still possessed, something me and Aliya must have lost years ago. Because Salma was quiet and gentle, the kids eventually followed suit, and by the end of the week, she would have them singing a karaoke song—Spice Girls and Back Street Boys—or fighting for smiley face stamps in their workbooks.

Aliya's intense socialising had paid off, as she had now become the law firm's favourite. This new-found confidence had encouraged her to seek the attention of the firm's other favourite lawyer—one of the senior partners' nephews. Jonathan had worked at the firm for over five years. His uncle was grooming him to become one of the youngest senior partners in the firm's long hundred-year history. His family was rich and boasted a royal connection through an illegitimate bloodline. Illegitimate or not, this was enough to interest Aliya who also boasted an Indian royal bloodline. Her ancestors, according to sources, were landowning royalty from a northern tea picking region. Aliya's ambitions were to reach straight to the top. She would never date an Asian boy, as she found them unattractive; although there had been offers, they were flatly rejected with the excuse that they would interfere with her law exams. I just imagined her in a state of infinite head-butting with her mother-in-law were she ever to marry a Deshi boy. I couldn't imagine Aliya playing at shy bride during the courtship or family inspection phase, as she hosted a Deshi tea dance for aunties while draped in a saree half-hanging off her head while she feigned modesty. I had never met Aliya's parents nor did my parents know anything about her family. Aliya would always talk of her colossal house in the country and her family's high political and social connections back in the homeland.

The following weekend, I had decided to invite a small group of my friends to my house for a Scrabble and curry party. This was a semi-regular feature that occurred monthly, and this time, it was my turn to host the event. Despite the disruption of having to entertain the two girls this week, I was determined to enjoy myself and spend some time with my good friends. As the guests gradually began to arrive, I frantically added the final finishing touches to my chicken curry with cumin, new potatoes, and peas. I prided myself on the dishes my mother had recently taught me to cook and with some help from Salma who was a culinary genius, my feast was taking shape. My mother was known to be one of the tastiest cooks in the community, and I was determined to follow in her footsteps. Her food was a sumptuous blend of mouth-watering spices that were never too hot, and the sauce was never too thick and oily. She would often mix ideas from other cultures. She was the first ever auntie to experiment with olive oil in our curries. I hadn't quite cracked her cooking method, but I was almost there. When you ate my mother's food, every grain of rice and every bit of meat tasted of a blend of luscious spices right down to the core.

Most of my friends were Deshi, but there were three non-Asian girls I had invited from work. Anya was a Norwegian doctor who had resided in England for over five years. Maria was a Croatian nurse who had arrived in the UK as a refugee and had been on the verge of deportation by the Home Office on several occasions. Each time she was on the point of returning to her homeland, courtesy of the UK border force, the universe had magically intervened. On the first occasion, the plane had been forced to return due to mechanical failure, followed by a passenger suffering a heart attack. Finally, two boys were spotted throwing their hands up in the air and speaking Arabic, so the plane was diverted and the young men were removed for questioning by Special Branch. Maria had finally gained British status when she married her plumber boyfriend from Sheffield.

My other guest Helen had been a good friend from my early days as a student; we had shared a house together during my first year, and she had married a fellow Asian student on her pharmacology course. Helen had taken on the faith, and her wedding was a beautiful affair set in an old castle in Wales. Today, she wore a saree and looked as elegant and regal as a mogul princess.

My two other uninvited guests Rozi and Dolly were upstairs and would not come down, despite repeated requests and coaxing from Salma. They were surprisingly intimidated by so many strong, opinionated and educated women. One woman not on my invite list was Nabila. Since the events of that disastrous party, Nabila had taken to her room. She had

80

claimed that she was ill and could not face anyone. As she didn't work anyway and lived with her parents, it was very little loss to Rikki and his housemates, but her love of fine dining with discount vouchers had used up all the money her parents gave her to allow her a social life. Her cousin Rikki had not forgiven her for causing such an affray and ruining his friend's housewarming party. Nabila had destroyed any hopes of Rikki attracting a decent, educated British-born girl, as Rikki was now the butt of many jokes, forcing him to search for a bride abroad. Any chance Nabila had of winning her cousin's heart was now completely shattered, and she had no option but to go to the country of her parents' birthplace and let them find her a suitor. Nabila's only alternative was to die an old maid, and that was a choice she was not willing to make. Nabila would go to see relatives for at least a year, look for her partner for life and return to the UK as a married woman.

Everyone loved my food. Several games of Scrabble were on the go and those who didn't participate gossiped over the plates of pilau in their clique corners. I was surprised to see that one of the final two competitors was none other than Salma, who was an undercover Scrabble genius. Aliya had decided she would only stay for a moment; she was still not keen on the two skinny guests and had decided her time was better invested with her lawyer friends at some elite London club with a rooftop and city skyline views. These were places I constantly heard about, but never had time to frequent due to the long hours of my profession.

The runaways Rozi and Dolly had still not emerged from upstairs, and truth be told, in retrospect, they were strangely quiet. I remember thinking for a moment how odd their behaviour was, or maybe they were genuinely just shy or asleep. I felt a pang of sisterly pity for them when, as if from the depths of beyond, came screeching and bellowing, followed by a thunder of feet down the stairs. We were all stupefied to see two flashes of lightning rush past us and head for the back door. There was no mercy as they fled past, and more than one person was knocked over. It happened too quickly to process what had exactly happened. Just as everyone had absorbed the shock, someone began pounding the door as if it would give way at any moment. With the noise and commotion of inside and the thunderous ruckus from the door, there was no time for fear. We all thought it was the girls again, and so when one of my guests opened the front door ready to reprimand them, we were unprepared for the following. Six unshaven, dark, alcohol-smelling boys burst open the front door and pushed their way into my house, yelling everything under the sun. Their time was up: the past had finally caught up with Rozi and Dolly.

It was just like a military assault or terrible parody of a Bollywood horror movie. Three men ran to different parts of the house. One covered upstairs, another ran to the back of the house, and the third ran through to the kitchen. The screaming and shouting had stopped just as the leader of this group stood boldly in front of my stupefied guests and shouted his orders with all the might of his tar-ridden lungs. It was only when he began shouting the name of the two girls and the image of them shooting through the house with such fear and panic in their eyes that the penny dropped. Of course, the girls were on the run from their brothers. As I was the only one aware of the situation, I stepped forward to explain the situation, but no sooner had I opened my mouth than I was shot down with:

"Shut up and sit down, bitch, or we'll cut you."

One of my friends stood up bravely, protesting, "Don't speak to her like that; she's a doctor, you know? If anyone cuts anyone …" I hushed her. I knew he was dangerous, but the girls took no notice. Suddenly, skills and qualifications were being thrown around the room like an episode of University Challenge.

"I'm a lawyer, and I will sue your ass if you lay a finger on any of us."

"And I'm a dentist, and I will extract your teeth with no anaesthetics."

"I have a master's degree in neuroscience and will frazzle your brain."

"And I have three master's degrees in physics, biophysics, and nuclear fusion."

"Shut the f*** up, you crazy bitches! Who are you, my mum?"

The power of his unhinged, thunderous voice forced me to take a step back. I had no doubts that something would make him snap, and he would attack one of us. I noticed now that the rest of the girls were either sitting down, hands on their chests or with their backs to the wall as if nowhere to go and nothing more to say. Others were beginning to shake, and that's when any traces of bravado dissolved away, and panic set in. I had no idea where this would lead and whether I had the means to protect everyone from our assailants. We were all boldness at first, but now we were just plain scared. The leader of the mob had also run out of options and kept repeating the same thing over and over, "Where are they, where are they? Those two little whores! I am going to sort them out," as if the natural next step would have to be something drastic or he would have to admit defeat. With new found courage, the guests began asking me a million questions. Sheer hysterical chaos was taking over.

"Who, who? What is he talking about? What do they want?" Everyone was shouting and screaming over my cries for calm.

"Be quiet! Where are Rozi and Dolly? Where are you hiding them?" The hairy man bellowed as he grabbed me by the shoulders and spat in my face. Everyone fell silent. I tried to stay as calm as possible as I repeated that I didn't know. His face was so repulsive and rough up close; I felt his sharp whiskers brush up against my skin, almost cutting into me. His breath stank of stale curry, alcohol, and cigarettes. He finally pushed me away. I didn't want him to know where the two girls were, not because I liked them but because this group of boys seemed so violent and mean. I genuinely feared what they would do to the two girls if they ever caught up with them.

"Now, everyone, sit down and listen," he ordered.

"Or what?" shouted one of my guests.

"Or this, you cocky cow." He smashed the sofa hard with the bat he held in his hand, and we all jumped.

Aliya broke in, saying, "We know where they are." I was furious with her.

"Aliya be quiet! Don't tell him anything!" I bawled.

"Aliya, Aliya … I know you." He studied Aliya with his menacing face.

"You know me how? Don't be so ridiculous!" she replied in the falsetto tone she would use when I knew she was either nervous or lying.

"Yeah, you were in my French class at school. I remember you."

"I went to an all-girls private school, so I think you are mistaken."

"No, I'm not. I can hear your Brummie accent."

Aliya had no time to refute his accusation. At that moment, we heard screaming from upstairs and a thunderous noise and crying as someone descended the stairs. Julie, one of my guests, flew into the room, followed by one of the other boys. Julie ran in and then headed directly towards the opposite side of the room. God knows what had happened upstairs, but she was shaking and looked terrified. She clutched at her chest area as if protecting herself from any further assault. Salma put her arm around her and comforted her. The other man stood in the doorway, laughing. Soon, there were three of them—smoky, unshaven, and threatening—all blocking the doorway.

"Where are they, then?"

"They were here," explained Aliya, "but they've gone; they ran away. We don't know where to but believe me; we're glad to be rid of them. They were pains in the backside."

The gang of men did eventually leave, but not before verbally insulting us. We tried to reason with them.

"You stuck up whores. You all think you are better than us." The gang leader threw a look at Aliya who pretended not to notice him.

At first, the room fell silent as our attackers had finally departed. There was nothing here for them. No one knew where to look or what to say.

Aliya broke the silence. "Fricking freaks, I've never seen that hairy man in my life."

I could sense the collective sigh of relief, and the short panic breaths radiating from all corners of the room. Julie sobbed gently, while Salma comforted her, caressing the top of her head with her fingertips. The worst was over, but my heart pounded; this should never have happened on my watch, not in my home. Suddenly from nowhere came a thousand micro explosions. Tiny shards of glass flew through the room, narrowly missing Aliya, who managed to cover her face with her arms just in the nick of time. Miraculously she was unharmed. The room was flooded with screams and cries. The assault was finally over. We'd let them win.

I apologised to all my friends with tears in my eyes. I don't think I would feel safe for a long time. All my friends were sweet and supportive, and a whole host of stories and woeful tales about muggings, robberies, bodily attacks on the underground and daylight insults suddenly emerged. London was not a safe place; maybe I didn't know this city after all. Being a doctor and seeing the victims of violent assaults that turned up at casualty made me think how naive I'd been. Salma was very supportive and when all the guests had finally departed, she gave me a long sisterly hug.

Chapter Eight

The Relationships - Laila

The siege had put a strain on us all. The slightest recollection of that evening could spark off a huge argument about who was to blame for the event. Salma would come home and disappear into her room and wade through education files and plan lessons, while Aliya spent a lot of time out with her lawyer friends. Aliya blamed the incident entirely on me for letting the two runaway girls stay at the house. What was I to do?

"How could I let those girls live on the street after that awful commotion at Rikki's party? God knows where they are now and how they are living?" I claimed.

"Oh, they've probably been kidnapped and trafficked by some mafia organised crime gang and are in the Middle East, already dancing on tables somewhere," asserted a smug Aliya.

Raj insisted I install a security system, and so he fitted the house with a video phone so that I could see whoever was at the door.

"If anything like this happens again, call this fast-track number for help. I've let the lads know at the station. They will be here within minutes."

"I'm hardly vulnerable. Aren't there more priority people?" I protested. "I'm more worried about those two crazy runaways and their psycho brothers catching up with them."

"Laila, my love, I'll hunt them down if it's the last thing I do. You shouldn't be living here on your own. You know I am ready to move in."

"I am not on my own; I have the girls and Kamal's always hanging around lately."

"Oh yeah, him," Raj grunted.

"Look, when the time is right, I will break the news to my parents, and as soon as we are wed, we can live together here, but living in sin is not an option."

After I had calmed Raj down and explained no real harm was done, he agreed to look into the situation and merely gather intelligence. Raj would talk to his crime unit and try to find out who were the boys that had barged their way into the house. If they were found, they would be questioned, but I did not want to aggravate the situation, so I merely wanted to forget it. I refused to visit Raj at his police station and make a statement or file charges. Taking the matter further would either place the girls in more danger or even worse, it could necessitate involving my parents.

What had happened to the passive peace-loving Deshi people from the 1960s, and how had the next generation turned into yobs? None of the Deshi men I knew behaved like those boys. They were hard working and ambitious. On the downside, young men of my generation could be spoilt or fussy when it came to choosing a bride; hypocrites, but not vulgar or violent like those boys.

Raj told me the gang problem was not just in the north and

Midlands but in London too; it was just a sign of the times. I wondered whether society was becoming too violent when it spilt over into peoples' safe, middle-class lives, or did I not see the harsh lives of others less fortunate? Raj described a whole new scary world I never knew existed. London was rife with gangs of Deshi boys; their crimes included drug trafficking, robbery, gang rivalry, you name it. Then there were other more sinister criminal gangs too that had grown from new ethnic groups settling in London who engaged in human trafficking, forced labour, or prostitution. A simple looking semi-detached house might house twenty girls who had been duped into coming to England for a job as a nanny or in the beauty business, but they had been drugged, raped, and sold into slavery for paid sex.

My parents were good, kind people, and for my father, religion was his compass for life. He couldn't see how I could ever marry someone outside of my faith. I had tried to approach my parents on many occasions and tell them about Raj, but I knew full well what their reaction would be.

It came down to choosing between the man you loved or parents and faith. For my parents' generation, faith and belief was a crystal-clear issue; a true believer showed their faith through their actions.

My father would say, "Faith can only be continued by bringing our children up in a pious household; marrying outside is out of the question."

His crucial argument was, "How would your children follow traditions and beliefs if both parents were not of the same faith?" My father would declare.

"Aba, do you not think it's more important that my partner and I share the same values? I would share the same faith of a Taliban, and it doesn't mean we would follow the same moral ethical code or have a marriage made in heaven." I replied.

At this point, my father would sulk, hide under this flat cap and read the Guardian. Unfortunately for us—the second generation—we were brought up in a multicultural society and had grown up without these barriers. We spent most of our childhood wanting to be accepted and yet had been told we weren't allowed to belong. Arranged marriages had been a way of taking away our choice, and I know that some girls were resigned to this, whereas others vowed to choose their partners when the time came. The ambassadors for arranging marriages were the aunties; dads kept out of the matchmaking. My parents' marriage was built on years of mutual trust and respect. Things had slowly changed as three decades had passed by. We girls demanded that arranged marriages no longer just meant marrying a person your parents had chosen from the Desh with a questionable biodata, or someone who had nothing in common with your dreams and aspirations and no idea of what made you laugh or cry. As we girls grew up, then so did the boys we'd fought with at our parental curry parties. Most of us struggled to find the perfect balance to please our parents who had showered us for so many years with such love. To break their hearts would be to break our own. I always remember what my mother had once said to me:

"Parental love is the only love where you give and never expect anything in return, and it lasts for all infinity, no matter what."

Perhaps that was our trump card; no matter what we did, no matter how many cultural values we defied in the name of 'freedom to choose', our parents would never really abandon us.

In times of doubt and confusion, I would turn to Salma for advice and her sense of integrity, but I was surprised by her response.

"Why do so many of us not see this as the ultimate sacrifice by allowing our parents to choose our partner? We should be free to choose!" I protested.

"I wonder why western people find it so strange. Just over a century ago, polite classes in this society would arrange marriages between people of the same socioeconomic group. Look at Lady Di and Prince Charles. What was the difference?" Salma explained so eloquently.

"Well, our parents tell us they are trying to protect us, but I think deep down they are protecting themselves and everything they believe in," I replied.

"That's because they've sacrificed a life in their own country for economic gain. They're worried about their customs and culture becoming diluted and dissolved by society, and they realise they may have paid a high price." Salma's explanation of why parents did what they did to us made breaking the news about Raj to my mother and father so much harder.

Aliya's ethos in life was that you get back what you put in; it's not about where you are from. Aliya didn't buy into what she called the immigrant sob story. If you're a hard-working lawyer who works long hours, flirts with the right people and earns lots of money, you'll have a good life. If you're not successful in life, it's because you aren't putting the hours or effort in, and you deserve your lot. Her attitude toward immigrants was the same.

"They should stay in their own countries and not drain all our resources and learn to speak English, or be deported," she cried.

Reminding Aliya that we were daughters of immigrants and calling her narrow-minded and elitist did nothing to sway her or soften her resolve.

Chapter Nine

Kamal – Laila

Kamal had been hanging about the house a lot lately. Ever since I sent Salma home in the taxi with him and his date, Salma would leave the living room as soon as he would turn up, whereas Aliya would tease him about the two girls, Rozi and Dolly. While the girls had been staying at the house, they had flirted unashamedly with Kamal. Like two very ridiculous school girls with a huge crush, they would constantly ask him silly and very personal questions. Despite all the flirtation and a solemn promise to take Rozi and Dolly out on the town, it had all ended in nothing really because before he could take them anywhere, their brothers had turned up, and they had run away.

Kamal and I had been frenemies since our teens. His arrogance about his sense of worth and entitlement irritated me, and then there was his inconsistency with the women and girls he dated, but as adults, we had found something in common, as we both worked in medicine. My negativity towards him had mellowed, and we occasionally hung out together, although my tolerance threshold would last about two hours, and then I would wish him to be gone. As teenagers, we were also often thrown together at parental social events; as adults, we often found ourselves moving in similar social circles at the university. I was witness to his flirty antics and drinking, and he was witness to my relationship with Raj. We both agreed to a vow of silence when it came to our social lives at university. His mother was actively engaged in arranging my future, and I knew for a fact she had her sights set on me for Kamal at one time. I had the sneaking suspicion she was now considering me for her younger brother. I just thought, *NO WAY! Mrs. Rehman keep your passport seeking, younger brother far away from me.*

She had to tread carefully because any rejection from my family would jeopardise the long-time friendship she had enjoyed with my mother and father. Her husband was not a doctor, and she felt this inadequacy deeply, so she made sure all her female friends were doctors' wives, which guaranteed she would never be excluded from any of the important social gatherings or weekend trips to Europe.

Kamal Yaqoob Rehman and his family had originally lived in the north of England somewhere, but Auntie had become ill over some incident that had occurred when Kamal was about 8 or 9 years old, and so they had moved to London. This had always been her wish anyway. For years, Kamal's mother had insisted they move to London so that she could live in a big house and therefore socialise with her London doctors' wives' friends. Her accountant husband was just happy leading a quiet life in Cheshire; he also owned one or two businesses that were run by family friends. Due to problems with the businesses and his wife's illness, he gave in to her wishes and finally came to live in the south. How uncle kept up with her constant demands of gold, jewellery and sarees, I would never know. What also shocked me about this family was that they even had a live-in servant from the homeland. Even with a servant, Auntie would never hang her washing out on the line in the garden; she would always use the tumble dryer. I would often tease Kamal about it.

"Kamal, your family's going to get arrested for keeping a slave, you know that's illegal. You should be washing your own underpants at your age." "I wash my underpants and dry them on the radiator at work. No, actually, I have mine dry cleaned."

"But seriously, Kamal, if Auntie doesn't behave with a bit more humanity and provide better living quarters than a shoe cupboard, she's going to be sued for human rights abuses.

"It's a box room, Laila; that doesn't constitute a shoe cupboard. It's no smaller than the room they give us to sleep in work between shifts, and if you have issues with my mother, speak to her directly."

I suspected Aunty Rehman or even my mother had possibly put Kamal up to hanging out at my house so much, or maybe he just genuinely wanted some company. I know they harboured hopes that one day we would fall in love, marry, and have beautiful, genetically perfect kids who would also be doctors.

"So, what's up with you and Salma since the party?"

"Salma? Who is Salma?"

"Shut up, Kamal! You know very well who she is. I catch you staring at her when she's washing up, and every time you walk into the house, she leaves the room and goes upstairs. What did you do to her in the taxi?"

"Oh, her, your housemate. Yeah, I made out with my girlfriend in the taxi, and she got all judgy and freaked."

I threw the remote control at him. "What is wrong with you?

Chapter Ten

The Weekend – Salma

Laila had been invited to a 16th birthday party that would last all weekend and so begged me to keep her company. We set off on a Friday to help out, party all Saturday and leave on Sunday. Laila was attending as a special favour to her mother. I was nervous about spending the weekend at the house of strangers, but Laila had promised to stay by my side all weekend and not abandon me. The family lived in a huge house south of the M25, which boasted a large and beautiful garden with a lawn that stretched as far as the eyes could see and a wooden summer house. The bushes and shrubbery separated one posh neighbour from another. How this family had managed to buy such an enormous, expensive house was beyond me and everybody else in the community. I had never seen anything like it. I lived in a dreary terrace in the north of Manchester with nothing but a concrete yard for a garden. The party house was to be found in a pretty chocolate box village with a clock, a church, coffee shops, and thatched cottages. Two golden lions sat on either side of a huge wrought iron gate and down a sweeping tree-lined driveway were two very posh cars: one a Mercedes and the other a Toyota 4-wheel drive. They had been carelessly parked in a haphazard angle adjacent to the house.

The party we were due to attend was for the family's teenage daughter. According to Laila, she was pretty spoilt, but we would have endless supplies of cake, curry, and en-suite facilities all weekend. Laila explained that the girl in question was her mother's god-daughter, and

Laila had been undemocratically elected to be the girl's mentor and to set a good example for her now and then.

"They want her to study medicine, so of course, the role of tutoring her has now fallen on me. But she's spoilt and bratty and what her mother doesn't understand is, grades do not make you a decent human being, nor will they get you into medicine or make you a competent doctor. It's also about being a kind, caring human being and having the ability to communicate with people." Laila pulled our suitcases from the boot of the car and dragged the already worn wheels toward a mammoth dark wood door that looked like it had been stolen from a 15th century Castilian palace.

"Laila let me carry something," I protested.

"No, no you are here to relax and keep me company."

Laila's hands were occupied with the bags, so I knocked on the door with the wrought iron knob.

Laila continued her rant. "From the day she was born, this young lady has been given everything she has ever desired and more, and as a result, she has emerged a spoilt, self-indulgent little horror."

I wasn't too sure how enjoyable this weekend would be. After Laila's glowing description of the birthday girl, I just thought maybe it's I who needed to support Laila. The house was truly beautiful. The hostess greeted us at the door. She was about 16, tall, slim, pretty and had very long black hair down to her waist. She wore jeans and a black crop top; her face was soft, and her skin was like delicate porcelain.

"Come on; I'll show the garden. You can see the stage. Nope, I should show you your room first. You won't have to share with my friends. We're all crashing in my room, all 20 of us. OK, not all 20 of us in the same room; I mean the ones I don't really like. Well, they're in the guest rooms, and you're both in the attic."

As she stopped to breathe for one Rimi minute, she stared at me.

"Who are you? Does mummy know you've brought a friend with you, Laila Apa?"

"Don't be so rude, you cheeky lady," replied Laila assertively. For such a young and obviously westernised girl, it was strange to hear her call Laila Apa.

"This is my best friend Salma, and if it weren't for her, I wouldn't be coming at all. What does your mum expect me to do all weekend with a group of twenty, 16-year-old babies, hey! Rimi? I am a grown up. Anyway, Happy Birthday, brat," she whispered under her breath.

This was not the Laila I knew; she was behaving a little impolitely towards Rimi. Laila then handed the present to Rimi's impatient waiting hands.

"Well! You can always go and hang with the aunties," she replied, giggling.

"Umm, where's your mother?" replied Laila. She was trying hard to maintain her serious composure.

And with that, Rimi ran off, shouting as she flew up the stairs to join her friends. "She's out buying me sarees and a suit."

"She's a bit of a brat for 16, isn't she?" declared Laila. "I mean, she hardly acts like someone on the brink of womanhood. I can't stand it when her mum brings her to my house. She's always sneaking into my room and rummaging through everything. Rimi's so cheeky; she tries on all my clothes, and then I find half of them here. It's like I was blessed by not having a younger sister to bug the hell out of me, and instead, I was cursed with Rimi. At least I could beat the hell out of a younger sister. With Rimi, I have to grin and bear it. I am going to have to say something soon because it's beginning to drive me around the bend."

Rimi rushed past us again.

"Can't stop, more guests. Just do what you want, go where you want; I don't careeeeeeeee!"

We carried our cases up three flights of marble staircase and then finally found our rooms at the very top of the house.

"Wow! How rich are these people, Laila?" I asked, eyeing up every exquisite detail of this Bollywood mansion, located slap bang in the southern outskirts of the M25.

"Well, Auntie gets all her fancy stuff imported cheaply from Spain; she has contacts, and so it's all a bit of a façade."

It was a pretty attic room with beams and dark wood furniture, a real Victorian fireplace with a reddish marble surround. It wasn't at all like the Asian houses I had seen in London: 1930s semis patterned with ruby carpet, Italian velvet sofas, Formica kitchens, and green or baby pink bathroom suites.

"If you like this, wait until you see the rest of the house," whispered Laila.

"It's impressive. Auntie's very stylish; I have to hand it to her. It's all period stuff with just a hint of the tasteless. Oh, and the garden, God knows what they have devised for the brat's birthday. It's huge; they even have servant's quarters, well, a box room and a real servant freshly imported from the homeland."

I was shocked at the way Laila spoke so candidly about these people. She was either very familiar with the family or didn't like them.

"The last servant, a poor man from Auntie's village, ran away. He couldn't take it anymore here. I think he ran off to Scotland or somewhere because they were so mean to him and didn't pay him any money. This time, they made sure they brought a young girl—well, a woman—over, because a female would be too inhibited and scared to run off into British society all on her own, so they told her stories of rape, kidnap, and sex slavery. I told Auntie to send the girl to FE College so that she could meet other girls, and Auntie nearly flipped her lid at the thought of giving her ESOL classes. Keep them ignorant, I think, is Auntie's motto."

As Laila unpacked our bags and folded them neatly in the chest of drawers provided, I stepped onto the bed and peeked out of the skylight. The heavens were completely fresh and clear; I could see thousands of stars set like perfect diamonds in the black night sky, like a pure ebony silk bejewelled saree. Laila was mumbling in the background about something she should have told me before we came. My mind had wandered; I was admiring the fabulous view from the skylight. It was like nothing I'd seen before and the sight of such a beautiful, magnificent garden filled me with a familiar warm sensation I had felt only as a child. It reminded me of when I could run the full length of a summer lawn with my friend Kal and then still have enough breath left within me to run even further. I wanted to fall asleep under this almost supernatural starry night and feel its seductive glittery swirls wash over me, while its intoxicating ethereal symphony lulled me to sleep.

I was excited and savoured a yearning to explore this marvellous magical garden. It smelt like a fresh June summer's evening. I had never sensed such a feeling as strong as I had now. At first, it was just a feather-like twinge in my belly, and then all those wonderful childhood memories came flooding back into my mind's eye. Perhaps it was the sight of the ethereal stars, but a powerful sense of my childhood and father's memory filled me with sheer happiness and joy. Why was the feeling so strong? Laila had promised me we would go downstairs and explore the rich Auntie's garden once we had unpacked, rested and freshened up.

Everything in the house was immaculate. The bathroom was beautifully tiled in Moroccan blue, the suite was white, and the taps were ultra-modern with single lever handles, the likes of which I had only seen on adverts in those posh house magazines that feature London penthouse flats or refurbished stately homes. We descended an enormous, winding iron staircase into the hallway and then into the garden. There was a catwalk set up for what would be the fashion show, which would be followed by some traditional Indian dancers. A few of Rimi's specially chosen girlfriends would arrive this evening; they would relax and preen themselves and engage in girly activities before the big party on Saturday. I stood for a moment, gazing at Rimi and her classmates sitting on the grass, relaxing and gossiping, dressed in pretty cotton dresses. Rimi had made all her friends promise to wear Indian clothes at the party. Scores of posh English mothers had descended en masse on the likes of Southall, Green Street or Wembley to buy their daughters sarees and salwar kameez for the party. The London curry mile had never seen so many crazy middle-class non Deshi women all at once and wondered what new fashion trend or Hollywood film had led these mothers to wreak havoc on their little Asiatic enclaves.

The grass was neatly cut, and a high old moss-ridden brick wall surrounded the whole garden. It sloped gently downwards, and then towards what seemed like the end of the garden, where there was a very small summer house made of part wood, part glass. It reminded me of the seaside or shelters in Victorian times, or the summer house in the Sound of Music where Liesel bellows out twenty rounds of "I am 16 going on 17" with her Nazi sympathiser boyfriend, Rolfe. Beyond that, there was a vast number of trees, shrubs, and plants. Laila was a regular visitor here and so didn't share my excitement. I had been worried about visiting a household that I wasn't familiar with. My family and I barely visited anywhere, so I was grateful to escape from the noise and chaos of London after so many months. It felt liberating, and something in my soul promised me it would be an enchanting weekend.

We walked about the mini forest of trees and bushes. I could hear the girls from the lawn laughing and talking. It was only June, but it had been a hot and humid day and felt like an Indian summer. As I walked across the lawn, shafts of light shone through the herbaceous clearings, and I allowed the evening's cool southerly breeze to envelop my face and arms. All I could hear now was the tranquil sound of nature. I found a broken tree trunk and decided to sit down on it to take pleasure in the last of the afternoon's warmth. It had been a stressful week, and London could be an arduous place in the heat when you're stuck on the underground or suffocating on a bus with only a paper fan to keep you cool. It then struck me that I had lived in London for nearly a year. It had broken my mother's heart when I had left, but I had planned to eventually send for both my mother and my sisters once I had settled down and found a place where we could all live. However, London was expensive, and all the nice leafy places were way beyond my financial capabilities. My two sisters would be starting university within the next few years, and we needed to be together as a family. How beautiful this house and garden was; how lucky it was that God had blessed the family with everything they had. I dreamed for a moment that I could offer my mother and sisters anything even remotely resembling this house, just as my father had always wished. But then I remembered how he valued honesty, compassion for his fellow man, and above everything, he treasured us, his wife and three daughters. Just months before he had died, we had visited the Desh. I was only 9 or 10 years old, my other sister was five, and the youngest was yet to be born. My father had to return to the UK early, as he managed a restaurant for two other friends who were partners in the business.

I remember watching him go through the glass screen that divided us from the air passengers. Suddenly, I felt a sense of panic and dread; my young heart felt a terrible sense of foreboding as if I would never see him again. I began to cry out his name. "Aba, Aba!" I screamed uncontrollably. I could not stop; they begged the guards to let me through customs so that I could say goodbye one last time. It took my aunties an hour before they could calm me. My mother told me I was always a calm child, I would hardly ever cry, and I would sleep ever so silently for hours. Perhaps a child instinctively perceives when she is about to lose a parent.

While we were in the homeland, my father had sold fields and property that he and his family owned, so that he might buy into a business and become a third partner. My father sold a large share of the family assets, but he genuinely believed the business in England would succeed. He managed the restaurant for his friends, and he knew it was a growing success. With a share in the profits, he could easily send money to the Desh for his family, send us to a good school and even contemplate buying a nicer house and moving us to the leafy suburbs of Cheshire. Certain friends had helped him long ago when times were challenging in the Desh; they had even helped my father pay for his passage to England. My father wanted to pay back the debt and, I suppose, to prove to his friends and family in the Desh that he was a success in England. He was once a promising young journalist.

My father was naive and much too honest. A large amount of money from the business and a necklace went missing, and all suspicion pointed in the direction of my father. He was too honourable to bicker or even defend himself, and it wasn't the first time he had wrongly been accused of dishonesty. He explained plainly and simply that he had no reason or benefit for doing such a thing. They did not believe him, so he was accused and shunned by the people who claimed to be his dearest friends. Soon after, my father became unwell and then died of a stress-related complication. Everything he had owned, he had put into the business, and so when this large amount of money went missing, he was stripped of everything he had contributed. My mother and sisters were thus left with nothing but the house we lived in.

Even our home was nearly taken from us, with its five tiny rooms and a concrete yard. After my father's death, some of my relatives came to England with a Deshi lawyer demanding the sale of the house and that all the money be taken back to the Desh to buy back the land he had sold. The fact that we were all in mourning, in shock, penniless, and my mother was heavily pregnant, was not an issue to them. According to my relatives, anything my father left behind in the event of his death meant that his 'tiny estate' should rightfully pass on to the first-born boy in the family, who was my cousin Pintu. Luckily, an old college friend of my father intervened and paid for a British lawyer, who then put my greedy relatives straight and told them they had no rights under British law to claim a penny. Who was that man? I would so much like to thank him. I loved my father and will always cherish his memory and all the things he taught me.

I had been sitting in the same spot for at least forty minutes, and my mind had wandered to a melancholy moment in my past. It was a lovely summer's evening, and I was determined to enjoy myself this weekend and forget work and all the other humdrum aspects of everyday

106

life. Suddenly, I was overwhelmed by a strange wave of emotion and apprehension; there was a sudden change of direction in the summer's evening breeze, and it swept right through me and filled my lungs. Panic, excitement, and an imminent sense of fear; something huge and out of my control was about to happen in my life. It was a sensation I didn't recognise.

Chapter Eleven

The Birthday Party – Salma

Rimi the birthday girl was having a fabulous time; her mother and father had agreed to stay away that night so that she and her friends might settle in and relax around the house for a girls' night in. Laila was the token responsible adult to make sure they didn't sneak boys into the house or get drunk on secret bottles of cider. For 16-year-olds, they seemed to be surprisingly girly and immature. I could hear them screaming and running down the landing corridor like six-year-olds in the playground. When working with secondary school children, it worried me how grown up young teenage girls were in Britain, even at thirteen, fourteen years old, they looked like women, even dressed as women, and they physically matured so early. On the non-uniform day, it was difficult to distinguish between staff and pupils. The garish makeup often gave the game away. These girls had forty to fifty years of womanhood ahead of them, so what was the rush? I had approached my twenties with apprehension. I was a 26-year-old woman, but I still felt like a child. What I was entering was a new world of adulthood, but only now was I beginning to realise that it was a vast and daunting place where nothing made sense or followed any logic. Outside the safe cocoon of university life, the real world was a completely different place, and I'm not sure I was quite ready for it.

"She's so spoilt," Laila whispered under her breath. "I never behaved like that at her age. Look at all those CDs strewn across the floor; all scratched with no covers on them. She doesn't care."

As Laila took me from room to room, there was a banquet type buffet laid across an enormous table near the kitchen. There were samosas, bhajis, salads, crisps, and an international mixture of all varieties of snacks.

"Her mother must be a fantastic cook," I said to Laila.

She chuckled. "Auntie, a good cook? My mum hates her cooking; she's awful. My mum says her cooking tastes like Paracetamol; that's why she always takes a dish along with her just in case auntie has cooked something disastrous," she whispered. "They keep a servant, but we're not supposed to mention it. It's like it's there in your face, but everyone pretends she's invisible. We do that very well in our culture; we pretend scandal will disappear if we ignore it long enough."

After touring the beautiful house and witnessing twenty odd teenagers party to snacks and pop music, Laila and I retired to a small and comfy TV room. We chatted for a while about some issues: Aliya and where she was headed with her wild ways and high spending power, how school and my work was progressing, and finally, poor Laila and her predicament with Raj. She was stressed and suffering deeply but constantly tired of hiding her real feelings.

"I do love Raj, but I don't have the guts to tell my parents. I can feel his patience is at breaking point. He's threatened to turn up at the front door and introduce himself. I know the shock would kill mum and dad. I wish I hadn't played the saint all these years and had been a bit more like Aliya—breaking all the rules and not giving a damn. Maybe I shouldn't have feigned the role of a perfect daughter in front of my parents and the aunties for so long."

It's called balancing the imbalance—well, that's what Laila called it. To shock Laila's parents now with this—that their favourite daughter's life had been far from what they could ever have imagined, the news would destroy them completely.

"Salma, so many of our fathers have suffered heart problems from an even smaller crisis than this; the risk of telling him about Raj is too much. I have created this world of deceit myself," Laila wept.

I tried to console Laila but in vain. "Parents' expectations of their children are too unrealistic. They've brought us up in a small, protected world and have not prepared us for the universe beyond. We aren't robots; surely, love existed even in our parents' time." Society and suffocating rules saved our mothers and fathers from scandal; not even our parents' wise teachings could save us from this world. Laila was right, we had nothing to protect us.

To be fair, maybe things were changing. The days when girls would fear the approach of womanhood and the imminent visit of a shadowy man from abroad with a strong accent and huge moustache, whose real age was hard to define, seemed only to apply to Bollywood movies and not to real life. Then again, many girls had married their serious, moustached man from the Desh and were perfectly happy, and he had turned out to be completely kind and agreeable. For others, it had not worked out so well, and there had been scandalous divorces that people whispered about in quiet corners at weddings and birthday parties, but if you were important enough, it was soon conveniently swept under the carpet and forgotten. There were no set rules or guarantees that any marriage would work out anywhere in the world. My parents' generation seemed perfectly happy; my mother loved my father, and her world collapsed when she lost him. Laila's parents seemed perfectly compatible and loved each other too. And that myth that Asian women were subjugated—that woman at Laila's house last autumn, the mother of the snobby boy Kamal, defies that theory.

Marriages among the young Asian community had changed a lot or more like evolved. You married within your community, and it was someone you liked the look of at a wedding or social occasion. Though, the boys still called the shots. If he liked you first (no matter what he looked like), then you were one of the lucky ones. However, you had to be approved and vetted by his very fussy mother. If you failed to meet all the mother-in-law's criteria or her approval, then you were doomed, no matter how much the boy liked you. No girl could be tall enough, clever enough, or pretty enough. And if your skin was too dark, well, the only hope was that you would meet someone, fall in love, and there was no mother in the way. The mothers' brigade was a powerful force indeed within our community. No son would dare confront his mother's wrath on pain of being cursed for fourteen generations to come, from village house to queen of her empire.

"Have you never thought of marrying a man your parents chose for you or met someone you like at a wedding, Laila?" I probed as I searched my brain for a solution.

"The problem is, Salma," Laila explained, "the boys have turned weak on us, and their mothers have the last word when it comes to their future bride. A lot of our boys date non-Asian women at university, you

111

know? Like Kamal. But even he, as stubborn as he is, would never contemplate the thought of eventually introducing her to his family. On the other hand, there is a whole new generation of Asian women marrying outside their community, like me. Daughters are more like our dads when they first came here. We have become strong, resilient and tough like our fathers in the 1960s, while some of our young men have just emerged as a generation of boys tied to their mother's apron strings."

Laila popped out of the TV room for a moment; there was a horrendous noise of screaming girls, and she had to check if they were trashing Auntie's house. My thoughts turned to Aliya who cringed at the thought of marrying a man from her own country. She had never taken to her parental culture or the food. She had visited the homeland as a child and had suffered greatly from the heat. She had contracted chicken pox and had made everyone's life hell: she refused to eat, use the bathroom— and on one occasion, Aliya had insisted on wearing six woolly jumpers in the sweltering heat of the rainy season so that she could become ill and be sent back to England. England and America were the only nations she would ever consider living in, as she believed that these were the only two civilised nations in the world where you could be anything you wanted to be.

Laila, on the other hand, had no aversion to her parental country; she loved visiting it. She adored the peace and simplicity of the village, the lemon and the grapefruit trees, playing, swimming competitions in the lake with her cousins, even when the oldest of the group Mustapha had tried to drown her for being a better swimmer than him. She loved the buzz of travelling on a rickshaw in the dusty capital city or the danger of riding in a paper-thin *nowka* boat on the murky river at sunset. To Laila, the Desh was the most beautiful country in the world. Every time she left, her paternal cousins would shower her with kisses and tears. On her visits, she would lend her services to the International Red Cross or Médecins Sans Frontières. Laila's mother's family were a little snobby. Laila's aunties and uncles could not understand why she would spend so much time with the poor and not prefer to indulge in shopping sprees or visits to the beauty parlour with her cousins, where malnourished 16 year old girls or Filipino women skillfully removed facial hair with merely a piece of string.

Most of Laila's female cousins had studied at university, but their ambition in life still centred on marrying into a good family, looking as white as you could on your wedding day and having children. Even in the Desh, you couldn't get a first-class husband with the perfect bio-data unless you had obtained a first-class college degree. Laila was the type of person who would be sitting in the city's best Italian ice-cream parlour and then she would walk out onto the street and give her stracciatella to the poor little boy who had spent the best part of an hour squashing his face against the window, sadly yearning to know what ice-cream tasted like. She would then force all her cousins to reluctantly give up their ice-creams to the multitude of other poor little children who would suddenly turn up from nowhere. Her cousins hated taking her to the ice-cream parlour for that very reason; they were never allowed to enjoy fully enjoy their gelatos because she would make them feel guilty as hell. However, they loved taking her to the Korean karaoke restaurant because she would sing all their favourite pop songs in perfect English. They especially loved to hear her sing Madonna songs. On one occasion, the other Korean karaoke singers in the restaurant had refused to give Laila the mic because she sang the songs so well, she put them all to shame. Laila's twenty-odd cousins almost caused a riot in the restaurant.

"Give Apa Laila the mic back, you witch! Just because she can sing better than all of you. She is the real Madonna."

Word got around, and they were banned indefinitely from most Korean restaurants in the city.

When Laila returned from checking up on Rimi, who was now causing riots with her friends all over the house, she decided to do her bit as the responsible adult and reproach her, "The house is a mess; there are girls, clothes, and makeup everywhere. I give up." Then we both continued our analysis of parents and our plans.

"I have considered taking a year out from medical school and spending time in another poor continent like South America. I could practise some Spanish, help people and gain a better understanding of another culture. No one would bombard me with silly marriage questions or why the heck I was doing this: I would be like any other voluntary doctor. I hinted at it with my parents, but they were horrified at this suggestion. They said I would be kidnapped by mad Colombian lefty rebels, Sandinistas, or Mexican drug barons and taken off to the hills in exchange for a hefty ransom. No, was their answer, especially if I embarked on such a thing before I was married. Even Raj disagreed with the idea of me spending a year in South America." Laila looked sad and forlorn; her destiny was not hers to choose. She had no choice but to put

114

away such a thought for the time being.

She was tired now after our evening's analysis of Deshi boys and their mothers. She was going to check whether Rimi and her friends were still up and causing havoc around the house. They were indeed causing some mayhem, but it was now mostly confined to Rimi's room; most of the girls were lying on top of the duvets and gossiping in the dark. An old style black and white film was still running on our TV: it was Tiger Bay. I loved the film, but on this occasion, I hadn't been paying attention. I remembered that Laila had something important to tell me but had forgotten. She had just popped out to phone Raj. It was something about the family, but what? I was sure she would tell me in the morning. I was surprised to see no evidence of any other brothers or sisters, and who were her parents? I suppose I would meet them in the morning and thank them for inviting me, although the thought of meeting this auntie who couldn't cook, and her servant terrified me a little. It was a late 1950s bittersweet movie; the Polish man had grown to love this young girl and had sacrificed his freedom for her.

I was suddenly taken aback by the voice of someone in the room.

"Oh, Salma, what are you doing here?"

I looked up and, to my horror, saw Kamal. There was a look of confusion on his face as he observed me. My throat went completely dry, and I suddenly felt sick and dizzy; nothing seemed to come forth from my mouth. He sat down on a sofa opposite me.

"I'm not looking forward to this weekend. I hate teenage girls," Kamal seemed ill at ease and annoyed.

I was hoping, no praying, that perhaps he had been dragged to the party to babysit too. I hoped he wasn't staying the night. I felt so at ease with Laila, but all he would do is ruin the evening by making me feel awkward and uncomfortable. I still had a horror of the taxi journey home fresh in my memory after the disastrous house party. Laila had forced me to take a taxi with him and his girlfriend. She spent the first part of the journey trying to make out with him in front of me, and I suppose, out of some warped sense of respect, Kamal had told the taxi driver to change course and drop her off at the nurses' quarters. Then I had to endure forty endless silent minutes in the taxi with him until I was dropped off at Laila's. Kamal walked me to the house and grabbed hold of the front door handle, he pondered for a moment, his mind preoccupied with something but thankfully, just when I thought he was about to accompany me into the house, he changed his mind and continued his journey home on foot.

"Laila wasn't too keen on being dragged here either. Laila says this family is rich and the party girl is a bit spoilt, but she seemed nice enough to me. Her mother is very bossy as well, so I've come to keep Laila company." I immediately regretted what I had said. It wasn't in my nature to talk about people like that, but Laila's casual sarcasm had rubbed off on me that evening. Then something horrible occurred to me—what if he knew the family? What if they were his friends?

Kamal didn't reply; he just looked at me strangely and scrunched his face up a little. He stood up and walked towards the door. Perhaps I had been a little too rude about the family, but he was rude first. Just then,

116

Laila walked into the room and whacked Kamal on the arm.

"Oh, you, what are you doing here? I thought you'd be at the hospital flirting with the nurses? If I'd known you were coming, I probably would have stayed at home and knitted a jumper or something!" exclaimed Laila.

"Laila, it's always a pleasure to see that pretty face of yours. Give me two minutes, and I'll be back. I am here to grab some things from my room. I am travelling back to London tomorrow morning. I might be forced to stay for the party."

His room? Oh dear! I realised this was Kamal's home, and Rimi was Kamal's sister. What had I said?

Laila leant over and whispered, "Sorry, that's what I'd meant to tell you. I didn't know Kamal was coming home for the weekend, so I thought I could get away with it. I know you aren't keen on him."

The image of his screwed-up, annoyed face just repeated in my head and I felt wretched. Kamal returned and sat down with us both.

"You girls make yourselves at home. I've been at the hospital for over 48 hours. I'm off to bed in a minute. So, Laila, how are the staff at Evelina's treating you?"

"I'm tired all the time, but I love paediatrics. I suppose I've just got to get used to it. Not so keen on this pay deal they're planning for junior doctors. It sounds a bit ill thought out to me."

"It gets worse, so do you think you're cut out for it?" He spoke with such an air of superiority. I could tell Laila was livid with anger, but she answered with her usual calm and composure.

"Well, if you've managed to get away with it all these years, I can't see why I won't cut it as a doctor. Anyway, I went into medicine because I wanted to serve my community, not because mummy told me to and because I like nurses' uniforms."

"You don't still want to work in some squalid refugee camp in Lebanon, do you?"

A message had just beeped on her mobile phone, and she left the room. It was now just Kamal and me, and there was an embarrassing silence. I wanted to say something or be polite, but no words would come to mind when I was in the presence of this person, so I was wildly searching my brain for a way to fathom this horrible situation I was in. *Why would Laila want to subject me to a weekend with two people who were rude to me?* I thought. I had just insulted this man's family. I felt uncomfortable in his mother's presence.

"Are you watching this, or can I turn over?" He had already turned over the channel before I had time to reply.

I choked as I answered, "No, you can watch it … I think I'm going to …"

"You stay," he replied coldly. "I think I am too tired to watch this. I'm off."

When Laila returned, she screwed her face up apologetically. "Now

118

you know why I didn't say anything. I needed your support, please."

I tried to make her feel less guilty, but she needed to know how awful he made me feel.

"I feel so ungrateful; you've been so kind to bring me here, but I don't think Kamal particularly likes me. He hardly says a word to me when I'm in the room. I never know what to say, and now I've just called his sister a brat and insulted his mother."

Laila was silent for a few moments, and then she burst out laughing.

"Good for you, they are snobby and annoying after all. Don't worry, I'll protect you. Kamal can be quite rude and direct, I know, but he's a teddy bear really, it's just a facade. You heard what he said to me. He deserves everything he gets. Oh, I laugh at him, so you should tease him too. He loves to play the serious, sultry doctor."

I don't think she quite understood how self-conscious he made me feel. He never volunteered any conversation. I always feared being ridiculed or laughed at, so generally, I tended to keep quiet, but the silences were so long and tedious I was always left feeling strange and insecure. My defence when he visited Laila's home had been to go about my daily business, read a book, iron, mark books, but with no such armour, I felt vulnerable. The first few occasions Kamal had visited the house, I had offered him tea. Sometimes he accepted, and at other times he had refused and just helped himself. Our conversations had tended to end there.

Chapter Twelve

The Conversation - Salma

My weary eyes had felt ready to close hours ago, but I couldn't sleep. The moonlight beamed through the skylight on to the foot of my bed; it was early summer, so the night felt cool and fresh. The millions of stars in the night sky still sparkled like diamonds set in a saree of pure black elegant silk. I could sense Laila wasn't sleeping but was in deep thought about her problems with Raj. How could she find the courage to tell her parents and break their hearts? It would destroy their belief system and make them realise that their only beautiful, intelligent daughter had been living a lie all these years? This would kill the very essence that made her parents who they were. Laila had kept aloof in her teens and listened to her parents. She had studied hard for her exams and never frequented the pubs or discos like her other friends or concerned herself about boys. She had all along believed she would meet the right Deshi male who was brought up in England and up to standard with her way of thinking. Before Laila had even a chance to leave her adult life, Raj had appeared. He was kind, funny, strong, honest and dependable. Raj had lost his mother when he was just a baby, and this had touched Laila's heart. When other mothers came to collect their children from infant school, he was often left all alone and waiting for some stranger or taxi to pick him up. Laila could never abandon him now. Raj, her mother, her father; she held them all equally within her heart. Fully aware that she was awake and that her eyes were still open, I decided to speak.

"Laila, no matter how much you love your parents and don't want to disappoint them, at the end of the day, they love you and would never abandon you. As adults, there are so many tough choices we will have to make."

"But I can't; I just can't do it," she replied.

"This is just the beginning, the stage in your life you have to make a choice. Your parents can't make that decision for you; you will have to. It doesn't matter what tradition says, if tradition gets in the way of your path in life, then do the inevitable—go it alone. They'll always come back to you, no matter what you do. Whatever decisions or mistakes you make, your parents love you, Laila; it's so obvious. You see, that's the difference: our parents never really abandon us."

"I'm so surprised you're talking like this. I thought you were much more traditional. I always thought you disapproved of me … deep down."

"I know I probably wouldn't have a fiancé as you do. I don't know, it's just a set of rules I've been brought up with … It's probably nothing to do with rules. I lie. I think it's most likely because the opportunity has never come my way." There were no rules. I knew I wasn't pretty like Laila. I was plain and invisible, so to avoid disappointment, I hid behind a rigid set of beliefs.

Laila sighed. "I've been brought up with those rules too, and I believe you should stick to them, but … God! This is punishment. This is my punishment for doing what I do, for taking this path … for not getting married before."

I could tell she was desperately traumatised and needed words of comfort.

"Laila, I see it every day at school; I see the Asian girls I teach, and we're all in the same boat together. Who's to say if I wasn't as gorgeous as you, some wonderful man could have swept me off my feet, and … well, where would my belief system be then?"

"Oh, Salma, you're so sweet and kind," Laila sighed.

"Listen, we don't live in the 19th century anymore. Yes, we must hold on to our beliefs and morals; those are what sustain us and keep us protected. But the pressures we have on us, in the west and this year 1999—it's not what our grandmothers had to sustain, it was a hundred times easier for them. What if they had been brought up in the era of Sodom and Gomorrah? I think they would have found it hard not to fall from grace," I explained.

"No! Our grandmothers had to marry a man they didn't know, put up with some wicked mother-in-law and have multiple children … Oh, and cook for the whole village on one of those little clay stoves and mill rice on a wooden dhenki. So, you think I'm a fallen soul?" she whispered.

"No, not at all. I admire you. Look at what you've achieved: you help people and save their lives, Laila. Don't you think God sees that? And who's to say women didn't fall in love and had tumultuous lives centuries ago? All those historical or famous women throughout time who have refused to play by society's rules. Think of Cleopatra, Helen of Troy, Hurrem, or Frida Kahlo, who lived by their own rulebooks and made their own decisions. And Lady Diana too. OK, she paid with her life, but she followed her heart—she was the Queen of Hearts. When we are all dead

122

and gone, who will society remember, the rebels or conformers? Will anyone care about the sins committed in our lifetime? No, they will admire us for them, even celebrate them. Look at it this way: at least you, and we, have a choice now."

"Do we?"

"Yes, Laila, we do."

She lay back in her bed, clutched the white duvet in her hands and looked up at the ceiling. "You have a special job. Educating our future doctors and lawyers is not an easy task," Laila said wearily.

"Yes, and our upcoming hooligans, dictators, or even future world terrorists too," I replied.

I must have fallen asleep. Laila's voice called over to me in a loud whisper. "Salma, Salma, are you awake?"

"Um, are you feeling better now, Laila?" I asked, still half-comatose and woozy from my slumber. It must have been at least 3 a.m.

"I am, but I can't seem to fall asleep. I want to phone Raj, but there's no signal here. Come to the garden with me."

We tip-toed down the stairs; there was surprisingly still a lot of noise coming from Rimi's bedroom. The girls were singing Spice Girls anthems and laughing very loudly.

Downstairs near the kitchen, there was a servant's room or

cupboard. The servant had kept a low profile, as the sight of her would prompt questions from Rimi's English friends. Inside the house had felt hot and sticky, so the night breeze felt refreshing. My body began to feel comfortable and cool again. As we looked back at the house from the garden, a light could be seen from Rimi's room.

"Auntie will be furious if those girls get no sleep for tomorrow's party. They're going to stage a fashion show, and there's some teeny pop group coming: the Kent version of the Back-Street Boys. Oh, and Rimi's got a special dance planned. I suppose she won't be doing any of that if she stays up all night."

I suggested we might have a word with the girls when we returned to the house.

"It'll be quite funny if she's too wiped out to do her stupid little dance thing." Laila chuckled mischievously. Her mood had lightened; it was nice to hear her giggle.

As we approached the far end of the garden, Laila walked off to the left to talk to Raj. As he was on nights at the hospital, and as it was a Friday night, Raj would be in A & E or wrestling drunks in Leicester Square. I found myself alone in this mammoth dark garden. As I walked towards the bench at the bottom of the lawn, my mind heavy with thought, I observed something move. I noticed a tall, dark figure emerge from the bushes. My heart seemed to stop for a moment. There was an awkward few second's silence. The night covered me, yet I felt curiously exposed.

"So, why are you up so late?" a deep voice inquired.

I stood still in front of this unfriendly man - Kamal. As I was open to the elements dressed in just a cotton white nightie, I wrapped my shawl around me. I longed for the anonymity of my room, but there was nowhere now to turn. "Laila … Laila needed fresh air."

"They're making so much noise; I can't sleep." Kamal sat down on the grass and then pointed his cigarette towards Rimi's bedroom window.

There was not much more to say. I wished I could sit down; the alternative was to make some excuse and go back to my room. We were both uneasily silent. I thought how rude Kamal was not to offer me a seat, but then again, I had offended him earlier.

"Take a seat, I'll be off soon," Kamal stood up to leave just as I settled down on the grass. I imagined Kamal would get up and leave, but he didn't. He was usually so quiet, moody, even distant, but the night made him seem more relaxed and conversational. "Is Laila upset about that man she's seeing? Raj, I mean."

How much did Kamal know? I had to be discreet about what Laila had divulged. Yes, Kamal did know, as I had heard them talking late during one of his recent visits. "Yes, Laila needs to sort some things out."

"They'll never agree— Laila's parents. Mixed-faith marriages never work."

What a hypocrite! I thought; what had he been doing kissing that nurse woman at that party months ago? "It depends on a lot of things," I replied.

"On what?" he replied sharply. I think he was surprised I had a voice, never mind any point of view. I imagined Kamal would be even more surprised if my opinion were to hold any reasonable liberal argument.

"Well, it often depends on who is the dominant partner in the relationship or who the child will spend the most amount of its time with. Even if the child is born into a family where the wife has taken on the father's faith, unless he spends a predominant amount of time with the child, he or she will take on the religious beliefs of the mother."

"You seem very convinced by your theory," murmured a perplexed Kamal.

"I minored in RE and English." Kamal was looking at me strangely.

"Why an English teacher and the RE thing? Why not something more?"

"You mean sciences or the Deshi top three?"

I spotted a hint of a grin emerge through Kamal's normally serious composure.

"Because I adore books," I replied, a little cross with his narrow view of the arts. "I always have, I love to read and to lose myself in a world very different from my own. Learning about other faiths, diverse worlds and culture is a life line for me. I like what we can discover about people of historical significance and what we can learn—their flaws, their triumphs, and their failures."

"Why?" replied a curious and thoroughly captivated Kamal.

"So, we never again commit those mistakes again in our lifetime, and we learn from the past."

"I just think people who do the arts aren't very good at sciences." Kamal still needed convincing.

"You know the world needs its fair share of journalists, teachers, and arty people; the universe requires balance. Arty people are always society's biggest threat. Who else do all the dictators kill when populations rise up against the status quo? Well anyway, we weren't all born to be doctors and dentists." I replied with indignation. "Art is a lie that makes us realise the truth. Art washes away from the soul the dust of everyday life." I whispered.

Kamal rested his head in his hands and repeated what I had said. Having a conversation with this man was strange. It was like talking to a completely different person, or was it that I was behaving contrary to my usual self? I dreaded any moment Kamal would say one harsh word, and I would return to my quiet, inhibited self.

"Which arty person said that?" Kamal replied.

"Pablo Picasso."

"What did he mean?"

"Without art how can we see the bare truth of our humanity and our flaws? Art refreshes and recycles the soul. I think that's what he meant."

"Where did your art gene come from then, Salma?" I had never heard Kamal say my name out loud before.

"My father was a literature graduate; he loved to read and study books."

"That's unusual for one of our dad's generation. What did he do here then – lecture?" Kamal enquired.

I felt ashamed to tell the truth that my dad amounted to nothing but a disgraced waiter.

"My father never did anything related to his degree when he came to this country. Times have changed since the 1960s and 1970s. I'm doing what he never could."

"Your father, is he a doctor like you?" I wanted to change the subject.

"No, no, he's an accountant."

"Oh, so ..." What I wanted to ask was whether his father wasn't very good at sciences either, but of course, I would never really say it out loud. "Why did you study medicine then?" I asked.

"I suppose I became a doctor because that's what my mother always had planned for me. I don't often think what else I would have done. My mother had my life planned out from the womb. I think I wanted to be, you know ... I don't remember what I wanted to be when I was young, but I know it's wasn't medicine. I probably wanted to be a train

128

driver or an astronaut or something. I was ill for some time when I was young and lost my memory: I hardly remember anything before my 8th or 9th birthday. Sometimes I sit on this lawn and remember running up and down it like some demented little monkey, hiding under tables and stealing onion bhajis and samosas. I don't know; it was a long time ago."

For just a second, I almost felt a tiny ache in my heart. Kamal almost seemed like another person, a little-lost boy full of doubt and pain. He was quiet for a moment as if his mind had wandered to another time and place. He bowed his head, stretched his arms and then turned his head towards me. "OK, but that was then, a long time ago. Whoever I was before nine years old, I am not that person anymore."

The clouds were now hiding millions of stars. I couldn't work out if Kamal was staring at me or whether I was too short-sighted to make him out now the moon had decided to hide behind the ephemeral night cloud. Laila had finished her conversation and was walking towards us. I stood up very quickly to leave and tried to hide the fact that the story of Kamal's childhood had actually touched my heart. Laila's eyes were still red, and I knew she would need comforting. We walked to our room, leaving Kamal still sitting in the garden, smoking his cigarette. If there had been any chance of leaving, I would have taken it, but for Laila's sake, I would stay as long as she needed me.

When I told Laila of my conversation, she replied that Kamal was his mother's son. For a moment during our conversation, Kamal had seemed reasonably friendly.

"Oh yeah, Kamal's a total charm with the uncles and aunties, but I have had the privilege of studying with him, and we've coincided at social occasions; I know exactly what he is like. He can be rude and brash. He's left many a broken heart at university and the hospital. That's because he is relatively good-looking, so he gets away with behaving like a jerk. But no one escapes from anything long-term. Kamal's time will come," Laila assured me.

"One day Kamal will fall in love with some gorgeous, brainy girl, and she'll break his heart, I guarantee it. To tell you the truth, I don't think Kamal is capable of love; I think he is a narcissist."

Once back in the house, Laila suggested to Rimi that and her friends get some sleep, or she would make sure all the aunties and uncles came to her party. Rimi and her friends protested, giggled, and then agreed.

Chapter Thirteen

The Mean Auntie – Salma

When the morning of the party arrived, Laila and I were both shattered, but there was much to do. Kamal was nowhere to be seen. Rimi and her friends refused to get out of bed, despite her sixteenth birthday party now only hours away. Rimi's parents had agreed to leave her alone in the house with her friends and would come for only part of the evening to watch her dance and cut the cake. On Sunday, once all the guests were gone, the family would have a birthday meal together.

It pained me to see the servant in the kitchen cooking breakfast for so many fussy young girls. Kushi was a small skinny thing and wore a tight-fitting red and green saree. I wondered whether that was how Kamal saw me: not as a skinny servant girl dressed in 6 yards of emerald cotton, but as some lesser person not worthy of talking to and not part of his jet-set doctor life. Perhaps that would explain why he behaved so superior and aloof in my presence. The servant girl said nothing; she just cooked and cleaned on automatic pilot. It was as if Kushi were just a ghost existing in another dimension, oblivious to anyone around her and the fact that she was now living in a completely different world to her homeland.

"How are your mother tongue skills?" asked Laila.

"Not very good. What about yours?" I replied.

We asked the servant whether we could help in broken, awful mother tongue. Even the most illiterate villager from the darkest corners of the Desh would have laughed. Kushi seemed horrified at the prospect of two Memsahibs helping her in the kitchen, but Laila and I insisted. We compromised by carrying plates of toast, coffee, juice, and other sweet delicacies into the dining room.

The girls arrived in dribs and drabs. Some ate a lot; others merely sniffed and pulled faces at what was on offer.

Laila complained that with all that was happening in her life, the last thing she needed was to have to organise some sixteen-year-old spoiled brat's party for Kent's finest. Laila was determined that Rimi would have to do her part.

"Where the heck is Kamal? Smoking in the garden at 10 in the morning, I suppose?" Laila remarked sarcastically.

A little later, I heard Laila shouting at Rimi and telling her to get ready and attend to her guests.

Laila screamed up the stairs, "Get ready, lazy pants! Who do you think we are? Your servants?" I suppose this is what Laila would have been like had she been an older sister. Although sometimes I wondered, had Laila had a real sibling, she would be nothing like Rimi.

Despite the protests, Rimi did eventually heed Laila's request. The stage where Rimi was to dance had still to be decorated, and people had been contracted to do exactly that—adorn the stage. Even before breakfast had barely been cleared from the dining table, the pizza was about to arrive for all the guests' lunch. The party caterers would then arrive around half-past six to set up the party food in the large dining room. The band had been substituted at the last minute for a disco. All this needed to be organised. Kamal had escaped, so Laila and I were the only responsible adults left to take on such a colossal task.

The evening arrived; Rimi had been practising her dance all day. Her coordination had been somewhat off because she was tired and so she had occasionally taken out her frustration on the poor servant girl by screaming at her in such a high-pitched octave that I am sure only dogs and cats could hear her in the Yorkshire Dales. The garden trees were adorned with white, pink, and blue fairy lights. There were balloons and flowers on each table and a banner that read "Happy 16th Birthday Rimi." The chairs were laid out, and the other guests would soon be arriving, including Rimi's mother and father and some of their very close friends.

"Now I know why they invited me," complained Laila. "Unpaid bloody labour! At least the servant gets some kind of wage. It's the last thing I need right now. If I don't tell my parents this weekend, Raj has threatened to visit them himself. Do you know how much time I've bought already?" she scowled. Laila observed the poor, small-looking servant girl and added, "I hope she learns enough English to sue them for every penny they have. It's disgusting having a servant in this day and age. It's nothing short of modern-day domestic servitude. I am sure there is some slavery legislation coming out soon from the Home Office. We should get Aliya on to this case or, better still, report them to Amnesty International or the UK border control."

It had been a long hot day, and I could tell Laila was exhausted and had just about enough. I had tried to give her as much support as possible with the organisation of things, but very little could console her now as regards matters of her heart. "Oh, look, Auntie and her gang are here. I am going to wash my hands of all this now, and she can take over. And where is that infuriating son of hers?" A fatigued Laila walked towards the house. I could tell she yearned for solitude, so I did not run after her.

I stood alone by the brightly decorated stage where Rimi was introducing her dance. She was dressed very prettily like a traditional village girl and wore a green and red crisp cotton saree, and a garland of delicate white flowers in her hair. Unlike the real village girl slaving in their kitchen, this particular more privileged village girl also wore a vast amount of gold jewellery, from her hands right down to her ankles. There was also a large gold chain that hung from her ear right to her nose. Rimi jingled and jangled across the stage to everyone's delight. They all laughed and smiled as they clapped their hands together in glee. Her English friends seemed to enjoy the traditional music and danced towards the front of the stage. They managed to blend a whole host of rhythms and dance cultures into some very beautiful moves. I looked over at the group of older women. I could not distinguish Kamal's mother from the many faces. I thought I would remember her from our first meeting in Laila's house almost a year ago.

And then I spotted her: the mother of all mothers—the lady of the house. Auntie Lamb Chop had the same shiny ebony forties style bouffant, so black that it would be possible to absorb us all and the universe deep into its abyss. As an added attraction, there were now ringlets hanging over each ear. She also wore a silky green and red saree, with an Indian style sleeveless saree blouse and piles of copious gold bracelets along her thick, strong arms. As I watched the dancing, she walked up behind me. Laila was trying to remain inconspicuous.

"Salma," Laila whispered into my ear, "I'm sneaking out for a bit. I don't know how long I'll be, but I've got to go. I promise I'll be back as soon as possible."

"What shall I say if anyone asks after you? I don't know anyone here," I explained, a little nervous at the thought of being abandoned.

"Say it's a medical emergency. I'm on call or something. Look, I must go."

I felt anxious, but I knew Laila had serious problems that needed to be sorted out. I looked around me. I could get away with being invisible; I'm sure I could. As long as Kamal didn't turn up and start interrogating me about why I called his sister spoilt and other weird things about the arts versus the sciences. Anyway, there was no reason why I couldn't just be one of Rimi's school friends.

It truly was a beautiful summer's evening. It had been one of those glorious sunsets when all your senses seem heightened by the warm winds and spice coloured sky. There were masses of delicious food laid both inside the dining room and on another table outside in the garden. There were samosas, bhajis, salads, tandoori chicken, and kebabs. The smell was truly awesome, and everyone was devouring the food with delight. I filled my plate discreetly and ate in a quiet corner. Rimi had finished her dance, and there was birthday cake and some speeches to get through before the disco started.

As I stood to the side of the stage, I noticed Kamal skulking at the back of the garden. He stood alone and looked serious; no one seemed to wonder where he was. I was tired and couldn't face another conversation with him. Most of the girls were dancing, and the aunties and uncles were already in their groups, chatting away. I would become conspicuous if I loitered any longer. I would go to my room, have a lie-down and wait for Laila to come back. I could look up at the skylight, contemplate the millions of stars and listen to the music from the disco from afar. As I walked through the kitchen, I noticed the servant girl sitting on a low circular wicker chair. Kushi was motionless, staring at nothing; she had an absent faraway look in her eyes. Perhaps this was all too alien for her, perhaps she was thinking, *What the heck am I doing here? Or What is that strange raucous hullabaloo?* Or perhaps Kushi was just lonely and missing home. *How inhumane,* I thought, *to bring her here, only to leave her in the dark on a kitchen floor.* As I began to ascend the stairs, I was confronted by a short, stocky lady in a saree. She stopped in front of me and so I acknowledged her. The stocky lady grabbed me by the chin, squeezed my cheeks and looked deep into my eyes.

"Hello, darling, who are you?"

"I'm Salma"

She continued staring intensely at my face as if studying it.

"Do I know you? Who are your parents?"

"No, I don't think so, Auntie. I'm from Manchester, in the north."

"Yes, I know Manchester" she replied.

"OK, enjoy the party," she added, and then she was gone.

I must have been sleeping for at least 2 hours. It was about midnight. I could still hear the party from inside my room, but there was no sign of Laila, so I decided to freshen up and look for her in the garden.

As I walked down the attic room steps, I was curious to peek into some of the other rooms on the first-floor. It was a vast landing, and many doors came off it. I went into what I assumed was Rimi's room; there was a huge wrought iron bed in the middle. There was a dreamy white fluffy duvet huddled into a mess and hanging off the end of the bed. The room was peach and complemented by other fairy-tale colours and enormous Mexican rustic wardrobes and cupboards. There was a door that led to a gigantic long dressing room with dozens of brightly coloured spangley shalwar kameez and various English outfits. The dressing room led on to another en-suite bathroom which was also peach in keeping with the bedroom colour scheme. There were makeshift beds all over the floor and fluffy toys everywhere. What also struck me was a pink stereo system and the vast collection of CDs this young girl possessed. They were all strewn across the floor. On one dresser, there were pictures of Rimi as a baby, and others as a toddler posing with her older brother Kamal. In the picture, he looked very loving and caring towards her. Kamal was laughing for once in his life. I noticed that when he smiled, there was kindness and charm I had never seen in him before. Rimi was sitting on Kamal's knee and looking straight at him and smiling; it was a really cute joyful type of laugh.

I then entered what must have been a boy's room once. There was an old BBC style DOS computer in a corner on the floor that looked like it belonged to the stone age. There were A Level study aids and masses of science books, some medical related. I guessed immediately that this bedroom belonged to Kamal. On a table in the corner of the room there was a more up to date laptop and printer and immediately above that sat a TV and video recorder. In contrast to Rimi's room, this room seemed old, dark and abandoned. It looked like a space someone just used for sleeping in; it had no character, no warmth, no life. I presumed Kamal still used this room and had not officially moved out of his parental home. He had done nothing to the room to make it seem his. There were no photos of his family or friends and there were no posters or pictures to brighten up the room, nothing. I don't know why I was so inquisitive and nosey; it was as if I was play-acting at being a detective. I was looking for evidence of something—an answer to a question that was nagging at the back of my mind. I could tell the owner of this room desired to be long gone. I felt uncomfortable as if I was invading his privacy. There was one last door that lay at the end of a lengthy corridor. It was a long walk towards the entrance, and I imagined that this door would be mysteriously locked and that whatever questions lay dormant and unanswered deep in my subconscious, I would find the answer to everything in this room.

As I walked down the corridor towards the light, it became apparent that several voices were coming from the master bedroom. It was a familiar sound; it reminded me of a very long time ago when my mother was well and would sit with the other aunties, and they would all chit-chat

138

and gossip about a variety of things all evening while dousing each other's hair in coconut oil. I felt nervous about approaching a room full of people I didn't know, but a powerful sense of curiosity drove me toward the noise, and the familiarity of the sound made it almost impossible for me to break away from my present course. The door was slightly ajar, and although I could hear words, I could not quite catch the sense of what they were talking about. The voices were high pitched, higher than Rimi's when she bossed the servant girl in the kitchen. One voice in particular reminded me of one of those old whistling stove kettles wobbling dementedly on the hearth. Several people seemed to be speaking with ferocity, competing for a spot so they might air their opinion above the rest. They seemed angry at something, and other women seemed to be trying in vain to appease a lady with a loud and most hysterical, shrill voice.

"Why is this girl here in my house? Who has invited her? This is an insult to my husband, my family and me. She must leave. I want her to leave."

"But she is not responsible for her father's bad ways. Of course, it cannot harm to let this girl stay. She will be gone in the morning, and Rehman Bhabi, you can forget everything."

"This girl does not know what happened. Please, Rehman Bhabi, just let her stay; don't be so hard on her."

"Why should Bhabi let her stay? Her presence in this house is an insult to Rehman Bhabi."

"No, no, you cannot blame the daughter for the parents' mistake; she seems like a nice girl."

"Chowdhury Bhabi isn't well; she has not been well ever since the incident. We must not curse Chowdhury Bhabi."

"Chowdhury Bhabi is fine; she's probably ill from shame."

"And this girl should be embarrassed for coming to my house, eating my food, insulting my generosity. I curse her; I curse her mother and 14 generations of her family. I want her out, out of my house." The hysterical kettle woman continued her vicious attack. "Her father is a liar; her mother is a liar." Her voice was now loud, shrill and full of emotion. "And I do not have to host a liar's daughter in my house!" she shrieked. "What's Chaila Bhabi thinking to let her daughter mix with this girl, this liar, this low-class girl from nowhere?"

"But she is a teacher, a school teacher."

"Is that all, a school teacher? My son is a doctor, a consultant. I cannot breathe!" she shrieked. No one seemed to come to her aid, so the angry auntie miraculously managed to find some more breath to rant on. "Every family would want my son for their son-in-law. He has a first class honour in medicine." The aunties were silent and let her go on; I think they wanted her to blow her own trumpet until the angry auntie was too exhausted to blow any more. They probably also thought it would be good quality fodder, so they could then gossip about her overconfident and yet arrogant outburst for months to come. Angry auntie was about to rupture a blood vessel or at least something if she carried on in this manner. "Her father was useless, and so is she. A school teacher. What is a school

140

teacher? My son is a doctor."

Why was Kamal's mother so angry with these people? What had they done to her and her family for her to speak with such anger and venom? The aunties knew now she had passed the point of any reasonable argument, and she was now in just insulting mode. They had not stopped angry auntie ranting abuse, and in many ways, they had fed her with more food to fuel her anger. But now it was time to stop; she was very close to insulting everyone. Despite most of the aunties' husbands being doctors, not all their children had made it into the same profession as her son.

It took me several minutes before I realised all that anger and disgust was directed at my family and me. "Chowdhury Bhabi isn't well; she has not been well ever since the incident." She must have been speaking about my mother. The lady on the stairs who grabbed my face earlier must have known of my family's misfortune and had told Kamal's mother. I knew I shouldn't have come to this house; I had a strange foreboding that something would happen this weekend. It had been nagging in the pit of my belly, forewarning me of this. It's funny how sometimes your body picks up on things even before your mind does. As I heard the words these aunties spewed out with such malice, I realised that my face and body were burning, and I sensed a tight knot in my throat. There had been all the warning signs that something was not right. The door had been ajar, and my eyes had rested on a family picture on the dresser. The first part of the bedroom was a dressing area, and so the aunties had not been able to see me, but I was able to hear them. Amongst the mass of voices, it was not always clear what they were saying, but make no mistake, their tone was angry, and the name of my family was mentioned on more than one occasion.

Chapter Fourteen

Rolf and Liesl – Salma

As a child, I had never really cried much. I prided myself on not being a crybaby, except for one occasion at the airport and then at my father's funeral as they removed his body from our house. This would then be the third time I had cried in my life. The pain was too strong, and it was more than I could bear. I ran down the steps, blinded by the tears. All I wanted to do was get out of this marble, gilded fortress, feeling like a fool and a fraud. I had a sense of unease from the moment I entered the house. The whole weekend had been a dream-like experience, and now the dream was turning into a nightmare. I ran into the garden, past the stage, the chairs, and the mess left from the party, just so long as I could get as far away as possible. I could lose myself amongst the trees and bushes, to hide all the shame and torment of my past. I could hardly breathe from the gush of tears that poured down my face. I was shaking with shame. Who was I to come to the home of respectable people and believe all could be forgotten? It couldn't be. My past, my future, everything that I am, all lay in the hands of those women in that upstairs room. The mean aunties were judge and jury, and I was now forever condemned to live under their scrutiny and their approval. My community hated me, but where else did I fit in? Without my community, I had no identity, no sense of belonging to anything, but I had to fit in somewhere.

Summer raindrops spattered on the mosaic paving; the storm was sure to follow next. I would take refuge and disappear amid the colossal garden, because I didn't want to be in a house filled with such venom and hate. Had I known where the heck I was, I would have packed my bags and walked home, but I was in the middle of nowhere. My feet were tired, my eyes were sore, and my heart ached. I just thought of my father and wished him here; his comfortable lap, his soft reassuring voice of calm and reason. How could those mean women destroy all that was dear and sacred to me? I was powerless to fight back and defend my father's memory. What a wretched, horrible daughter I was. My head felt heavy, and I buried my humiliation in my shaking hands. I sobbed uncontrollably on a bench at the bottom of the garden for at least ten minutes. I knew there was a negative mood towards my family from the community and especially towards my father, but it was never blatant or obvious. It was mostly just a feeling or the fact that very few people mixed with us and that my parents' close social circle from all those years ago had abandoned us during my father's death. We never had any reason to have to confront people; we had simply disappeared off the social scene and the face of the earth. My mother, sisters, and I had all kept a very low profile for many years.

I planned my escape from the house this very night, but what would Laila say if I were to have disappeared in the morning? I would have to explain to her why I had left—it was all too humiliating. Laila knew very little about my past, and I would be devastated if I lost her friendship and respect. Laila was like a sister to me. I was trapped and in a no-win situation. What could I do? I couldn't bear the thought of going back in the house and having to face a shameful and degrading confrontation with a mob of angry saree ladies. The whole experience was crushing my insides; I felt lost, my throat hurt from crying, and my belly ached from emptiness. The helpless feeling of being incapable of defending those that I loved most dearly filled my heart with shame and remorse. I was a terrible ungrateful daughter. As I continued to sob into my trembling hands, a feeling of panic suddenly struck me: I was not alone in the garden. I could see the glowing end of a cigarette dancing in the dark, not very far from where I was sitting. I didn't know who it was, but they must have been watching me for at least ten minutes. I was embarrassed, as they must have seen me crying. A deep voice called out to me: it was Kamal.

"Salma, Salma, what's up?"

"Nothing," I sobbed. "Absolutely nothing."

I felt the presence of a soft hand almost caress my shoulder and then retreat as I flinched. An overwhelming ache enveloped my body; I dared not look at him. My face was swollen, and my nose was running furiously. I know I must have looked a hideous sight. No one had ever seen me cry, and I was determined not to let this arrogant man be the first. If Kamal were ever to come to know the source of my pain, then I would be subjected to even further humiliation. All I wanted right now was for someone to soothe me and take the pain away. The warmth of a kind hand, even Kamal's hand, would have been a welcome comfort. I had no hankie to blow my nose on, and I knew I looked a sight with stuff running down my face, so I buried my head in my hands.

"Something has upset you. What is it? I mean, can I help?" Kamal must have seen all the contents of my nose running down my face and handed me a cloth. "Wipe your face with this."

"It's just the ... It's just something not very important ... Well, not very important to you ... but important to me." I was blubbering. I looked down at the cloth he had handed to me; it was his posh designer shirt, and I had left him wearing just a scruffy over-washed grey cotton T-shirt. "It's of no consequence, and I just want to forget it."

"OK, then; come and sit down here and dry your face. Oh, and where's Laila gone to? Have you both quarrelled or something?"

"No, she popped out to see ... you know, who called her a few hours ago and she's not come back yet."

We both sat on the garden bench, speechless and motionless, staring into the night sky.

"Has someone said something to upset you? Was it me? Have I been rude? Was I impolite with you before? You know my sister is a brat; Laila tells me all the time. I wasn't offended. I thought it was funny. You didn't realise this was my house?"

"No, of course not," I replied. "I'm just not ... not very good at large social gatherings; I feel a little overwhelmed. And I am sorry about that misunderstanding earlier, I didn't realise."

"And that's what made you cry?" Kamal seemed shocked at the thought. I didn't reply; my silence must have made him uncomfortable, so he started rambling. "We used to live in the north years and years ago; I hardly remember. It's funny, when I first saw you at a wedding in Ealing last September, I thought for a moment I recognised you from somewhere, but I realised I couldn't have known you. We don't mix in the same social

146

circles, do we?" Kamal fiddled about with his cigarette lighter. "And then I saw you a couple of times on the tube."

"Really? When did you see me on the tube?" I replied. I heard the words, but they weren't registering. Everything those ladies had said in that room was spinning around incessantly in my head.

"You were fast asleep; I didn't want to wake you. On another occasion, I nearly warned you because I thought you might miss your stop, and then you woke up just in time." This was not the Kamal I knew—sociable, chatting, even caring. "You need to socialise more, then it won't seem such a trauma. I hate socialising, it is tedious. All these pointless weddings my mother drags me along to—so she can parade single girls in front of me. I work long hours at the hospital, and I've got hordes of exams to get through."

"You look like the type of person with lots of friends and non-stop social life," I added.

"Not really. I date a lot. Too much. I need more time on my own to take stock of what I've achieved in my life up to now and where I will go from here. You know, I was thinking about our conversation last night, about what I wanted to be when I grew up, and then I remembered."

"What was it, then?" I asked, curious to know what jet-set job the younger Kamal had aspired to be.

"I wanted to be a driver Bhai."

"A driver Bhai?" I said with a giggle.

"Yes, I loved cars as a child. You know, when I was a junior doctor in A & E, patients would visit the aftercare surgery and tell me they had caught a cold or sore toe, and I would think, *Just go away and leave me alone.*"

"No!" I replied in horror. "If a child came up to me and said, 'Miss, how do you spell launderette?' and I said, 'Go away and leave me alone,' I'd get the sack."

"Actually, how do you spell launderette?" Kamal replied.

"I don't have a clue." This seemed to amuse Kamal greatly, and he spent about two whole minutes laughing.

"I thought you were a prude. You know, a traditional type that wears a long plait at the back of her head and has no opinions. You've surprised me. I like surprises."

"Well, I think you're not particularly friendly."

"Oh, and has Laila told you what a ladies' man I am?" Kamal laughed.

"Yes."

"But it's only until I find the perfect wife."

"And you openly admit it?" I asked, shocked at his candour.

"Yes, yes, I do." Then Kamal seemed to stop for a moment and paused. Kamal's following question confused me. I was baffled because I hadn't ever really thought about it even in my mind. "She has me all

148

wrong—Laila." Kamal had stopped laughing and was now staring at me strangely. "Salma, are you arranged, you know, with someone?"

"No, no, I'm not, I ... I don't have time to think of that side of things. I'm so busy with my new job and looking after my family. My mum doesn't get many queries about me. Thank God! I suppose it looks like a horrendous experience—if you're in love with someone else, that is." I paused for a moment, "I think I will always be master of my own path, no one will ever choose for me."

"Then you are very lucky. And yeah, you're right; it is a horrendous experience if you are in love with someone else," Kamal replied softly. I could feel his eyes burning into me and was too mortified to look up at him. I could sense he was somewhat self-conscious too. I was silent. "If I've embarrassed you, I apologise." The tips of his fingers gently touched my arm. It was like an electric shock discharge through my body, and I instantly pulled away.

I wanted to go back into the house at this point, but it had started to rain, and so we were both trapped in the Sound of Music summer house. But I was no Liesel, and Kamal was no Rolfe, the Nazi sympathiser. The frame had no door and was open to the elements. The warm rain forced its way in and beat gently onto my face, washing away whatever remnants of mascara and lipstick were left on my skin, which felt raw and sticky under my fingers. The thunder clouds roared like angry gods of Olympus, and the lighting illuminated the trees with powerful explosive strikes. We both sat very quietly and awkward as the rain beat heavily on

149

to the roof, trapped in a small space by nature's most powerful force. I could feel Kamal's presence so close I could hardly breathe. My mind was blank, and I desperately searched for something to say, but I felt profoundly self-conscious.

Kamal decided to break the silence. He leant towards me, extending his hand. "Salma; there is something I want to ask you."

I looked at him, too tired and confused to process what might come next.

"There you are, Salma!" Laila cried as she emerged from the shadows of the garden. "I've been looking for you everywhere."

It was very late, about three in the morning. Laila had turned up from her rendezvous with Raj. She approached me in the garden as I sat still in awkward silence with Kamal. Laila approached us, blurry-eyed but determined to smile. Kamal took the hint and said that he would see us both in the morning.

"What were you doing with him?" Laila asked, but without waiting for an answer. Then Laila informed me how it was now officially over between her and Raj. "I chickened out, Salma. I couldn't do it. When it came to it, I couldn't tell my parents about him, so we split up. Raj was angry as he walked off towards his squad car and drove off into the night." I caressed Laila's shoulder as she told me the rest of the night's events. "I could see Raj rubbing his eyes. He was crying—silently. I made him weep like a lost little boy." Laila's eyes were filling with teardrops again and she blew her nose. "I feel too raw to give intimate details now. I can't stay a moment longer."

Laila knew it would seem impolite, but she couldn't face a barrage of questions and general queries from the mean aunties about why she wasn't married yet, after what she had just experienced that evening. A traumatic and emotional event such as this puts everything else into perspective, so being rude to the aunties didn't seem such a big deal anymore. Laila's suggestion to pack our bags and leave without a word was like music to my ears.

The whole weekend at Kamal's parental home had been so strange. First the insults from the aunties, which all seemed like a dream I'd imagined, then my conversation with Kamal. On the one hand, I had confirmed to myself that he was a flirt and egotistical, but on the other hand, maybe he wasn't so bad. He had opinions, fears, and ambitions like everyone. Under no circumstances would I tell Laila about what had happened that evening.

Sure enough, Kamal's mother complained about Laila sneaking off, but Laila's mother defended her by saying she must have been on call. Funnily enough, Kamal's mother mentioned nothing of her annoyance at me for staying at her house 'uninvited', unless Laila's mother had been just too polite to mention anything to her daughter. All in all, I was just happy to have left that house.

On the car journey home, as Kamal and his family home faded into the distance, Laila and I had, at last, escaped our Rocky Horror weekend. Despite the unbearable event with his mother and the aunties, I thought how surprised and wrong I had been about Kamal. What he had said that night circulated over and over in my head. Kamal wasn't happy in medicine; he just wanted to drive cars or be an astronaut. Underneath the egotistical exterior was, in fact, a man who was possibly not that happy with the choices he had made in his life. It gave me a guilty sense of comfort that even under the most polished and confident façade, there was sometimes just a mere mortal like the rest of us fighting whatever life threw at us. I supposed our newly found friendship would be short-lived now his mother would tell him of my past, but it was of no consequence now. I was beginning to contemplate my life; constantly on the fringe, on the outside looking in, never belonging to anyone or anything.

Chapter Fifteen

The Break Up – Laila

I felt guilty for leaving Salma at the mercy of Kamal and his mother. The weekend had been a disaster: Raj had given me a deadline to tell my parents, and when the time arrived, I had been incapable of telling my mum and dad the truth. Raj went off in a terrible rage, and we haven't spoken since. Raj asked me several times if I had explained our situation to my mother and father, and each time I had told him that now was not the right moment, but I would be telling them anytime soon. Days turned into weeks, and then into months, and Raj had no more patience left in him. He was keen to set up a family and a home but did not understand that things were not that simple. During the weekend that I had attended Rimi's sweet sixteenth, Raj had accused me of giving more importance to silly parties and Kamal than to our relationship. I explained that it would have been rude had I not attended the party and that I had promised to help and was there representing my family. This was not enough; Raj set me the impossible task of telling my parents that very weekend. I was trapped and had no choice but to leave the party and meet with him to talk about the future.

"You talk of always standing up for what you believe in, of following your heart's true belief. I don't see you fighting for us. I put up with you being ogled at—like a prize for auction—and how many times have I told you how much it hurts me knowing you've got to meet other men?" Raj protested.

I explained how they meant nothing; I was going through the motions to please my parents. I tried to explain things to Raj the best way I could. "I can't hurt the people I love most in this world. They love me, they adore me. My parents would lay down their lives for me. How do you expect me to change who they are in an instant? They're the kindest, most generous people in the whole world. How do you expect me to destroy them?" I defended my parents' point of view for so long that Raj had become deaf to anything I had to say.

"Why can't you let me be part of that, then? Why can't I be loved too by your family? You say they're good people, so why can't they accept and grow to love me?" Raj's protestations broke my heart, but I was powerless.

"They are good people, but I can't change them. I don't want my mum and dad to be so westernised that I can't even recognise them. They wouldn't be my parents, would they?" I replied.

"So, your parents' observance of their customs and identity means not accepting someone like me, a man that loves and adores you and would offer you everything? Is that how these wonderful parents of yours show their love towards you? The daughter that loves them so much, and they repay you by selling you off to a man who could never love you the way I do?"

"I don't know!" I shouted. "I don't know." Oh, how did it get so complicated!

Raj threatened to phone my parents then and there. The shock would have been too much for them to take.

Too many deadlines had come and gone, now Raj would never believe me if I were to put events off any longer. The desperation to be recognised and accepted ate away at Raj every day. His family consisted of just himself and a drunken old father. His mother died when he was little. When his mother passed away, his father drowned his sorrow in drink. Raj believed that once my parents had met him, he was sure they would accept him, trust him and come to love him as a son. Despite all the love I possessed for my parents, the cruelty of the faith issue would be something I would never come to terms with until my dying day. We weren't different species of life forms; we were both human beings designed to love, hate, and procreate, yet the way we worshipped separated us from ever living as man and wife. It's the cruellest of all things I can imagine. The harsh irony was that not even I was fully convinced that the strength of our love could survive the sacred duties and convictions that develop with age and maturity. I wasn't a great practitioner of religious beliefs, even though I did deep down believe. In years to come, I knew I would embrace my faith with more solemnity, and I would also seek to pass on to my children what my parents had taught me. Could Raj be part of all this? Although from a mixed-faith background, he had no real religious convictions and saw himself very much as an agnostic.

So, Raj dialled my parents' number amidst a flood of rage, betrayal, and tears and spoke to them. My father answered, but on hearing my father's voice, Raj froze. No matter how much he tried to get the words out, Raj couldn't bring himself to say them. Once those words were spoken, there would be no return. Whether it was from fear of hurting my father or, worse still, the possibility of rejection, Raj could not utter a word. In his frustration, he threw the phone at the car windscreen. When it ricocheted clumsily off the glass and landed on the floor, Raj picked it up and threw it out of the window with all his force.

"Happy now?" he sobbed indignantly. I was terrified at this sudden show of violence from a man who I was expected to spend the rest of my life with. I stretched out my hand to calm him as I did in the hospital when people were distressed or troubled, but he flung it away with his arm. He began to drive very fast. I was primarily concerned with our safety rather than Raj's career. My instinct told me that it wasn't a good idea to talk at this point. I felt confused. Was I more concerned about his hurt and disappointment, or about the consequences had he succeeded in telling my parents? I couldn't face him right now; I feared my silence made me transparent, and Raj knew exactly what I was thinking, plus the fact that he had hurt my arm when he had forcibly pushed it away. I had to get out, get home and take it all in. For the rest of the journey, we continued in silence. Raj was breathing heavily, trying hard not to cry or maybe even shout. I did not look at him when I left the car; I daren't.

Raj and I made no arrangements to see one another, and nothing was said. Now back at home, and the prospect of exams and long hours at the hospital ahead of me, it was finally time to dull the pain and get on with everyday living. Was I heartless by not shedding a tear over my breakup yet? Everyday life was so stressful and fast that sometimes it was too difficult to get bogged down with real feelings; they just got in the way. I knew the moment I took a second's rest, it would all come tumbling down on me like a mammoth avalanche of pain.

Salma was kind and reassured me that everything would work out. "Give the whole break up some breathing time. Time to heal and reflect and then when you are ready, you'll know when the moment is right to speak to Raj."

I thanked her for her concern. It worried me how calm and even nonchalant I felt about the whole event. I wouldn't sit around crying about my loss. I planned to get on with things. I would lose myself in my work. My Pre-Reg year was coming to an end, so maybe I could even start thinking about applying for a year abroad in South America—where I could visit my little adopted boy, Eduardo. I loved the soothing sound of Andean flute music. Not long ago, a Peruvian group was playing in Hyde Park. It reminded me of my visits to Retiro Park in Madrid and watching the summer evening fall on the lake. Beautiful couples walked hand-in-hand down the many dusty paths buzzing with peddlers, artists, and fortune tellers. On hearing the sounds of the flute, I would feel unexpectedly uplifted and a sensation of sheer joy and liberation. Suddenly, I felt a rush of adrenaline and a desire to organise and plan a thousand projects for the next ten years of my life. I could pick up learning Spanish again and take up where I left off at A Level: I was pretty good at the language. The following advice from Salma seemed to clarify things for me:

"All the bad experiences, the hurt and the pain, they make up only a tiny part of our whole life. Every fresh venture we embark on is like starting afresh, and then so many things can happen. We can learn amazing things about ourselves and the people around us; we can make new friendships, fall in love. Every experience is like a rebirth. We can't change the past, but we can enjoy our present and take pleasure in planning our future."

After a week of behaving like a zombie, I decided to be proactive. I'd been invited to a football match/picnic. Two rival groups (doctors' sons vs non-doctors' sons) would be playing against each other somewhere in a park in Berkshire. The organiser assured me no parents would be there, just us young single people and some recently married couples. I had neglected my community long enough, and now it was time to keep busy and mingle again. I'd ask Salma and Aliya to join me. Salma would say yes, as she never really had any social life of her own; Aliya would say no, as her social life was so full.

Things had taken on a new phase with Aliya's relationship. Her romance had reached a new level, and things seemed to be serious between herself and Jonathan. He constantly asked her, and no one else, to accompany him on several social occasions. She had been invited to numerous weekend parties at Jonathan's family home, and he had introduced her to his most intimate old school friends. Jonathan was a charming, well-mannered type of boy, and it was easy to see how a girl like Aliya could have captured his curiosity. Jonathan had a positive influence on Aliya, as she seemed much more mellow and friendlier than usual. Aliya's normal self-was cool and calculating, and she only had harsh words to say when she opened her mouth. She tended to be extremely jealous and would seek out and often orchestrate the downfall of any rival that may get in her way. On the other hand, she was strong and assertive. Aliya was sometimes a little dismissive of Salma and would on occasion attempt to put her down, but Salma was oblivious to anything around her, as she kept her thoughts to herself and her head in her books.

About two weeks had passed since Kamal's bratty sister's party and my breakup with Raj. I had still heard nothing. The good news was that Aliya had become engaged to her lovely, posh boy Jonathan. She illustrated her emotions of happiness most bizarrely. I would have thought that any would-be bride who had landed such a colossally rich beau despite the odds would have been positively ecstatic. However, Aliya remained incredibly cool. Her false posh southern accent had suddenly become even more snobbish. Her speech was slower and more deliberate as if she were pretending to be a Home Counties debutante.

"Jonathan's grandmother lives in a castle in Ireland with its own stream, and we were wondering whether that would be a good venue for the wedding, or perhaps a chateau in the south of France."

Aliya managed to mention every hope and dream she had imagined for her wedding and her happily ever after life together, but not once did she mention the huge mother of all engagement rings she was wearing on her finger. However, Aliya did manage to wave it several times in front of my face, and she even managed to accidentally hit me with it and scratch my nose.

"Aliya, your engagement ring is spectacular. Yes, it's really pretty," I commented while nursing my now wounded nose.

"Jonathan bought it in the Big Apple because I told him I loved the film Breakfast at Tiffany's. Can you believe he snuck off and bought it in New York?"

"You're a very lucky girl, Aliya. I suppose you're a bit like Audrey Hepburn in the film. Aren't you into endless shopping and hunting down rich men?" I ridiculed. But Aliya rightly pretended not to hear my comments.

"When are you going to tell your parents?" I continued.

Aliya was silent for a moment, and then she suddenly changed the subject.

"I've wanted to be engaged forever, but a wedding this summer is definitely out of the question. Oh! I'm meeting Jonathan's parents this weekend."

I had never met Aliya's parents, but I imagined them to be pretty wealthy and liberal enough to allow her to marry someone English and from another religion. That was normally the big sticking point in most mixed-faith marriages. Anyway, I was genuinely happy for her and wished her all the best. What I hadn't realised though, until she had later let it slip, was that neither anyone at work nor both sets of parents knew anything about their plans to get married. Jonathan had asked Aliya not to wear the ring at work until he had spoken to his parents first. Word could get to them through work because the law firm bosses were his uncles. It had just occurred to me that Aliya had aimed for the top in her career and was very nearly there. Jonathan had told his parents he wanted to talk to them about a very serious and personal matter, so they were not to go off golfing in Marbella that weekend.

160

Chapter Sixteen

The Picnic – Laila

It turned out to be another warm early summer's day in June. I'd convinced Salma not to go back to Manchester yet, as I had heaps of things planned for the summer. I know she was missing her family; I was being selfish. I needed her support to get me through these difficult weeks after my break-up with Raj. Salma said the Northern town where she lived depressed her, it was dull and grey, and it brought on melancholy thoughts. She couldn't afford to become too depressed, as her mother was already ill and showing signs of early dementia. Salma was the head of the household and her family all relied on her strength and her salary. As the only breadwinner, she had to hold it together for her younger sisters. She planned to bring her family to London as soon as both her sisters finished their A-levels and had secured places at London universities. As things stood, Salma felt she would never be able to buy a house or make a home for her mother and sisters. A strong pound, demand for housing, and low-interest rates had caused prices to soar, and each month, everything she earned became less and less. It was sad because she did work hard. Even the East End of London was out of her price range, and West London was just impossible.

We drove in convoy to the picnic. Salma seemed distracted and pensive; I worried whether I was keeping her away from her family and was being somewhat selfish. I know Salma worried about her mother and sisters constantly; she would phone them nearly every day without fail and always send money for bills, food, and course books for her sisters. I had heard nothing from Raj for over a month, and although I felt some degree of guilt, I also began to experience a sense of relief and liberation. I believe my feelings for him had always been sincere, but he was beginning to suffocate me, and I was quite honestly not ready to give up my parents' love for a lifetime with him. No more sneaking or tiptoeing into my own bedroom after a night at the hospital while Raj slept off his shift. I would do my best to be as quiet as a mouse but would always manage to drop a heap of my things on the floor and wake him up. "Sorry!" would be my daily mantra. When Raj had moved all his things out of my room, I could finally make a star with my outstretched arms and legs in my own bed. When it came down to it, I chose my freedom and my parents over a life with Raj.

It was a crazy drive to the park in Windsor. The girls had insisted on taking an alternative route to the boys, and so both the females and males raced to see who would arrive at our first destination. Sofia, the driver, suddenly stuck her two fingers up at the boy's car as she sped off; even Salma momentarily woke from her quiet thoughts and stared in sheer amazement. The use of bad language was deemed as vulgar, and yet here we were twenty-five years on, no parents in sight, breaking national speed limits and swearing at one another.

It was a light-hearted game of football. Each side represented a region of the Desh. It was northerners against southerners. For the first hour of the picnic, we spent our time talking about work, and then we began to talk non-stop about weddings, caterers, venues, and sarees. Venues were top of the list. We had progressed from school halls and were now venturing into new exciting and interesting locations: country manors, gardens, marquees, and even castles were all the rage now. The only hitch was that we ate curry at our weddings, and most venues insisted on their own caterers. No matter how much we tried to negotiate, the quality of food could never be compromised. One hotel had insisted their chef had received the best curry training, but no way did the curry taste the same.

"My mother even adds curry and spices to the turkey on Christmas day or the roast lamb on Sundays," claimed one girl.

There were no new novelties in wedding sarees; brides still liked them red, covered in gold and expensive, although some were daring to try new colours like blue or cream. All this talk of marriage made me think that maybe I'd been looking in the wrong direction and avoiding a path in life that was not so bad. These would-be brides all seemed happy enough to be marrying within our community. What struck me most of all when watching these couples was how at ease and in love they seemed with their fiancées. One girl stroked the hair of her husband-to-be as he laid his head on her lap, and they weren't even married yet. I had known many of these boys since childhood and saw most of them as rivals or playmates, not as potential husband material, but suddenly I felt like an outsider, suddenly I wanted to feel as happy.

I could have consoled myself by talking to Salma, but she was pretending to read her book. I could tell Salma wasn't focusing on her story or the words.

"Salma, do you want to go for a walk?" I beckoned.

Salma and I walked around the town for around an hour. We looked through a quaint shop window and discovered a beautiful coffee shop called Café Milano. It was like entering into a continental European parallel world. But this was not the Mediterranean full of tacky tourists, this was gourmet Europe; a stylish coffee shop painted in mint and peach—even the air conditioning pipes were part of the trendy decor. The owners were an Italian man and a Spanish woman. Both had been fed up with their endless dead-end jobs, so they had decided to trade everything in and set up shop, or should I say a coffee shop. The first shop had originally opened in Madrid, and now they had decided to venture into the English market. It was true that the British were becoming more Mediterranean in their behaviour, although I frankly had not seen any evidence of this yet, as people still seemed either over-polite or on edge. But this coffee shop was continental bliss; it was like they had picked up a piece of Madrid and transported it to this touristy spot of old-fashioned Britain. The people sipping coffee and engaging in chit-chat at the tables looked suspiciously tanned and non-Anglo Saxon. Maybe they were summer exchange students. It had a strong smell of coffee, real coffee, and the taste; it was creamy and sweet without leaving a bitter aftertaste in your mouth. They called it 'Café con Leche'. I tried explaining these thoughts and feeling to Salma, and while she listened with interest, she had only been abroad once, and that was the Desh. In Britain, Salma had only visited the Lake District (as a child) and London, so she knew very little outside her hometown.

As we arrived back from our walk, it was halftime, so the team members were resting and happily stuffing samosas and biryani as the picnic was being served. I ran to the car to offer the readymade samosas

164

Salma had fried the night before. I couldn't cook, although Aliya was even worse than me, that's why she always ate out, ordered home deliveries, or bought microwave food. Nila, a bossy newlywed, jumped on us as if we were two naughty school girls who had snuck off on a school trip.

"Where have you two been? You left all the hard work to us."

"Oh, but we're leaving all the entertaining to the married girls," I answered. "I could never be as good a hostess as you, Nila."

"She can't even fry an egg," claimed her husband. Nila nudged him in the waist. "I cooked that byriani," her husband laughed.

"And where did you learn to cook such a delicious byriani then?" I probed, waiting to hear some cooking tips from Nila's master curry chef husband.

"Well! You can only water down your mum's curries for so long before they go off," he replied.

"Yuk," we all screamed. But Nila's husband was right. Living at home and not going into halls at university was creating a generation of girls who were becoming spoilt and useless in the kitchen. We didn't have the culinary expertise our mums boasted, and we took their delicious dishes for granted. Suddenly, panic struck. What would we do when our mums weren't around? Who would cook that mouth-watering, spectacular food—recipes that had been passed down from mother to daughter for generations? It was no good going down to the local curry house; that food was nothing like my mother's. For one thing, it was cooked by men.

165

Salma could cook tasty authentic dishes, she had the knack and knew exactly how to blend the spices, so the meat and vegetables would soak up all the delectable flavours of the spices. Salma had spent a lot of time at home, but she had been forced to practically run the household, as her mother had been unwell since her father's death.

I looked at all the couples around me; they seemed at ease and lost within each other's company. One husband was tickling his wife, and another ran around the picnic chasing his fiancée, others were a little more conservative. The couples certainly wouldn't have behaved like this in front of our parents. I was no prude outside my community, but within it, I kept a certain level of decorum. I suppose these young couples were married now, and after years of mild-mannered oppression and tyranny at the hands of our parents, they should be allowed a little flirtation. Suddenly, I felt a pang of jealousy for what they had. Even the snobby girl from the Desh with the headband and strong accent was having fun as she fed her husband onion bhajis with her fingers. I was missing out because of my obstinacy.

As a child, I had promised myself to marry for love, not money, not good looks or even education. Salma was pretty, had a heart of gold, was intelligent and a good cook and yet had never had a proposal. What more did these mothers want? I was quite fed up with the constant inspections by the aunties making comments behind my back and the long line of suitors that meant nothing to me. Some of the men were arrogant, others sad and pitiful, or obsessed with alien life forms. Maybe I hadn't given any of these boys a chance because I had failed to see past their annoying mothers, just as they only wished to see as far as my parents' good name and wealth.

I was suddenly surprised to see Kamal run on to the field. He sprinted across the lawn and began kicking the ball around with one of the teams.

"What's he doing here?" I whispered to Salma. She shrugged her shoulders. As Kamal showed off his skills with the ball, he began looking our way and grinning. *Why is Kamal smiling at me so much?* I thought. I looked at him suspiciously; I hoped his mother had not put him up to this. Before I could say any more, he was sitting beside us. "Why are you so happy?" I asked Kamal. "… And shouldn't you be playing around with some bimbo somewhere? Oh! Where's that 'I've been to Saudi' nurse you're always kissing? Yes, Kamal, Salma saw you kissing, or should I say snogging her at that party, you shameless hussy."

Normally, Kamal would call me names back like a tart or even worse, but this time, he was quiet and looked genuinely embarrassed.

"I don't have a clue what you're talking about, Laila." He turned away from me and looked straight at Salma. "I'm off down to the North of Spain next weekend with some friends. We're going to stay at a property in a fishing village. Would you like to come with us"?

"What, Marbella?" I replied excitedly.

"No, it's the very western tip of Spain overlooking the Atlantic Ocean. It's not the Mediterranean; it's an oceanic climate. Wild rainy winters but pretty nice warm summers, and it's got panoramic views. My friend has got a boat moored in the fishing village, and they're thinking of taking it out to sea. Are you going to be joining us?"

"We'll think about it," I replied. "I'll tell you in a few days; we're very busy at the moment, partying and stuff."

"Well, that Spanish doctor Francisco I told you about, the one who's a top paediatrician in Spain. He works for Médecins Sans Frontières; he'll be there."

"Really?" I replied enthusiastically.

Kamal had me in a corner; I had to go. I'd wanted to meet this Spanish doctor for a long time. He had bought a stash of books for Eduardo the South American boy I sponsored, and I wanted to thank him. Why was Kamal so friendly to me suddenly? I had been asking him for months to introduce me to this doctor, yet he never seemed to get around to organising anything, despite constant promises. Kamal must be taking an interest in me. I'll go for the weekend, meet the doctor, and then I would make it clear I wasn't interested in Kamal.

The Spanish doctor Francisco was supposed to be very attractive. One of my colleagues who had met him told me he had intense dark eyes with long, girly lashes, olive skin, and thick black hair. When Dr. Francisco spoke, it was with a strong Spanish accent that made you feel self-conscious and go weak at the knees. He had spent a few years working in Eastern Europe and spoke all the languages of that region perfectly, including Russian. He had married a Bosnian girl, and they had eventually come to live in England. Stories like that made me green with envy. I wished I could catch the eye of any intelligent and rich foreign man who would suddenly take me away and save me from all this. Francisco's mother was a famous doctor turned Socialist politician from the Mediterranean Levante region of Spain, but Francisco had trained as a doctor in the windy Atlantic north of the Iberian Peninsula. He was very clued up on world politics and issues and would have long extreme discussions about globalisation and third world debt. I mainly wanted to meet him so that he could point me in the right direction concerning working in South America and which organisation would be best to work for.

As the game of football continued, I left Kamal and Salma chatting; he seemed friendlier towards her now. I made conversation with some of the other girls I had neglected for most of the afternoon. They spoke of married life and pregnancy, but I had little to say on the subject except from a medical point of view.

"You are so lucky to be single; you'll get the cream of the crop," explained Nila with a hint of pity you only hear from married women.

"Well, most of you have already taken the cream of the crop, so what exactly is left for us?" I answered.

"Oh, but you are so fair skinned, tall and a medic," replied Nila.

"Nila," I retorted, "if I went on Shaadi.com every five minutes, then maybe I might have found a life partner by now. But unlike many of you, I didn't choose that route. I want to fall in love." Nila was too incensed to reply and pretended not to hear me. She threw me one last look of disapproval and then sauntered over to the married girls.

On the one hand, I felt left out and on the other hand, lucky not to be tied down just yet. As I watched Kamal speak with Salma, I noticed something different about him: he seemed more mature and increasingly relaxed. Kamal was smiling, which made him look handsome. I don't deny he was ever bad looking, but he was moody and arrogant at work, which gave him a dislikeable quality for me. Women at work loved him for being like that. He had them all falling for him, and he had broken many hearts along the way and showed very little mercy. Kamal had a hard heart, and once you lost his interest, there was very little chance of changing his mind, even if you laid it out on a plate for him. He had always seen me as a bit of a challenge, and out of respect for my family, I suppose he would never mess around with me unless there was a serious commitment. I kept him constantly at arm's length, so maybe I'd overlooked him. I know Kamal's mother had been chasing me for years. It would possibly take some effort on my side to see Kamal other than as some annoying, vain and distant relative.

I looked at the girls around me chatting happily. They seemed content with what they had, and they hadn't complicated their lives with conditions and impossible situations. Kamal had listened to my advice about Salma; he was now friendly with her, chatting away and smiling sweetly. A few months ago, he had been ignoring Salma or giving her dirty looks every time she walked into the room.

Chapter Seventeen

The Lake – Salma

Laila and I were to spend a long bank holiday weekend on the northern coast of Spain. It was only one hour away by plane and sixteen hours on the ferry from Southampton. I had never had the chance to travel abroad. I needed to go home to Manchester soon, but Laila was depressed about her break-up with Raj, and I know she needed me to be with her for a couple of weeks at least. She had been so kind to me; I could hardly abandon her now. I was on school holiday, but Laila still had to slog away at work. The horrible incident at Rimi's birthday party still preyed on my mind, but fortunately, the unkind words the ladies had uttered about my father had not emanated from that room. Neither Kamal nor Laila seemed to know anything about the incident. Kamal was much friendlier and had newly found sociability towards me, although I still felt a little nervous about him. I felt this civility that he now showed towards me was somewhat tenuous and could disintegrate at any time.

Aliya had now met her prospective in-laws, but all had not gone as she had wished. The parents had been polite enough, but they had asked very little about her, and this made her feel that perhaps they were not taking her relationship with Jonathan particularly seriously. They had spent the dinner evening talking about themselves, although it was mainly Jonathan's mother, as his father had hardly uttered a word. Their house was a beautiful four-storey Georgian townhouse on an exclusive road in Chelsea. On hearing this, Laila had asked Aliya if she knew what she was getting herself into, to which she replied:

"I know exactly what I'm getting into. I didn't study law and manage to work for one of the best law firms in the city to end up sweating over a clay stove in the Deshi back of beyond and be ogled at by my in-laws and some old village idiots. I'll leave that life to you two."

"Well, if you're happy having a couple of cardboard snobs for in-laws, then that's your choice. Can you imagine them at one of our weddings?" replied Laila tauntingly.

"What on earth makes you think I'm going to have an Asian wedding? The fact that your parents would expect you to have one doesn't mean we are all condemned to that fate," exclaimed Aliya.

Aliya later confessed to me that she had just planned to get married in a registry office and had no intention of telling her parents, but Jonathan had got back to her after the meeting with his parents and said they would like to meet Aliya's parents before any wedding vows were exchanged. I concluded that Aliya hadn't thought all of this through properly and just wanted to marry as quickly as possible. Neither was I convinced she was going to manage to marry this man without parental consent on both sides. Aliya seemed nervous and tense and in a quandary about something. "Salma," she whispered so Laila wouldn't hear, "do you think I could manage to marry Jonathan without his mother and father meeting my parents? Like if we eloped abroad or something?"

"I don't know. Maybe."

"No, it's a silly idea. I'd never get away with it," Aliya mumbled under her breath. I was surprised that she was so nervous about her parents meeting her future in-laws, as she had described them as being so liberal in the past. And why was she confiding in me and not Laila? "Don't mention anything to Laila on the matter. She is a bit of a prude," she whispered.

"I promise I won't. Your secret is safe with me."

It was about one week into my summer holiday and time for me to take stock and reflect on the year that had passed. I was beginning to think London was not the ideal place for my family to settle. On the one hand, it was a fascinating city, vibrant and alive with shops, theatres, cafes, historic sites and endless numbers of handsome-looking people. On the other hand, it could be fast, cold, dirty and unforgiving if you were poor. It was strange; when I was with Laila, it felt cosmopolitan, continental and fun, and when I slogged my way to work on a school day, it felt unfriendly and hard work. I had worked at several schools around London, and especially in the East End. I supplied regularly at a secondary school in Hackney, and on the odd occasion, I would be called to cover primary schools, which I loved to do. When the children were high as kites and not able to settle, I would sing them into submission. The school in Hackney had offered me a permanent position. The pupils were great; many of them were of Asian origin, and I think they enjoyed having a teacher with whom they could identify. I had to decline the offer because I had to be flexible in case, I needed to take a train back to Manchester for my mum or some other family crisis. Furthermore, I wasn't sure which London Universities my sisters would be attending. Once all these things were settled, I could look for a permanent job, visit the banks and try and get a mortgage to see whether we could finally settle down somewhere away from all of our painful past, unhappy memories and start afresh.

Time in school was sometimes enjoyable if the pupils were motivated, and the staff were friendly, but on the other hand, if the children were difficult, it could be mentally and physically exhausting. I would sometimes sit in a staff room and feel completely invisible, and no one would talk to me throughout the whole day. Then again, there were a lot of young newly qualified teachers working on supply, and when I met one in the same situation as myself, it was nice to compare notes, share experiences and know I was not alone. I had had a hard time during my teacher training experience and lost a lot of my confidence. One school had been supportive, and the staff and girls were great, but at another school, my mentor had been a bit of a battle-axe who had not helped me that much. She was a perfectionist, and her classroom had to be left just so, or she'd call me at home and demand I come in early to put everything back in its place. She gossiped about other teachers to me and seemed very friendly, and then she would be cold and ignore me as if I had done something to upset or offend her. She would never accept any of my teaching ideas as adequate and would quote out of the National Curriculum as it were the Bible: anything to make me believe that I was irrelevant or not adequate. She had been annoyed that I had managed to pass my teaching practice when she had recommended that I fail. I had been too upset and overworked to mention anything to my college tutor, but a friend, on seeing how upset I was, spoke to my tutor and as a result, an independent inspector was brought in to see me. I then passed. It had been a hard year of work, but I managed to put some money aside for a house.

Living now in a world of her own, my mother would often sit us down and tell us stories of when she was a child in the Desh. She had a thousand tales to tell us and could quite easily sit for hours at the table, telling us her amazing stories. Her eyes would light up, with a childlike expression on her face. It was strange; my mother had hardly aged at all in the last twenty years. Her hair was still jet black, wavy and fell to her waist. Her skin was soft and a beautiful shade of golden brown. My grandfather had worked on the railways, he was a station master. By coincidence, my paternal grandfather also worked on the railways and was a station inspector. On one occasion when my mother was a child, she was playing by the family pond, when she saw what she thought were two giant yellow bananas walking towards her. They spoke to her in a way she didn't recognise. They smiled and laughed, but she still could not understand a word of what they were saying. They were so tall and thin, they dwarfed her. They sat on the edge of the pond, and one of the bananas sat her on his knee. She led them to the family house, where my grandmother gave them food to eat. They sat with my grandfather on the veranda, and to her amazement, my grandfather was able to communicate with the two bananas. My mother had never heard her father talk in this strange tongue before. Years later when she first came to England, she realised the two bananas had been English or American geographers. We laughed so much when we heard the story. We were never tired of such stories.

My mother had convinced us that there were ghosts in the Desh. In the village, everything is so raw and close to nature you can feel the spirits hanging around the water's edge. When my mother went to live in my father's village, she found she wasn't allowed to enjoy the same freedoms she had delighted in at her own parental home. The men of the village used the main lake towards the front of the house. The lake designated for the women was towards the back of the house and surrounded by willows and other thick foliage. At night when no one was around, the young women of the village enjoyed sneaking into the men's lake to bathe. The lake was larger, more open and more pleasant for bathing. Not very far from the lake was the local house of worship built by my great grandfather for the people of the village. As my mother and her sister-in-law bathed one night in the lake, they saw a figure moving in the distance. They hid behind some willows and held their petticoats over their bodies. The two women found themselves mesmerised by this incredibly tall shiny figure that walked towards the door. They raised the hurricane lamp in a bid to recognise the night time visitor. To their astonishment, as the man approached the door, he did not open it and walk in as any normal human being would do; instead, he slipped under the door like a sheet of light. Both women were petrified by what they saw. They blew out the flame in the hurricane lamp, but still the light shone from this unearthly figure. They began to pray frantically. The next day, they told everyone in the house what they saw. It was believed to have been a jinn, which is a kind of organism that is neither human nor angel: it is something in between. They roam the world in semi-human form. Some are good, and some are evil. When my mother told us this story, my sisters and I would end up feeling so petrified we would all sleep in the same bed for days. Of all the stories, it was our favourite. We would constantly go back for more.

Chapter Eighteen

The Atlantic – Salma

I had packed my bags and was now ready to spend a weekend on the northern coast of Spain with a group of strangers and Laila. We were travelling by car and ferry across the English Channel, as Kamal insisted on taking his big posh Mercedes soft top. It was late, and there was still no sign of Laila. She told me that being a doctor in your Pre-Reg year, meant spending long periods in hospitals and working on weekends and even nights. Laila would have to spend two or three days at a time staying at the hospital. Laila was a house officer, and in doctors' terms it was the lowliest member of the team; they carry out routine chores, admit patients and deal with day-to-day problems on the wards. Laila then went on to explain that house officers traditionally worked very long hours and often complained about not being properly supported. Most of Laila's colleagues suffered from high levels of stress and even depression. Things were steadily getting a little easier for her, but it was certainly no picnic. After this year, Laila could finally begin to choose a suitable career path and apply for full registration. There was even an opportunity to spend some time abroad. Where was she? We were due to go in less than an hour.

Aliya's parents were coming to London as she had something to tell them. Her mother and father would meet her fiance's parents and they would all get on, then she would live a happy and fruitful life with the man she loved. Aliya was very lucky she knew exactly what she wanted, and I admired her courage and the way she was never afraid to go for what she wanted or to speak her mind.

Kamal had arrived, but there was still no sign of Laila. I had felt lost for words when I opened the door; his confident, arrogant manner always left me feeling somewhat tongue-tied. I think I was afraid of uttering something silly or irrelevant or perhaps it was the fear of no sound coming out of my mouth if I spoke. I don't even know why I even cared, but people with a sense of great self-importance just made me feel that way. I always tried to be polite; sometimes I even over-compensated my levels of civility. It often left me unprepared if people were rude or nasty.

I mumbled under my breath that Laila had still not returned from the hospital and that she would not be too long. Kamal gave me a prolonged hard stare, then walked straight past me and up the stairs into the living room. I followed him, but he was already sitting down on the sofa and fiddling with the remote control. I repeated that Laila had not turned up from the hospital yet. At the picnic, Kamal had been polite and in a good mood, but now he was his usual quiet, moody self. He also seemed a little abrupt. Just as we were about to leave, the phone rang. It was Laila.

"Listen! I haven't got time to explain why I'm late; just put Kamal on the phone. Is he there? He can explain everything to you."

I handed the phone to Kamal. He gave very little away with his non-verbal communication and just spent the conversation nodding his head. Kamal paced about the living room, grunting and nodding every so often. He then hung up the phone and sat back on the sofa.

"We are not going to Spain, we are going to spend the weekend on the coast near Brighton. By the way, we changed the plans."

"Oh!" I tried to hide my disappointment. I just read a Lonely Planet Guide on the witches, shipwrecks and mermaids of Galicia.

"Really!" He seemed surprised. "Did Laila not tell you? My good friend Francisco Javier is on call and so needs to be in the UK. He's on call for an emergency pioneering operation on conjoined twins from Venezuela."

We spent most of our journey in silence. It seemed so quiet in the car. I thought Kamal could probably hear me breathing, so I tried to enjoy staring out of the car window and watching the changing face of London. It was fascinating to watch this great metropolitan melting pot gradually change from city to town and then from town to countryside.

"Are you staying another year in London?" It was Kamal who decided to break the silence.

"Yes, I'm planning to bring my sister and mum. My sister is starting Uni next year, so it just makes sense for us all to live here," I replied.

Kamal began to laugh. "The way you say 'mum': it's so northern."

"That's because I am northern."

Kamal rapidly changed the subject. "Where will you live? It's not cheap here."

I wondered whether he was implying I was poor. "I don't know, I'll just have to sort it out when it happens."

"What will you need, a three-bed place?"

"Laila's already told me about all the no-go areas, and I just don't think I can afford all the places she suggests. I'd like to stay in North West London, it's got everything: the park and the lake, but most of it is out of my price range." Who was I kidding? Kamal knew I was poor, so it seemed pointless pretending I had money like him.

"'I'm taking the scenic route so that you can see the countryside on our way."

"Is that because you think us Northerners have never seen the countryside and live in inner city two-up, two-down hell?"

"No!" Kamal laughed. "Because I thought you might like to see the South coast of England, Salma, since you are going to miss the North coast of Spain."

"So, you are the main breadwinner in your family, then?" he asked.

"Yes, I suppose so." I just wished Laila had been here, so I wouldn't be forced to make conversation with this man. Kamal just made me feel so on edge and uncomfortable.

I found the more we talked, the more at ease I felt, and I didn't have to initiate the conversation. Kamal seemed interested to know more about my sisters, their plans for university, and my plans to settle in London. I didn't want to tell him everything about my past, so I gave him a brief overview. "My father died when I was young, and it's been up to me to look after my family. My mother took my father's death badly, and now she needs constant care as she lost the ability to live independently. My mum can walk and talk, but she is still traumatised about losing my dad," I explained reluctantly.

I couldn't read Kamal; it was hard to read someone's silence, but I decided to carry on, telling him about my family to fill time. "My mum is independent enough to go out on her own. We still allow her a great deal of freedom, but we have to be careful she is in her right mind. On one occasion, my mother didn't return for hours, and we had to call the police in case she'd been kidnapped or forgotten her way home. We found her sitting in a rose garden, chatting with an elderly war veteran, and he wouldn't stop talking about his recently departed wife—his 'Nelly.' On another occasion, she had given a pound to two homeless boys and then brought them to our house to make them a sandwich. As touching as the gesture was, my sister put her foot down and said that we couldn't allow my mum to start bringing strays into the house.

"And have you never thought of getting help for her or sending her to a ..."

I didn't allow him to finish his sentence. "No, we are her help," I replied abruptly.

"So why are you living in London and not in Manchester, looking after your mum?"

I felt perhaps I'd told Kamal too much about my life. He'd lived a 'jet set' type of existence, drove a fancy, fast two-door car and would most probably find the story of my life somewhat pathetic and pitiful. I'm not sure whether my family perils had left him surprised or whether he was a little disgusted at my poverty. Kamal was silent for the rest of the journey, so I spent my time playing the alphabet car registration game or dreaming of what the North of Spain might look like with its lush landscape, mountains peppered with forests of pine and eucalyptus. I imagined standing alone in one of its craggy coves by a deserted finishing village as the unforgiving ancient Atlantic sea gouged away at the rocks. I imagined our conversation had we visited the magical wild northern Spain of mermaids, witches, and sailors lost at sea.

"What is the house in Spain like, Kamal?" I asked.

"The house is an old converted farmhouse and has a real Aga stove."

"Sorry, what is a real Aga stove?"

Kamal laughed. "Think Deshi village but Europe – like Poldark on the Cornish coast. Anyway, we are all cooking or bringing a dish. There'll be plenty of vegetarian food, so don't worry, and I'm cooking the chicken curry. It's halal so that you can eat it."

"How do you get halal to the northernmost corner of Spain?"

"No, I am talking about the flat near Brighton. That's where we are headed to now and where we will be eating the halal curry, but my friend Francisco can get anything, anywhere."

"I know, I realise we aren't going to Spain anymore." I protested defensively.

But I continued to dream of what the trip might have been like had we crossed the sea. Back in the car, we would turn a corner on the cliff's edge. I would be greeted by a panoramic view of the town below: I could see the houses, the beach, the sea and all the tiny people going about their business. Just beyond was the ferry with its jaws wide open, waiting for us, only to then cast off onto a wide open, unforgiving Atlantic sea.

I had never travelled abroad and would have felt both excited and scared at the thought of finally fulfilling my dream. Then I remembered the words of a song I had once heard: "That was the river; now this is the sea."

Back in the real world, Kamal was still driving in silence. I studied the contours of his face; the floppy black hair that fell over his forehead, the smooth, soft golden skin, the lashes that were long and black like an Andalucian Spanish señorita. It wouldn't be long before Laila was here, and the pressure to converse would be less. For the rest of the time, I just sat quietly and enjoyed the trees, the flowers, and the pretty village houses. England was a different country out of the city and on a sunny day. I felt that as a community, Asians refrained from ever venturing out of their ghettos. Instead, they went to the typical places like the Lake District, Wales, or Blackpool, but there was so much more to see. We needed to travel to Europe and explore the fascinating continent that lay before us while buying boxes of fresh Mediterranean fruit and vegetables as we passed from one tiny village to another. We needed to stay the night in hotels or country inns and not give a damn how many local people might stare at us behind their pints of dark, malty beers. Perhaps it was a money thing or fear of travelling too far from the familiar that had stopped our parents from venturing into no-go areas. Of course, not all Asian families were like that. Laila had been lucky enough to have seen most of Europe with her parents, and she could afford to go on student exchanges. The doctors' families were an elite hybrid of our community who would often organise various trips to Europe. They stayed in five-star hotels, and the wives would spend all their time shopping and dining in fancy restaurants. Kamal and Laila had been on many of these trips. His parents weren't doctors, but his mother was an intimate friend of most of the doctors' wives, and they were rich, so they were regarded as honorary doctors. So long as Kamal's mum had enough gossip stuffed up her lamp chop sleeves, the doctors' wives would always welcome her with open arms.

We were coming to the end of our journey and I could now see the coastline. The hills were gently undulating, and the rock face was steep, white and chalky. I'd never been any part of the south coast of England. I had only watched repeat episodes of Poldark on BBC Two on a Wednesday afternoon and would race home from school just in time to watch a fiery haired pregnant Demelza battle the Cornish sea in her tiny boat. The Sussex coast was of course different to the rocky coves, headlands, dunes and sandy beaches of Cornwall; here there were bold cliffs of chalk and sandstone, pebble beaches and multicoloured terraced houses that hung perilously on to the cliff's edge, ready to tumble at any time and be claimed by the sea. Kamal pulled into a pub on the way. It was built very close to the cliff edge, and it had distant views of the sea, which gleamed and glistened from the sun's strong rays. The sea looked almost silver and mercurial from such a distance.

"Are you hungry?" Kamal asked.

"A little," I replied.

We sat by the window with a fabulous view of the sea. Most of the coastline had been eaten away by the sea at an alarming rate, and a line of cheerfully coloured turn of the century terraced houses hung precariously from the cliff's edge. They were due to disappear into the sea at any moment, and the pub was rumoured to follow not long after.

"My parents would bring me here as a child," Kamal explained. "I loved the sea and the dramatic landscape. I have a place here, well, down there," Kamal pointed somewhere towards the shore. "I bought it with a friend as an investment. I am thinking of buying abroad too. The place I am considering is different from your typical tourist place; it's at the very edge of Spain. The coast is lined with fishing villages and dramatic coves and, best of all, not often frequented by your British tourists. A place to chill and just look at the sea."

Kamal owned a lot of properties I thought. I looked at the miniature town below the rocks, currently hanging on for dear life. I imagined how the happy Mrs. Kamal might be married to a property mogul with a dramatic house by the raging sea in Northern Spain. Samosas and sarees in a forgotten corner of rural Iberia where they probably ate pig's feet and rubbery octopus tentacles, especially if Kamal took his mother there to visit with her doctor lady friends.

There were dozens of new building blocks scattered along the English southern coastline. Developers had spent millions converting what was once shingle and marshland into an impressive-looking marina development, apparently the largest in Europe. London people would cotton on to the fact that just over an hour away from the capital, it was possible to buy a luxury apartment in Brighton for half the cost of a London one. As more people in the city bought holiday homes here, prices would be pushed up, and Kamal and his friend would make a good profit from a resale property. He had bought more than one and had already managed to sell and pay off the mortgage on his first property. Now Kamal wanted to buy this new property abroad in Spain and wanted to show it off.

"I haven't lived all my life in the south," Kamal confessed. "My family spent a short time in the north near Manchester, but I was very young at the time." Kamal went on to explain that his mother had also been ill for a while. However, Kamal remembered very little of his life there. They came to live in the south where the weather was a little milder, but the main reason had been because Kamal's father could earn twice as much money in the south. His London-based clientele was wealthier and had larger accounts, and so Kamal's family moved south to be where the money was.

After telling me this tale of his family's history, Kamal became all moody and quiet again. He had an unpredictable character; sometimes he would be cold, quiet and moody, and at other times he would open up and show a much warmer, more human side to his character. I still wasn't sure

186

he would make a good match with Laila; she was too independent and strong, and they would cancel each other out or end up having some sibling-type fight and divorce after a week. What Kamal needed to put him on the straight and narrow was a woman who was either so strong she would finally kick his ass into gear, or kind, traditional and quiet on the outside but incredibly strong on the inside.

I ate a salad for lunch. I wasn't very hungry, and it all felt a little surreal. I was eating at a restaurant with Kamal, a man who had been so rude and dismissive of me in the past. He watched me as I picked at my salad.

"No wonder you're so skinny. You're just picking at that, and it's not even a proper meal; it's rabbit food," Kamal said. I was too tired to answer and carried on playing with the food. "I'll have to start feeding it to you myself," he added. I stared at him in horror and began gulping the food down as fast as I could. He smirked and then quickly changed the subject. "The pub's not due to fall into the sea this year, so you can take your time eating that meal, Salma," he smirked. "We're all cooking or bringing a dish. There'll be plenty of vegetarian food, so don't worry. As I mentioned before, `I'm cooking the chicken curry and it's halal so that you can eat it." He must have read my mind.

"I am not that strict about my food, it's just religious, even cultural conditioning I guess," I replied.

Back in the car, we turned a corner on the cliff's edge. I was greeted by a panoramic view of the town below; I could see the houses, the beach, the sea and all the tiny people going about their business. It was the most beautiful, breath-taking view I had ever seen.

Chapter Nineteen

Sea Views - Salma

Kamal carried my bag up to the apartment. As we entered the living room, there was a huge window that looked on to a garden where the sea lay beyond. The sun was setting, and the late summer winds thrust the sea waves back and forth against the harbour walls. There were two men and two women sat casually around a glass coffee table, sipping tea and playing a board game. I was quickly introduced to everyone and within minutes I found myself standing on a balcony overlooking a mock Venetian waterway. Kamal joined me on the balcony; he said he had to leave me with his friends to pick up a work colleague from the station. He promised he wouldn't be too long. "Look after her!" he yelled to one of the boys, who promptly raised his alcoholic drink, nodded his head and made his way towards me.

"Hi, I'm Nigel. I didn't catch your name earlier," he enquired in a melodic southern Irish tone.

"It's Salma."

"Oh, as in 'Salma Hayek'?"

"Salma who?"

"You know … Mexican actress, beautiful face, the snake dance, etc.?"

"No, no, I've never heard of her. Who is she?"

189

"Oh well! She's pretty gorgeous. What do you do then, for your sins?"

"I'm a teacher, a secondary school teacher." I knew I was coming across as rude and quiet, so I tried to make an effort. "I suppose you're a doctor?"

"Yes, I certainly am. I did my Pre-Reg year with Kamal, and, well, now we've gone our separate ways, but we're still fine friends. How do you know Kamal? Are you two …?" He shook his glass from side to side.

"Oh no," I answered in a panic. "No, I just know him through my friend Laila."

"Oh, Laila the doctor. I know her. Are they together?"

"No, we're all just friends."

"Oh, I just thought those two had a thing going for a while; maybe I was mistaken." There was a short awkward silence. "Well, if you need anything, Salma Hayek, I'll be around, so give me a shout. Look around the flat if you want." He left to re-join the game.

I took my bag to one of the rooms. I noticed the two beds in the room had already been claimed. A tall girl with jet black wavy hair walked into the room. "Oh, we're sleeping in the other room now, so make yourself at home. The other bed is for Laila. This room has a bathroom." She opened a tiny door that I thought was a cupboard. I peered in, a little relieved I wouldn't be brushing my teeth with four men I barely knew. The dark-haired woman and her friend would sleep in the master bedroom; it also had its own bathroom, and there was another room for the boys and a

190

sofa bed in the lounge. I dreaded the prospect of having to sleep on the floor in some smelly sleeping bag in a room full of men. That was the life I had conveniently avoided at university. Luckily, I had lived at home during my university days. It was nice to see that I was going to spend the weekend with clean, well-groomed adults.

Kamal's friends had decided to go for a walk, so I lay on the bed for a moment and rested. *Gosh! He's so English,* I thought, *and so much friendlier and at ease around these people.* I decided to take a walk around the harbour by myself, but just before I left for my tour, I took a quick look at the apartment. It was pleasant but very mannish and testosterone infused with very few, if any, feminine touches at all. There was a chrome theme running throughout the apartment, and each room had a view of the waterfront. The master room had breath-taking views of the English Channel. The waves were dangerously close to the apartments and I wondered how the view would look on a windy day or during a storm.

As I made my way to the front door, the handle began to move by itself. It was Kamal, accompanied by a slightly shorter but very handsome-looking man with olive skin and very dark eyes.

"Are my friends looking after you, Salma?"

"Oh yes, they're treating me very well. I was popping out for a walk. They've all gone out somewhere."

"OK," answered the foreign olive-skinned guest. "Let's all go for a walk together. Show me this harbour of yours, Kamal."

The man's accent was strong, and he sounded Spanish or Italian. I realised it must be the Spanish doctor Laila was always hassling Kamal about. Laila had wanted to meet him for months. He'd come alone because his wife was at a weekend conference. His name was Francisco Javier. I was only half-listening to their conversation, but I heard that they were speaking passionately about Middle East issues and what could be done to bring about peace in the region. Francisco had a theory that if a world war were ever to occur, it would kick off in the Middle East and that it had been predicted in many of the holy books. For a Spanish man, he seemed very obsessed with Arab affairs. Laila had told me that the Spaniards hated the Moors because they had occupied their land for 700 years. They called them Moros, which was a derogatory term, although those who used the word refused to believe they were being intolerant.

Laila had a Spanish pen pal she still kept in touch with. He had told us that one summer, he and his parents had spent the day in Tunisia. Their guide had warned them not to use the word Moro, as it would offend people; they preferred to be known as Arabs or Tunisians. He explained to them that it was like calling them Spanish Conquistadores, or even worse. Throughout the visit, all the Spanish tourists tried very hard not to use the derogatory word. However, by the end of the trip, her friend's father could no longer hold his tongue and began to rant and rave about how there was nothing wrong with using the term Moro. "I am a Spaniard, and that man is a Moro. What's wrong with saying this word? If these people aren't Moros, then what are they? And the biggest proof that they are Moros is that our guide el Moro has overcharged us for all of our visits."

Francisco was still sorting the world out; he waved his arms about

192

frantically, and his jet-black hair bobbed up and down as he spoke. I just tagged along, took in the summer afternoon air and watched the sights around me. It was really weird to hear this man talk; I could almost notice a northern twang mixed with a strong Spanish accent. The other bizarre thing that struck me was that if Francisco were to grow a beard, he would probably be arrested at an airport on suspicion of being a member of some dodgy insurgent middle-eastern group.

On the way back, we met up with the others who had been shopping at the supermarket. Everyone had to contribute or cook a dish for the evening feast. They all admitted that they were too lazy to cook, and so they had just bought most of the ready-made food. The Spanish doctor began banging on about how in his country, ready-made food or 'packet food', as he called it, was unheard of. "In my country, we have the finest vegetables in Europe. We only eat fruit and vegetables." He seemed so proud of his fruit and vegetables. He wanted to make us his famous Spanish omelette, which was just basically potatoes, eggs, and olive oil.

The only two people in the kitchen cooking were Kamal and the Spanish man. The two girls were in their room getting ready. One boy was engrossed in a Game Boy/PlayStation-type game, and the Irish man had gone out again to buy more wine. Kamal had asked me whether I would be offended or scandalised if his friends drank wine in front of me. As long as I didn't have to drink it, I didn't care what they consumed. The girl with black wavy hair was called Anastasia, and she was a doctor that specialised in tropical diseases. The other girl was her housemate and girlfriend of the man engrossed in the PlayStation. I wondered which of the boys had sold this property to Kamal. Both girls were incredibly tall and elegant. Although we had hardly spoken to one another, they seemed pleasant enough. They had offered Laila and me the better, bigger room, so they would now have to sleep in a double bed together. I wished Laila would ring and tell me whether she was on her way. I missed her. I didn't fit in; I felt like a loose end. Everyone was nice enough, but they were comfortable in each other's company. I felt somewhat the outsider. I was painfully shy, and I knew it would take a lot of effort on another person's part to get me to engage in a long conversation. Very few people had the time or energy nowadays to invest any effort in someone with very little to say for themselves. I didn't blame them. Time was a precious thing, and I was a firm believer in not wasting it with people with whom you fail to bond.

The omelette was finished, and Francisco Javier the Spanish doctor joined me on the balcony. Before long, I was chatting away, and I felt at ease as he was a very friendly man. He told me all about his wife and how they had met in Bosnia. Listening to Francisco Javier speak was like riding the cusp of a wave of steady rhythms and undulating r's.

"My wife, Sonya, was also a school teacher, but her village and school had been destroyed, and so she worked as an aid worker in a refugee camp. However, Sonya set up a temporary classroom for the children so that they wouldn't miss their reading, writing and basic mathematical skills. Even in the midst of war and suffering, the Bosnian people tried hard not to lose sight of life's necessities. There were children in the camp that had not given up the idea of being doctors, scientists, inventors, even firemen, and teachers," Francisco explained.

Francisco had met Sonya in the camp, and they had been married shortly after. Despite his parents and family welcoming her with open arms, he soon realised that Spain was not the perfect country for them to settle in. It was, by and large, deemed a Catholic country. In Spain, it wasn't weird to be young or old and be a practising Catholic. Being a young Christian in Britain was widely associated with strange mind-controlling cults. The Spaniards were warm-hearted and kind people, but they harboured negative views of the Moors, which was a kind of legacy left over from the Spanish Inquisition. Francisco didn't want to give his family the impression he didn't love his country; he loved it and was proud to be a Spaniard. There were many wonderful things people could experience in Spain that other societies lacked.

"We have the finest weather in Europe and one of the healthiest diets in the world, and once you had made friends with a Spaniard, you have a friend for life," Francisco explained.

However, Francisco couldn't risk Sonya suffering any more than she already had, and so, for now, they would live in England, which was a much more multicultural society. On a few occasions while living in Spain, Sonya had entered a coffee bar or a shop while wearing her headscarf; the shop assistant had followed her around and behaved very rudely towards her. On another occasion, Sonya had stopped the traffic because she had been wearing traditional clothes, and people were staring at her in the street. Francisco had even been asked when he was going to buy his wife some proper clothes, to which he took great offence. He was deemed to be bohemian and quirky for wanting to leave his hometown and travel abroad. Spanish people rarely moved from city to city or town to town.

They tended to love their community and had little inclination to leave, unless there was a necessity to study or work. The Spaniard would spend all their time dreaming about the day they could return to their place of birth or village. Francisco explained it was because the family always remained an important part of your life, and it was not strange for a young person to stay at the parental home until they got married.

"Why do you think Jesus Christ was a Spaniard?" Francisco asked.

"I don't know," I replied.

"Well, because he was 33 years old, unemployed and still living with his parents."

Only Francisco laughed at his joke because only he got it. When Francisco gave me a lengthy explanation of some of the quirks of Spanish society, I finally understood the joke. One thing didn't make sense.

"Didn't the Moors reside in Spain for over seven centuries? Weren't the Spanish people proud of their heritage?"

"My people don't see themselves as descendants of the Arab invaders; the expulsion of the Muslims represented a huge victory in Spanish history. We appreciated what the Moors had left behind, but my ancestors also celebrated how Catholicism had eventually triumphed over their supposed enemy. The golden age of Islamic society was a time of scientific discovery and creative time for art and literature. The downfall of the Moors in the Iberian Peninsula was because the leaders did not force people to convert. It was a society where three faiths—Christianity, Judaism, and Islam—existed together in tolerance and harmony."

I thought it a fascinating-sounding society, all the values of the East but with all the comforts of living in the West. Francisco kept on repeating, "I am 80% Arab."

I was so lost and intrigued by the sound of his amazing country that the fact that Laila had still not arrived had completely slipped my mind. Kamal was busy slaving away in the kitchen. I looked over to see what he was doing and was surprised to see him already looking this way. I smiled at him to acknowledge I hadn't forgotten him, but he didn't respond and kept up his stern look. Francisco also looked across at Kamal, and this seemed to make him laugh.

"I'm making your man jealous."

I looked at Francisco in dismay and confusion. "My man? No! We're not a couple."

Francisco laughed again and said, "I know, but he is. He is a jealous man tonight."

Kamal summoned Francisco into the kitchen, and they began to discuss something. Francisco came back for a moment and said he had to help Kamal, but he would be back, and then we would carry on our conversation. Time had passed so quickly while I was locked in this fascinating conversation with Francisco that I hadn't even noticed that the rest of the guests had come back from their walk. They were sorting out the table ready for dinner. I asked Kamal if he could check his phone to see if Laila had called. Kamal grumpily slid the phone towards me across the granite worktop. "You check. Just press the green button," he said.

Sure enough, there was a message from Laila, who said that she couldn't make it, as something very urgent had come up. Laila was so sorry and would make it up to me. However, there was the possibility that she might travel down tomorrow, although she doubted it. My heart sank; how would I cope without her, and what was I even doing here? If it wasn't for the nice Spanish man, I think I would have little desire to be here. I decided to go back to the haven of the balcony and feel the cool evening breeze. No one would notice me out here on my own and out of the way. Hopefully, here I could be invisible to all.

I sat in quiet contemplation on the balcony, hoping Francisco would come back quickly to rescue me and entertain me with tales of his country. I had a strong need to hear about faraway places and people. The school term was only a few weeks away, and I already had that feeling that summer had passed too quickly. I would have to go and see my mother soon. She would phone me every day and ask me when I was coming home. My sisters also missed me intensely, so it was time to go back to my roots. Now and then, I would look over at Kamal and Francisco to see if they were anywhere nearer to finishing their conversation. They were locked in a passionate debate about something. Francisco was patting Kamal on the back and would occasionally swing his arms in the air. A couple of times he would catch my eye, so I thought it wise to look away quickly.

There was no time for Francisco to come back to the balcony because dinner was being served. Luckily, he sat right down next to me. I noticed Kamal look our way; he still seemed annoyed with me. The table was full of dishes; Kamal's chicken looked and smelt delicious as did the omelette Francisco had made. There was rice, a variety of salads, cheeses, fresh bread, and readymade Indian snacks. We all began eating immediately. Nobody spoke for at least five minutes; a sign that everyone was hungry. The guests passed around the wine, but Kamal and Francisco refused. The Irish man Nigel gave the game away by saying, "Kamal! What's with the dry spell?"

Kamal looked at Nigel with a hard stare and replied, "It's a new leaf."

Francisco broke the awkward silence "I miss my Spanish fruit and vegetables and the Spanish wine, but now I'm giving up the alcohol out of respect for Sonya's religion. My friends and family don't understand; they like to drink La Mancha wine all day."

After dinner, the two couples offered to clear everything away and wash up. When I offered to help, I was told no way would I be washing dishes; I was a guest and would not be allowed to lift a finger, so I decided to go for a walk. Francisco offered to accompany me. I thought Kamal would join us, but he refused to go. He said had some calls to make and might catch up with us later. During our walk, Francisco talked a lot about Kamal.

"Kamal helped us both when I first arrived in England. He sorted out Sonya's immigration papers, accommodation, phone lines, internet access, transport, and so many other things."

I felt strange to hear such different side of the man I thought of as vain and selfish. Francisco continued his analysis of Kamal: "It is time Kamal settled down and found himself a long-term partner. I have told him exactly what kind of girl he should go for—intelligent, sweet, and sincere—and that it was time to give up the frivolous lifestyle." I told Francisco that Kamal's parents were keen on Laila, but she saw him more like an annoying brother than a life partner. Francisco was quiet for a moment and then asked me: "Are you courting anyone or planning to marry at all, Salma?"

I felt at ease in Francisco's company, so I told him my situation.

"Marriage is not on the cards; I have family obligations."

"How would a relationship get in the way of your family obligations?" replied the man who had defied generations of his family legacy and strict Catholic culture to marry the woman he loved.

I daren't mention that the real reason was that I was probably so painfully shy. I had zero experience with men and, above all, had failed miserably to attract anyone to ever ask me out because I was invisible. I wasn't glamorous like Laila and Aliya. I didn't wear particularly fashionable clothes, and I never wore makeup or contact lenses. Laila had tried on numerous occasions to pump me up with compliments, claiming that behind the glasses and the tied-up hair, I was very cute and pretty. Laila loved to dress me up, ruffle my hair and cake me with makeup. I drew the line when she had tried to shove contact lenses in my eyes. I realised Laila only said these things out of the kindness of her heart and to fill me with confidence.

When we returned, I decided to go to bed as I was tired. The rest of the group, including Francisco, decided to play a game of Trivial Pursuit. Kamal was in the kitchen, quietly drying the plates. I didn't understand one thing: if Kamal was so nice to Francisco, then why in the nine or ten months that I had known him had he always come across as rude and arrogant? For months, Kamal had ignored me and spent his time giving me condescending looks. He would visit Laila's house and sit there for hours, zapping from channel to channel and saying very little to me. When I eventually talked to Kamal, his character had softened, but he was still occasionally moody and unpredictable.

One moment Kamal would open up and be pleasant, the next he would dismiss me again and continue with the disapproving looks. Kamal had a reputation for breaking women's hearts and drinking alcohol, despite his efforts to disguise his habit. I had no clue what to make of him, yet he constantly preyed on my mind. Deep down, I sought his approval; I wanted to be his friend and understand the enigma behind the façade. However, according to Francisco, he was a wonderful, intelligent and generous man. What had I missed? I knew Kamal was someone who had never been denied anything in his life and that he was possibly privileged or spoilt like his sister. A weekend at his huge house and the sound of his mother's bad-tempered voice imprinted in my brain was enough to ascertain that. It was only a matter of time before Laila, Kamal, and everyone else came to know about my father's disgraceful exit from this life. My father's accusers would once again rob my family and me of any possibility of fostering relationships with people within my community. No matter where I turned or who I got to know, this painful event would always come back to haunt me. I would never be free from the wretched legacy my beloved father left me.

I went straight to my room and closed the door behind me. The window was wide open and with the imminent arrival of September, the weather was now hot and clammy. The boats rocked silently, abandoned on a calm murky green sea. I realised I was gazing over what was the end of England and the beginning of another world; a new continent lay before me, and I knew nothing of what existed beyond this sea. It was only the English Channel, but it felt as colossal as standing on the southern edge of Spain and looking out to Africa. Watching over the waterfront was a liberating experience. I felt a sudden desire to discover what society had always denied me.

Talking to Francisco had stirred that same yearning in me—a longing to escape this cage I had created called everyday life. Francisco talked of a world beyond Manchester and London, where people fought fate and carved out their path in life against the odds and against what life had in store for them. He depicted a world where borders did not exist, where life was not a dull, grey town; every street like the next, with no beginning and no end, and waste bins spilling with dirt and refuse. There was no greenery for the poor. The train was a strange inter-world that moved you from one wasteland to another. But this was no wasteland. This place was a perfectly crafted oasis for those who already had everything. It wasn't until this moment and meeting Francisco that it occurred to me that my life was not a rigid path; I could choose another way. Francisco had chosen another route and in doing so, he had changed his fate and that of his wife, Sonya. Now I understood why Laila was so desperately wanting talk to Francisco about working for Medicos sin Fronteras and why she would want to leave all the comforts of her life to work in a poor faraway country with people who had nothing.

I smiled as I lay on the crisp lilac sheets; they smelt of new, fresh from the sheet-making factory, not of sweaty student or stale cigarettes. I shook my head and purged myself of all negative and grey thoughts. They were still playing Trivial Pursuit in the living room and laughing out loud. I opened the door ever so quietly to see who was still up and playing the game. They were all so wrapped up in their fun that they didn't notice me. The boys were leaning on their elbows on the floor, and the two girls sat on the sofa with their knees up against their chest. Francisco sat lodged between the two girls. The ginger girl kept on falling towards him and gently pushing him with her hands, and the dark-haired girl had her head on his shoulder. They all looked dangerously comfortable. My eyes quickly skimmed the room; Kamal was nowhere to be seen. I switched off the room light, lay on the bed and let the moonlight flood in. I don't think I had been wrong in my decision to come to London.

I liked Francisco and I felt really at ease in his company. I didn't like him that way, though. Francisco's stare was hypnotic but warm, and his voice was foreign but kind with a confident edge. I think Francisco was trying to sell all of the virtues of Kamal to me, but how far from the mark he was, as I think Kamal was in love with Laila. Francisco's character description of Kamal made me see him in a different light. From tomorrow, I would begin to treat him differently and stop seeing him as some rogue, or a wayward Asian boy who had lost his roots. Yes! Tomorrow, I would make more effort and try to get to know him better. Maybe Kamal could be a good match for Laila. What a shame she wasn't here to bear witness to this glowing testimony to Kamal.

I had very little experience with men; in fact, the only men I had known in my life were my father and Kal, my childhood playmate. Laila's childhood playmate was her cousin from the Desh. They would beat each other up and try to drown each other in their grandparents' lake and play nasty tricks on one another. Laila was terrified of cockroaches, so when her cousin knew he was beaten, he would threaten her with a cockroach, which always did the trick and sent her screaming and crying in retreat.

Aliya's childhood playmate had been a servant boy called Topon. On this occasion, it was Aliya who did all the beating. She spent all her time kicking him and beating him up with one of those multipurpose Deshi jute brooms. He had a twin sister who looked the spitting image of him. Topon didn't even make it to ten years old: he died of tuberculosis.

Chapter Twenty

The River and the Sea - Salma

It must have been about 2 a.m when I woke up feeling very thirsty. It had been an unusually hot night, and I normally kept a glass of water by my bedside. I wandered into the bathroom and splashed water on my face; it felt hot and sticky, and then I tiptoed into the living room, worried I might wake whoever was sleeping on the sofa. There was a bed made up, but there was no one in it. As there was no one around, I proceeded quietly to the kitchen and poured myself an icy glass of water. I decided to sit on the balcony and wait for the last of the summer sun to rise.

Tonight, the sky seemed different. The night blue was gone, and in its place was an ebony blanket of silk and a million stars spangled across its fabric. In one corner of the sky, the midnight clouds had parted to reveal a brilliant white light that shone through; I'd never noticed the night sky look so black before. I thought I knew all the colours of the sky. I had a recurring dream: it was always about my father, my childhood, and summer parties on someone's lawn. The dream always ended with the sky turning a strange colour of spicy orange. I called it my saffron-coloured dream. I wonder whether it was my father's way of keeping his memory alive within me, but doesn't he know that I'll never forget him? The heat was oppressive, but the tiled balcony floor was cool and soothing on my feet.

I lay down on a sofa, and I could see the harbour and the sea through the aluminium balcony bars. At last, I felt I could lie down and be completely invisible. I could stand in front of a class of 30 strange children,

205

but put me in front of an adult, and I would lose all my ability to speak. I remember the little girl who would play with her friend Kal all day on green summer lawns. I wish I were still that little girl, with no inhibitions and no knowledge of how terrifying the adult world could be. I was still that child; I wish I was strong enough to calm her and assure her that nothing would hurt her. All of a sudden, my heart leapt right into my mouth. I noticed Kamal was standing upright in a far dark corner of the balcony. Although I couldn't see him clearly, I could see the cigarette tip in his mouth.

"Why are you up so late?" he asked.

"I'm just a bit thirsty. I can't sleep," I stuttered nervously.

He didn't reply for what seemed an eternity. I still couldn't see his face in the dark, but I knew he was staring at me, which made me feel exposed and uncomfortable. So, I stood up from the sofa, ready to leave.

"Can I ask you something?"

I sat back down for a moment. "Of course."

"Did you want to come this weekend, or did Laila force you to?"

Of course, I was forced. Why else would I endure an entire weekend with you against my will? I thought. I took some time in answering. "I came as Laila's guest."

"And had she said no, would you have still come?"

"No," I replied bluntly.

"You don't see me as a friend, then?"

"No, well, I'm not sure."

"Then you see me as something other than a friend."

"Yes! I see you as Laila's friend."

There was a silence. Where were these questions leading? I felt it was time to depart for my room again, but just as I was about to leave, more questions followed:

"Can I ask another question, and you won't be offended?" Kamal continued, but I didn't have any choice at this point. "I'm not always sure how you might take things that I say. You're like a closed book that no one is allowed to open, and I can't ever tell what you're thinking," he continued.

The king of duplicity and deception was calling me a closed book. I felt tired and just wanted to go to bed, but out of politeness, I had to stay.

"I was watching you while you were talking to Francisco, and I think it's the first time I've seen you look relaxed and smiling. It's true, I don't think I've ever seen you smile. You're not the type of girl that would flirt with a married man," Kamal whispered.

I was somewhat offended, but above all, I was embarrassed and felt exposed, blushing as I lowered my head; it was like a reflex action. I tried to hide it, but I couldn't. "Francisco is nice; he's interesting, and he was easy to talk to. I have never met anyone like him. Francisco is the type of person that makes you want to visit far away magical places." I explained with an ease that surprised me.

Kamal seemed deep in thought for a moment and then replied, "Magical places then!" Kamal paused again as if not sure what to say anymore. "You're never normally that talkative. Well, not when you are with me anyway."

"Oh, I hadn't noticed."

Kamal seemed determined to explore the issue. "You spent a whole year ignoring me. I thought you were a bit haughty and didn't like me. Then I thought maybe you're just one of those shy little Asian girls who have nothing to say for themselves, but I think I've possibly had you all wrong." He seemed determined to cross this barrier that had always stopped us from talking frankly with one another. I found his comment somewhat impertinent, as it was, he who had spent a whole year ignoring me. However, tonight I felt brave too, so instead of walking away from this awkward situation, I decided to stay and defend myself.

"So, you think I'm either shy or rude? I don't see myself as particularly shy. I think I can't be that timid. I do stand up in front of 30 kids every day and talk nonstop for 6 hours, so I must be just rude, then. Maybe there are some people who have very little to say to one another," I responded, feeling a sudden urge to fight back with a passion.

"You mean like you and me?" Kamal replied, a little confused.

"I mean like anyone, any two people. I don't see the point of wasting time talking to someone unless you have something kind or constructive to say," I replied.

"I must say I have misjudged you all these past months. You're not as …"

"Shy and pathetic?" I felt I had to defend myself.

"No, I didn't mean that," Kamal replied.

"Go on: say it. I can guess what you are thinking—I am shy, and I am a bit quiet. I know what I am. I like reading and staying at home and I only talk to people I feel comfortable with. I've never liked pubs or clubs, not just for religious reasons but because I genuinely don't like them, so I don't bother going out. The minute I enter a noisy, smoky pub, all I want to do is go home and curl up on my sofa. I prefer to spend my time reading, marking books and preparing coursework for my kids. Oh! I do go to a book club once a month." I wasn't sure why I was telling Kamal all this, but I knew he held a preconceived idea of who I was and had been judging me all these months, so I was determined to prove him wrong. "Anyway, at the moment, my priority is just getting my mother and sisters to London, so we can all start a new life together." I continued, no longer caring what he thought of this new bravado.

Kamal didn't seem to be listening. "How do you know what I think of you?" he replied.

"Well, I don't know what you think of me, and to tell you the truth, I don't care. I don't care what anyone thinks. When my dad died, I just stopped worrying a long time ago about what people think." I couldn't understand what had prompted this new dawn of honesty between us, but the sea air and that strange colour of the sky had made me feel bold tonight. I suddenly felt I could say anything to Kamal, and it wouldn't matter, as the raven black sky hid all my fear and infused me with the spirit of a warrior queen. "If we are going to be honest with each other, maybe I should tell you what I think of you, but I won't, because I'm a guest in your house," I continued. I waited for his angry and sarcastic answer or an invitation to leave his home, but it never came.

"Salma, I know what and who I am." Kamal was quiet for a moment and then added, "I wish I could be more like Francisco."

Kamal suddenly seemed like a young boy lost. I genuinely believed he was baring his very soul in front of me, and for a moment, I felt an urge to hold him and comfort him. But if this was about Kamal's inability to find his ideal partner, then it was of his own making.

Suddenly I felt irritated at his self-pity. "You know, I think we, as in people from our culture, are a community who are so obsessed with looks, education and social status, that we have lost all our passion and humanity. In our culture, our life partner is based on what university you went to, or how light skinned you are. And why do you have to mess about with non Deshi women? Why? Aren't they worthy of some respect?"

"No! Well, because the types of women I meet don't want long-term relationships," Kamal retorted.

I could tell he was making lame excuses. "Everyone should be treated with the same respect, no matter where you are from or what your background is. At the end of the day, what do you value most? Would you fight or die for the woman you love, or would you choose your family instead? That is the choice."

Kamal was deadly quiet, in deep contemplation about what I had just said. I wondered what was wrong with our community. Why had we become so superficial? If marriage was based on such fickle things as looks and social status, how could it ever stand the test of time?

"Why were you crying at my sister's birthday party? What would make you cry with such pain and in a stranger's house?"

I couldn't believe Kamal would bring the issue up. I was so humiliated. Why was he changing the subject suddenly? Kamal was playing dirty to avoid the subject, so I decided to play ignorant. "I don't know what you are talking about."

"Salma, I watched you sobbing for more than 10 minutes, and then we spoke for about an hour after."

"I don't remember, and why do you need to know? It's private."

"Yes, it probably is, but if anyone were rude to you in my house, I would like to know about it."

"Believe me, no one was rude, and it's not worth knowing why I was crying. It's very private; just personal stuff and something that goes way back. I told you at your sister's party that you wouldn't understand, and you wouldn't want to know. Why are you bringing the subject up again? It was months ago." I was so cross I just turned my head away from

Kamal. I could tell by the look on his face that he wanted to know more. I could see a look of pity, and perhaps even a hint of tenderness etched on his face. He knew I was annoyed with him, so he tried to change the subject.

"Francisco never really bothers talking to the girls I go out with; I don't think he approves. He's always trying to fix me up with some brainy doctor woman. I think Francisco approves of you."

I was still upset; I don't know why it was so exhausting trying to play the game and keep up the pretence of not being bothered by Kamal's inquisition. I didn't know how to answer his awkward questions. All I wanted to do was go home and crawl into a ball on my bed and disappear into nothing. He knew it was now time to be quiet. There seemed nothing more to say. On the one hand, I should have got up and walked away, but something was stopping me. Kamal and I both sat quietly, staring at the sea. I was tired now; it had been a very long day. My eyes were heavy, and dawn was about to break. It was time to return to my room and collapse onto my bed until late morning. He had noticed how quiet I had become. I could hardly keep my eyes open, and my head had begun to slump.

"You're sleepy, aren't you? You should go to bed." Kamal seemed to lean towards me and then took hold of the necklace I was wearing. He seemed fascinated by it but said nothing. He examined the jewellery between his fingertips. It was the type of necklace that would often catch people's eyes. It was like a tiny silver Arabic book with a black stone placed in the centre. It had dangly bits that hung from the bottom and a secret compartment where you could place a special prayer. My necklace was empty; there was no prayer in it. Its symmetrical circular patterns had become blackened by years of oil and soot.

Kamal held my shoulders lightly and guided me to my feet. It was a weird thing for him to do—cross that barrier again—but I was too tired to react. Kamal was standing so close to me, he smelt of incense and sandalwood, the aroma was intoxicating. I felt a sudden rush of heat in my head and the dizziness returned. I know his eyes were fixed on me, but I dared not look up. It was just for a brief moment that our eyes met. I recognised something familiar in him, as if from a forgotten time in my life. It was too early to allow my brain to process its meaning. As I turned to leave for my room, I thought I felt him caress the ends of my hair, but I wasn't quite sure if I had imagined it. "Goodnight!" Kamal called after me. I didn't answer; I was too dazed and too … Well, I felt strange.

The door closed behind me, and now inside the security of my room, I sat bewildered on the bed. I suddenly began to cry, but they were quiet, silent tears. I didn't know why I was crying: Kamal hadn't been impolite or misbehaved, he'd done nothing wrong and there had been no impropriety. I couldn't pinpoint what had upset me, but he'd invaded something, crossed some barrier he shouldn't have, and I felt very peculiar. Everything felt like a tired haphazard mess in my brain. My face was beginning to ache, and the muscles in my face locked. My head fell onto the pillow. I had to rest, as it had been such a long day. By 5 a.m. I knew there was little chance of me sleeping now. Dawn had long since broken, and a strange ethereal saffron light shone onto my bed. It was like I was having one of my strange dreams again, but this time, there were no ladies in blue headscarves, there was no smell of food, and my father's soft voice was not calling for me and Kal to come and eat. There was no hysterical, screeching lady desperately searching for her son. There was an early morning chill, and I clutched my tummy because it ached with pain and a dull hunger I had not felt before. I decided I would get ready to leave, and it had to be as soon as possible. I would leave a note saying that I had to get back for an emergency. It was time to go back home and see my family.

Chapter Twenty-One

Aliya's Parents – Laila

It was possible that Salma was annoyed with me. Maybe I shouldn't have left her to the mercy of Kamal; I know how much she disliked him, and he had very little regard for her when she was in the room, although I had noticed that at the picnic, Kamal had behaved very well towards her. I suppose throwing them together like that might do them some good. Each sat at the opposite of the morality scale, but as long as they could be civil to each other, that's all I asked. Salma had arrived back from the coast just after 11 a.m. She wore a serious look on her face and walked straight past me as I greeted her. After some time, I walked upstairs to her bedroom in the attic and asked her if all was well. I apologised for abandoning her and asked her a few routine questions about the weekend. Salma was not particularly forthcoming about how she had spent her time, although she did tell me that the Spanish doctor Francisco had been there and that he had turned out to be a charming man. I wanted to know all about him. Salma had decided to come back early and not bother with waiting for a lift from Kamal. She had left things too long, and it was now time to go home and visit her mother and sisters in Manchester. It was imperative that she go as soon as she could. However, before Salma was due to leave, I told her I had two pieces of unusual news to tell her. I chatted while she quietly packed her bags. I thought it best to tell her the first story when she had returned from Manchester, as it was too complicated and too weird to tell in a hurry. As I babbled on, her eyes rarely seemed to meet mine. She was preoccupied with something.

"Salma, is something bothering you?" I enquired.

"Ugh," she replied lamely while continuing her frantic bag packing.

"Is it Kamal? Was he mean to you on the weekend?" Something had touched a nerve because suddenly I had her full attention. She was staring at me and hardly seemed able to blink her eyes. I bet Kamal had been unkind to her, and as soon as she was gone, I would phone him and command him to stop behaving so horribly towards her once and for all. Salma stopped for a moment, then shook her head but said nothing.

"Anyway, you've got to hear this about Aliya, it's bizarre," I continued. "In truth, this whole weekend has been weird."

I continued to describe my meeting with the elderly mystery couple. I had arrived home after my shift on Saturday; it was about 7 p.m., and as I walked upstairs to my bedroom, I was shocked to see an old couple sitting in the living room. They were both possibly in their late 60s or early 70s. The man was wearing a velvety Russian style Arab hat, dark collarless jacket and trousers. He wore a long beard, and his hair was grey. The lady's hair was dark and a little grey at the sides, which she had in a loose bun. She wore a dark green polyester saree, and on top of that, a brown acrylic coat. They looked old and tired. They sat stiffly, saying nothing and staring into space. It freaked me out a little.

"Oh, maybe they were your parents' friends or something?" Salma replied.

"Yes, my thoughts exactly."

My first instinct was that my parents had invited some prospective

216

in-laws over and let them into my house without telling me, but they didn't look the type of people my parents would typically match me up with. Then I thought maybe they were distant relatives from the Desh, but then why were they not staying at my parents' place? And surely my mother would have phoned me to say something; she knew my 'No surprise relatives from the Desh' rule. No, something felt very strange.

Salma continued to pack her bags, but I had her full attention now. I continued to relate the whole incident with the strange elderly couple.

"Assalamualaikum. Can I get you a cup of tea or something?" I asked them politely.

The old couple both turned towards me slowly and shook their heads simultaneously. "No thank you," replied the man with a strong accent. "We're fine, we wait, Aliya."

"Are you her grandparents?" They looked at me and seemed to be half-nodding yes and half-nodding no, but I wasn't sure whether they had fully understood me. I tried to speak to them in my most shameful childish level of mother tongue: "Apnara Aliya Nana, Nani?"

From their answer, it emerged that they were in fact, to my utter surprise and disbelief, Aliya's parents. I also discovered that Aliya had gone out that evening and not returned for some hours. Her parents hadn't eaten but denied that they were hungry. Knowing Aliya and her non-culinary genius, there was no way she had fed them, and as she had left at around three or four o'clock in the afternoon, it was apparent they had not eaten for hours. Knowing my parents' generation, I knew they would never admit to being hungry, because they would feel '*lodga*'—shame.

I told them to wait and ran downstairs to ransack the freezer department. My mother was a saint; she always stacked my freezer full of samosas, bhajis, curries, and a variety of Indian flatbreads. She knew I led a hectic life at the hospital, so all I had to do was pop one of her dishes into the microwave, and voila! I could eat a healthy meal. She made me promise her two things: that I would never wear a mini skirt or eat pre-packaged microwave food from the supermarket.

I knew they must have been starving because a warm glow of gratitude crept across the face of the mother as I laid the food before them. They insisted over and over that I eat with them, but I tried to explain that it had only been an hour since eating my evening meal. I left them to eat while I phoned Aliya. "Why are your parents abandoned and hungry in my house?"

It was about 11.30 p.m. by the time Aliya returned. I tried to corner her and ask her what could be so important that she would abandon her parents to hunger, but Aliya just refused to talk and walked past me.

"Look, I'm not staying. Tell my parents, that they can stay in my room," Aliya declared indignantly.

"No, I will not. You tell them, and you should take some damn responsibility, for God's sake. I found them here starving, malnourished and sitting in the dark."

"Look, Laila! I've had a hell of a day, and you're not helping. So, get off my case; I don't care where they sleep."

I listened in shock as she continued to spurt out a list of heartless horrors about her parents. It emerged from Aliya's unfeeling rant that they had come for a meeting with Jonathan's parents. Aliya had at all costs tried to avoid such a situation, but Jonathan's mother had insisted they all meet—as a condition that she and her husband could acknowledge the engagement. Aliya's parents travelled down from Birmingham, not quite knowing what to expect. The meeting had been a disaster. According to Aliya, on sight of Aliya's parents, Jonathan's mother had refused to even talk to them. His father had made some effort, but Aliya's parents could barely speak English. Every time Aliya's mother spoke in mother tongue to her husband, both Jonathan's parents looked at each other in snobby disgust. Jonathan had tried hard to ease the situation with his mother by taking her to one side, but she flatly refused to make any effort at all. I think the gist of it was that Jonathan's parents were not at all impressed by Aliya's parents, and her mother and father were confused, and wondered what they were even doing having tea in the house of a well-to-do white British family.

Aliya did speak some mother tongue, but she had long since stopped using the language or even communicating with her parents. Aliya had, in fact, not seen them for a long time. She had several brothers and sisters and kept very little contact with any of them. She had on several occasions told me the story of how rich her family had been. They had previously lived in a beautiful mansion, far bigger than my parents' place in Egham. Aliya's parental home was so big that it made Kamal's family home seem like a Wendy House. Aliya's family were of noble descent from the homeland and owned acres of paddy fields, lakes, rivers and even a bit of the jungle where the tigers resided. I had noticed her expensive tastes in everything and the blatantly careless way in which she would waste her money. Every month, I would have to go through the humiliating role of chasing Aliya for her rent or contributions towards the bills. Aliya never really bought any food or contributed to the housekeeping, yet she would make a regular habit of eating all our food. My mother scolded me when I complained: "God has provided you with more than enough. You will never starve. Never deny anyone shelter or food. God will refund you four or five times over for your generosity."

My mother was right of course. I had to swallow my indignation on the subject and open my home and grant her unconditional access rights to my kitchen cupboards and food. Many things didn't fit her haughty, controlled 'I am a spoiled brat from a rich family' image. I searched for any signs of wealth and breeding in the faces of these two lost, old, worn-out people who looked as if they had just landed in Britain from some tiny Deshi tea picking village. They were not the parents she had described to me. Maybe I was wrong; appearance means nothing, but they hardly spoke English. I looked again for just one hint, one sign somewhere to prove that I was wrong—a piece of jewellery, her mother's saree or bag, her father's watch, something—but I saw nothing but a sad, confused old couple. I could sense the pain and sadness they felt in their eyes. Aliya all this time had played the part of Doña Superior so well it was hard to believe that it was all a huge farce, a façade, a charade of a life she had invented for herself. I didn't care whether she was rich or poor; I just wondered why she felt it necessary to lie about who she was.

Chapter Twenty-Two

On My Way Home – Salma

The one good thing about train journeys is that they give you a chance to relax and reflect on past and present experiences. I couldn't stop thinking about Kamal's friend Francisco: he was such a breath of fresh air. Yes, I liked this country. Yes, people like myself are lucky to live in the West and all the opportunities that are open to us, but it didn't mean I had to like everything about it. Most people here dream of going abroad and buying a huge house in some hot Mediterranean country. Even as a British Asian woman, I have every right to love and hate this country and move to some sunny getaway too if I felt like it. I suppose that meant that the whole of Europe was now open to all the Deshis that lived in Britain. I have the right to hate the weather but love the summer, to misunderstand the culture and feel nostalgic for the past.

I remember tears rolling down my eyes when I sat in a church on my last day in 6th Form. I sat staring at the stained-glass window and listening to everyone sing "Jerusalem". I tended not to join in the singing because I have a horrible voice, but I made an excuse—it was because of my faith I wasn't allowed to sing carols or Christian hymns, but secretly I loved singing them on my own in the privacy of my room. I found myself wiping away the tears from my eyes and yearning the loss of a bygone era. What era? It's not something my ancestors lived or ever experienced. I had no qualms talking about supply teaching in Christian schools; I'm not a Christian, but it made me wonder why I knew more about Christianity than most of the children in my class. It was nice to teach them about other faiths such as Hinduism, Judaism, and Islam. My expertise was my religion. I brought in samosas for Eid, taught them about the five pillars and the daily prayers. I showed them my late father's prayer mat and explained about fasting and giving charity to the poor. The children were delighted when I brought in a lilac and silver spangly saree and shalwar kameez. The boys protested, "That's not fair, Miss. What about us?" And so, I brought in my father's hat and waistcoat and a Panjabi. They looked so cute dressed in all the gear.

It made me smile when the naughtiest boy in the class, the one I was sure would grow up to be a skinhead and mug someone on the street one day, asked me, "Where's that book about the building with the stone, where the people walk around and around?" He was talking about the Kaabah. I told them to treat all books, especially books containing the words of God, with care and respect. He spent all his quiet reading hours turning from page to page, mesmerised by what he saw. "Look, Miss, I'm treating the Kaabah book with respect." World peace and mutual understanding lay in the heart of that little would-be hooligan boy. It was 1999 and the new millennium was looming. I had no clue what the future had in store for this young student of mine: one day he may come face to face with a person different to him, and whether he stands before him as friend or foe, he'll always remember that book.

There were some lovely songs they would sing in assemblies that were modern but lovely hymns. As the Christian tears welled up in my eyes, I would think how pretty the words to this song are, and how angelic the children sound.

My father told me always to be proud of my faith and to respect the faith of others. In Islam, a forced conversion was prohibited, and that had been the downfall of the Moorish empire. They lived side by side with the Jews and the Christians. It was so weird that Francisco had told me the same thing my father had told me when I was a young girl. My heart had leaped when he spoke to me of things, I had heard my father say. I felt this bizarre sensation as I talked to him like we had a connection from my past.

The route from London to Manchester is an interesting one. You can find yourself staring at two acres of perfectly patched yellow fields or peering into the backyards of run-down terraces. Some people say Britain has not the history, the architecture or the culture of other European cities. I disagree. European cities may have the museums, the cathedrals, palaces, and parks, but look beyond the historic centre of Europe's most beautiful cities, and what you often find are miles of faceless concrete tower blocks. We, on the other hand, have our churches, our country parks, and stately homes, our royal palaces and Roman ruins. There are also numerous museums and art galleries. When I was a little girl my father would take me by the hand as we walked from street to street, and he would explain the historical roots of every town and village we visited.

"Don't forget the Tudor manors and listed buildings. Look down most streets and you'll see Victorian and Edwardian houses that have stood for centuries through wars and revolutions. Have you noticed the train stations? They are inspired by Moorish arches and mosaics. Salma, my daughter, we don't just admire our history from afar; we live our history." As my father savoured the fine architectural details of the country that was now his home, I would stare up into the magnificent, timeless sky. "If one day I die, I want you to bury me here in Manchester, the city that made me a man. But most of all Salma my dear, it made me a husband to your wonderful mother and a father to my darling daughters."

So, England was a mishmash of the old, the very old, the decaying and the new, and it was because of my father I loved reading about its rich and bloody history. I always imagined that if I had lived in the past, I would have been an Indian princess, but more realistically, I probably would have been a poor servant girl brought over from the Desh by some rich English family.

I'd only been away a weekend, yet so many things had happened. Laila told me two of the strangest stories, and yet there was still a third story she had yet to tell me. She would spill the beans when I returned from Manchester. The first anecdote was about Aliya's parents. I had seen for myself that her parents were not at all how she had made them out to be. They were old and tired and spoke little English. We had gathered from Aliya's stories that her parents were young, posh, and as rich and westernised as she was.

I told Laila only the bare minimum about what had happened that weekend. Well, I told her a lot about Francisco, but not that much about Kamal. Laila asked me over and over again if he had misbehaved towards me. "I'll go and sort him out and kick his flirty disrespectful ass," Laila promised.

I could see she was hoping I would say yes, so she could fulfil a lifelong desire of hers. I couldn't answer because I wasn't even sure whether he had behaved rudely towards me or not. Kamal's mood had been on and off all weekend. One moment he was polite and attentive, the next moment he was mean and annoying. What had confused me most was his behaviour in the early hours of the morning when he had caught me on the balcony. Why did he grab my necklace? He fondled the silver jasmine between his fingertips and stared at it without saying a word. He made me feel exposed and vulnerable, whereas with Francisco I felt secure and protected. I had returned to my bedroom with a strange sensation in the pit of my stomach and a lump in my throat. All I wanted to do was run as fast as I could out of that flat and away from Kamal. I had completely lost my appetite since the balcony incident. My mind had acquired a life of its own and just went over and over the events with a kind of rebellious obsession.

Ever since I'd first met Kamal at Laila's house, he had come across as extremely aloof. If I was in the room, he never seemed to notice me; it was as if I were invisible. I don't know why I'd always come away feeling not very nice about myself inside. In company, he would talk to others but not me. About three months ago, he began visiting the house regularly, even when Laila was out working nights at the hospital. He would hang around the house and watch the satellite channels; sometimes it would be the football, strange aliens, the history channel and other times some American sitcom. As we were the only people in the house, he wouldn't exactly ignore me, but he wouldn't engage in any long conversations either. If Aliya were in the house, Kamal would occasionally go to her room. I could hear her giggling her girly, flirty laugh, and I imagined she would be flicking her hair and rolling her big mascara eyes at him. Aliya had a habit of doing this a lot in the presence of most men who visited the house. Laila would pinch Raj ever so hard on his arm if she found him caught up in Aliya's flirty sessions. It was Aliya's arm she wanted to squeeze ever so hard, but the fact that Aliya practised law became a huge deterrent.

By now, I was accustomed to Kamal's discourteous manner, so I made minimal effort to talk to him and just got on with my reading, planning and marking books. A couple of times he'd made a bit of effort and asked me general types of questions like what book I was reading or if I ever went out socialising with friends. But then the routine questions just ran out. I gave very little away, and I would eventually leave the room and go and sit upstairs and read. What had put me off Kamal from the beginning was not just because of his rude manner towards me, but because I had seen him in a passionate embrace with the nurse at the party that Laila had taken me to last autumn—the party with the two mad skinny girls. I wondered what had become of them. I don't know why I felt very uncomfortable when I had seen him kissing his girlfriend. It was just kissing, nothing else, but I remember thinking how impure it seemed. I am by no means an expert, but there was little love or tenderness in it. I think I was shocked because I'd not seen an Asian person kiss before. I read about kissing; I'd seen it on the TV, and even on occasion at university. I'd seen couples smooching on the lawn outside the Humanities building or in the Students' Union, but I'd never seen an Asian man or even a woman kiss someone. It was strange to think that so much ice had now been broken between both Kamal and me. This weekend, he'd almost become a friend to me, but then he had also crossed a strange line that had left me feeling very confused.

Chapter Twenty-Three

Kamal's Marriage – Laila

The thing with Kamal was that no one quite knew who he was. He was the master of duplicity—a character that from birth had been given two names, although I'm not quite sure which came first: the names or the schizophrenia. Kamal's cousin Ayesha, first born child of his American uncle, lived for a while in the Surrey house with Kamal's family; she was studying to be a doctor. She came across as a proud, strong, but in truth, she was the opposite—humble, kind and just a little insecure about herself. Ayesha had high, robust morals and would pray five times a day. Happily, she was to be married at the end of summer to a fellow medical student she had met while training in the city. Kamal's mother had a fit and fainted when she heard of cousin Ayesha's forthcoming wedding. "Oh, why are my children still single? I am cursed. My children are tall, fair, educated, but I cannot find anyone for them, anyone fit enough to suit them."

Oh yes! Kamal had great respect for his cousin Ayesha; he only showed the goody two shoes side of his character to her and, of course, the rest of his family. Kamal was, in fact, the golden boy. Attentive, open and a flirt with the aunties, but only just enough to make them blush and then run their soft hands over his thick black hair. Yet in real life, Kamal was quite a different character. The odd sharp Deshi girl saw right through him, but he was heavily sought after by the majority of false young equally arrogant women. I suppose Kamal did have all the right credentials: the one and only king of the mighty Deshi jungle. Kamal would always boast how tall he was and how unusual this was for a Deshi man, and that's why mothers-in-law sought him with such ferocity and passion. It was as if he was the one last remaining bachelor ever.

"And what about the real world, Kamal?" I would ask him. "You're not quite so unique there, are you?" And yet I thought, *why are women still stupid enough to fall for you?*

"Well," he would boast, "I suppose it's the boyish Kamal charm. They love the Asian charm, the manners, the respect of old values."

"Old values!" I would laugh. "You sleep with them, completely make them trust and fall in love with you and then run like the wind the minute they say the L word. Where are your old values then?"

Kamal would joke, "Ah, but I don't just sleep with them, Laila; they get the full Kamal treatment. Any woman lucky enough to experience the full effect of Kamal love, well … they can't get enough of me."

This is when nausea would begin to kick in. "Come on, Kamal" I would say disapprovingly.

His dark eyes would begin to sparkle and fill with intrigue and guile. He would then lower his voice and whisper, "It's just that none of those women are the one. I'll feel it when it's the right woman. I'll know it's her."

"I know you're looking for this great, mind-blowing love, but you'll never find it Kamal, because you won't look for it the simplest of places— your heart." When I knew he was feeling vulnerable, I would ask, "I'm sorry, how many women have you charmed?"

"I am not at liberty to tell you," Kamal would answer coyly. "I wish to respect the privacy of my former lady friends."

"What, Kamal? All three thousand of them?"

Kamal had once told me that he and his two other university friends had managed to have 'done', as he put it, the whole of the hall of residence.

"Don't you feel guilty when you break someone's heart? Don't you feel any obligation or loyalty towards them?"

"Look Laila, it's a mutual decision. There are women just like men who want to be friends and have a good time; they understand the rules."

"What women? Who are these women?" I protested.

"Most women I meet."

"Kamal, there's a name for that kind of woman, and that's a lady of the night. OK, maybe I am very stern on my kind, but seriously, don't kid yourself; women who pretend to want a good time … we all want the same—a good man and kids. Even if they fool themselves into believing they don't want all the commitment and security, the hormones soon catch up with them."

Kamal was silent for a moment; a look of revelation seemed to creep up on his face. It was as if he had suddenly come to realise something that had never been explained to him before. "Is that why they go all psycho bunny on me?"

I give up! I thought.

"You women, you're all the same. I knew it. All you want are my quality genes, so you can trap me and make me get married and have kids."

"You know, Kamal, it's not global warming that will end the human race: it's men like you. And seriously, those ginger-haired, green-eyed Asian women only exist in Bollywood films and photoshop."

Whatever Kamal was looking for, no matter how much he sinned, I sometimes think it wasn't entirely his fault. Kamal had been a naughty boy as a child and was constantly smacked and disciplined by his mother for not listening, showering, doing his homework, playing when he shouldn't or just not behaving himself. Normal kid stuff, I suppose, but for Auntie, it was too much to cope with, and she just had no patience with him. The beatings went on for a long time. Then one day, Auntie went ballistic and left him in the hospital, and that's when the hitting finally ceased. Now the boy had become a man, a dangerous one, who left a pile of broken hearts wherever he went.

I thought accompanying Kamal to the coast for the weekend would give me an opportunity to meet this infamous Doctor Francisco. I also wanted to prove to Kamal that there was more to Salma than he imagined and show Salma that Kamal was not always such a rogue, he could behave on occasion. Salma had seemed quiet and distracted when she had returned from the coast. She had hardly spoken to me, and I had so much to tell her. Kamal must have been so mean to her, so as soon as I bumped into him on my rounds at the hospital, I would have a serious word with him. It had to stop: Kamal would have to explain to me why he was so bent on being ill-mannered towards Salma.

Many months ago, I had engaged in a long conversation with Kamal about where he was going with his love life. It was obvious his mother wanted him to marry a Deshi girl and not just any bride would do; his mother would have to vet and approve her thoroughly. Every mother was obsessed with marrying their son and daughter to the right sort of partner. I guess there must have been a lot of peer pressure amongst other mothers when it came to the theme of marriage. Mothers tended to have a better choice when it came to be searching for a suitable bride for their sons. We were a community run by an army of matriarchs who revelled in giving us girls such a hard time. I still couldn't understand why so many of my gorgeous, intelligent, kind friends remained unmarried. They were approaching their 30s and were being usurped by younger models. Yes, I did say younger models because that's exactly how it feels at times. Second on the scale of shame of non-marital disappointment was your daughter marrying a white British or European man. As long as there was no scandal, no one seemed to mind.

Kamal knew deep down he would have to marry a woman of his mother's choice, and if he did not do as she wished, his mother would suffer some irreversible fit or seizure. So, Kamal enjoyed his freedom while he could. OK, he was very good-looking, but his arrogant character and the fact that I knew him so well made him unattractive to me. He was used to girls sucking up to him and falling all over him. He was superficial and found great pleasure in winding me up, so we would argue all the time.

Occasionally Kamal would have a deep moment, and we would have a serious conversation about life and the future. I always disapproved of his choices of women, which were usually empty-headed. I think they were like a trophy for him. He usually dumped them as soon as another girl looked his way.

I had once foolishly arranged a blind date with my Czech nurse friend; she was strawberry blonde, pretty, intelligent and in need of a passport. I thought maybe I could annoy his mother and make a match between Kamal and my friend Irina. It didn't work out because she was too intelligent and on the ball for him. She dumped him, although he had sworn it was the other way around. One day Kamal had been lazing about at my house, and we began another one of our regular talks about marriage.

"You should have said yes to that boy my mum brought to your house in September," said Kamal.

"I have someone, and it's serious, not like one of your little adventures," I replied.

"OK, but you'll never be able to marry him."

"How do you know?" I replied, knowing all the time that Kamal was probably right about Raj.

"OK, how about Aliya? Successful, attractive lawyer woman. Oh, and Salma; she's gentle and sweet. Aliya's too much like you. You need a complete change. A good person to sort you out," I added.

"Who's Salma?" He looked bewildered. Just at that moment, Salma walked into the living room to look for a book she had been reading. Salma didn't say anything; she just sauntered into the room, gave me a little silent smile and then returned to her business. "Her? You've got to be kidding me," Kamal replied.

I must say I was shocked by such an immediate rejection. "She's not my type. If my mum ever makes me marry a girl like that! No way. No!"

"Hey!" I protested. "You don't know her; she's a really lovely girl."

Kamal's mother married his father when she was only fifteen years old. She was exceptionally tall for her age, and her skin was fair for a Deshi girl, like café con leche. Kamal's maternal grandfather was a clerk for a Dhaka accounting firm. The boss of the firm had noticed her one Friday afternoon as he paid a courtesy visit to his employee's humble house. Despite her being only a young girl, he was determined to marry her to his son. Kamal's maternal grandparents at first refused, but eventually, they agreed. It would be unwise to refuse one's boss this kind of request, as such an offer for the hand of their daughter may never come their way again. Their only demand, once the nuptials had taken place, was that although Kamal's mother would go to live with her in-laws, the marriage must not be consummated until she had reached her sixteenth birthday. By her sweet sixteenth, Kamal had been born. The two years Kamal's mother had spent with her in-laws had been very traumatic for her. Her sisters-in-law were spoilt and greedy and took all the wedding gifts. Any gold jewellery or sarees that entered the house as gifts for the new bride would go directly into the grabbing, greedy hands of her sisters-in-law.

For the first year of Kamal's life, his mother would not let anyone near him; then in the following two years, she neglected Kamal due to the fact she had become somewhat emotionally ill from the stresses and strains of life at her in-laws. On occasions, she had to be stopped from beating him violently for no apparent reason. Things came to a head one day when the family was boarding a train. They were taking their annual trip down to the village some seven hours away from the capital. Kamal's mother, still unwell, had let go of his hand. The train was already pulling out of the station when Kamal's father noticed his only son was nowhere to be seen. In a crazy panic, his father jumped out of the train and ran furiously through the train station in search of his son. By this time, a member of the party had alerted the train inspector, and the train had been stopped. The whole family searched in vain for Kamal.

The station was jam-packed and chaotic; it would be almost impossible to find such a small child amongst such a multitude of people. They screamed his name over and over again in the vain hope they may find him. So many children were lost this way and would end up poor and as beggars on the street. By this time, realising the full gravity of what she had done, Kamal's mother had become hysterical and was screaming and crying in full view of everyone at the railway station. Just when all hope seemed to be lost, a poor elderly man appeared, with a child clutching his hand.

"Who claims this lost boy?" bellowed the elderly gentleman.

This event seemed to be a turning point for Kamal's mother; her attitude towards her son changed instantly. She recovered quickly and took control of her life. From that day, she never left Kamal's side, and they became inseparable.

Kamal's paternal family became hostile toward his mother and felt she would benefit from a spell in a psychiatric hospital, and so his father decided it was time to start afresh in another country, especially with civil war looming. While all family ties were not completely broken, Kamal's father's family did not feel she was a worthy, fit mother and, for many years, would not welcome her back into the family home. They sent money to England and helped Kamal's father set up a family business in partnership with some other Deshi family. This helped supplement his work as an accountant.

Kamal received the best public-school education money could buy and grew up to be a successful doctor. He was tall, confident and handsome and the obvious target of matrimony for many a would-be mother-in-law. Kamal's mother loved her son more than anything in this life. Her daughter Rimi received material affection, but Kamal had a monopoly on maternal love. And because of the nature of his mother's love for him, he grew up arrogant, vain and conceited. For years, there had been no signs of violence towards Kamal. She loved him deeply. He was supposedly her most treasured possession.

Kamal was about nine or ten years old when his mother had a violent relapse and hurt him quite seriously. Something to do with jewellery or missing money had triggered it off, and poor Kamal suffered the brunt of his mother's anger and frustration. Apparently, he lost consciousness and was treated by a family doctor friend, but the incident wasn't reported to social services or taken any further. Kamal's mother never suffered a relapse, and then soon after that, they moved to where they live now—in the south. Kamal remembers very little about his childhood before that incident and can only recall snippets.

During the 6th form when Kamal turned 18, he had applied to study medicine in America. He hadn't told his mother anything of his plans to study abroad because he knew she would be against any such arrangement. He was her dearest, most treasured thing in the whole world (after her collection of hand embroidered sarees), and the idea of her beloved son living so far away would surely break her heart. His father's brother lived in the States; he was a surgeon and had children: a daughter and two boys of Kamal's age. The plan was that Kamal would live in the university halls, so he was still only an hour and a half drive from his relatives' home. Kamal finally plucked up the courage to tell his mother, but he was not ready for her reaction. She cried, yelled, wreaked havoc on the kitchen crockery and finally fainted into a heap on to her bedroom floor. His mother didn't recover from this state for a whole week.

"Where will you live? Who will feed you? What if you meet an unsuitable girl?" screamed his mother. And so, it was evident that Kamal was going nowhere; he was to stay in London by his mother's side. He was a relatively well-behaved boy at his private boys' school, but he made up for this once he had reached university. He had found his forte in the halls of residence of Queen Mary's School of Medicine and Dentistry. Kamal was very popular with the female students and was soon busy dating several girls at a time. He liked the prestige of a good-looking, in-demand girl hanging off one of his arms. He was very calculated and always in control. Girls must have found this an attractive quality, for he was always the one being chased, but he was never the chaser.

During his first year at medical school, Kamal met an Asian girl. She was a few years senior to him. She was stunningly beautiful, independent, extremely gifted as a doctor and spoke her mind. Her parents were very wealthy and had businesses all over the Indian subcontinent, Pakistan, Bangladesh, and the Far East, and they were now breaking into the US markets. He was besotted with her as soon as he met her, but she was not so smitten with him. She left the hospital a year later to marry a cousin who was a computer whiz and had set up a software company in Silicon Valley. He was a millionaire many times over. Poor Kamal took a year to recover from the disappointment and rejection, but as soon as he recovered, he wasted no time in returning to his old habits. He had emerged from the experience not humble, but increasingly more arrogant and unfeeling. He granted his mother's permission to find him the ideal bride.

We argued all the time about arranged marriage. "As much as we hate the whole matrimony thing, why do we seem equally incapable of fighting against it?" I argued. "We advocate, permit and even nourish the very system that reduces us to mere prize cattle. Why do we put up with this, Kamal?"

"Laila, you overthink things. Just enjoy the now, live the moment, and it'll all just fall into place."

"Yes, Kamal, but we trust our parents who would never intentionally subject us to insult and injury or ridicule. They supposedly love us. Aren't we brought up to hold authority in great esteem, with respect for society, and above all, respect for the rules it lays down for us to follow blindly?"

"At the end of the day, I'll settle down. One day, it will just feel right, and I will stop," Kamal would reply calmly. "Anyway, it's just biology. Survival. They want us to carry on the best gene pool. Surely you should understand, Laila, you're a woman of science."

So, did the system of arranged marriage work? I would often ask myself. It was foolproof, a tried and tested formula, and it had worked perfectly for our forefathers over the centuries. What was the alternative? I was in my late twenties now, and the thought of finding my life partner via a method of catching someone's eye in a bar, and then this culminating in some passionate, physical embrace was loathsome to me.

Our parents encouraged us to trust their method of matchmaking, after all, the arranged marriage system is not unique to eastern cultures. The boy should have arms, legs, a head of hair and with all the right bits in the right places and everything functioning as it should. The girl could be kind, compassionate, and intelligent, but if she was the wrong shade of brown, she was possibly doomed to a life of sitting on the side-lines, waiting for a colour blind Deshi gentleman to look her way

My English male colleagues at work could not understand all the fuss and palaver surrounding the arranged marriage tradition. To them, it's quite a straightforward procedure: "If you can't find a husband, Laila, just put on a tight pair of trousers and top, go into town on a Friday night, and you'll pull in five minutes." This was advice from professional medical people.

Chapter Twenty-Four

Home - Salma

Mum was not getting any better and I could sense it was beginning to be a strain for my sisters. Leaving them to cope with university and A Levels all at once, I realise now I had not been completely fair. They had missed me, and we needed to be together. I knew I couldn't afford to buy a home for us all right now in London, and so I would have to rent. Deciding where to live in London was difficult. There was no way I could afford to live in Laila's neighbourhood, an entire house would cost me at least £3,000 per month, and my teacher's salary was half that amount. When my two sisters qualified, it would be a different matter; we would all earn enough to contribute towards a mortgage. The house in Manchester was debt free, and we could have easily stayed there, but the best jobs were in the South, and we needed to start a fresh new life at some point. Half of my mother's problem was that there were so many sad memories and ghosts still wrapped up in this house of ours. "I see your father everywhere," she would claim. The doctor had told us that my mother found it hard to move on because she was trapped in a time warp.

"Where do you see him, Ama?"

"Well he's in the garden mostly but sometimes he's at the kitchen table eating his favourite rice, dhal and aloo bharta." Then she would go silent as if lost again, haunted by sweet memories of days gone by.

Unfortunately, we would hardly get £30,000 for our house, which would go nowhere in London. We could buy a garage, and all live in that. I had several plans: sell the house and use the money to rent until we were all earning enough to buy a place. We could rent the house out in Manchester and get a few hundred a months in rent, which would help towards our rent in London. I had to make a decision soon, as time was running out. Sabrina, the older of my two younger sisters, was studying law at Manchester University; she had only completed a year of her course and could transfer to a university in London. The youngest, Soraya, would be finishing her A Levels next year. She was the brightest of all: an all-rounder, gifted at everything. Soraya was a talented writer and artist but took the practical route and decided to study medicine. She genuinely had the personality to be a good doctor because she was incredibly kind and caring—a real people person.

Soraya would spend hours talking to mum, reading her stories, combing her hair and calming her down when mum became upset and sad. My mother lived in a fantasy world, a world of make-believe, where time had stood still. She would follow my father's shadows through the house as if he had never left, thus she was living in total denial—denial that all her so-called friends had deserted her and that the man she loved so dearly, more than life itself, had also abandoned her. As my father lay dead in our house, she had cradled his head in her lap, rocking to and fro; her weeping and praying sounded just like one painful moan.

It's still too traumatic to dwell on what happened to my father and I'm so glad my sisters don't remember anything. Only I bear that burden of loss and pain along with my mother. None of my father's so-called friends came to the funeral; we were left to cope on our own. After someone dies, people usually visit with food and look after you for forty days officially, and many weeks after that. Whatever resentment or anger people may have felt towards my father, you would have thought that they could have put their feelings aside and helped us throughout the mourning process. It was just me, my baby sister and my pregnant mum. My mother's family couldn't all afford to come and help her, so just one brother came to assist with the funeral arrangements.

My father's family were all too angry to attend the funeral because they had felt he had cheated them. When they got wind of the fact there was a property involved and that money could be made by evicting us and selling our home, they planned to send a representative whose goal was to ascertain what inheritance was due to them after my father's passing. What my uncle meant was, could he sell my father's property, make us all homeless and take the money back to the Desh? The answer had been no.

My mother's brother had managed to get in contact with a family friend who had kindly paid for a lawyer. Everything was sorted out, and our family home was safe. As I said before, none of my father's friends came to the funeral, but the day was saved by the sudden appearance of a group of ladies in blue headscarves and flowing loose gowns. They cooked, cleaned and did general tidying. They reminded me of the flying nuns. They would swoop in, help my mother and then fly out again in their silver Toyota estate cars. They were silent and efficient and never asked for anything in return. My mother refused to eat, and we had to stay with someone else for a few weeks as she lay ill in the hospital. They had to feed her through a drip so that she wouldn't lose her baby. We believed Soraya was taller because she had been fed chemicals through a drip in the hospital, whereas we had merely been fed rice and dhal while in the womb.

242

Chapter Twenty-Five

Auntie Shayla – Salma

Laila was the picture of her mother, who we called Auntie Shayla, pronounced Chaila. Auntie Shayla was at least 45, and she was still very elegant, with intelligent, warm eyes and a strong motherly figure. Laila, I would say, was a skinnier version of her mother, without the maternal fat around the belly. Auntie Shayla was greatly respected and loved by the young people of the community, and you could talk to her about virtually anything. She was pretty unique. She was a magical cook who could muster up almost any international dish from anywhere around the world in virtually 10 minutes. Auntie Shayla was the first auntie to experiment with olive oil, a technique she had picked up from one of the many luxury European trips she had attended with doctors. Uncle took her regularly on exotic and expensive holidays. Uncle was also pretty approachable, but slightly more traditional than Auntie. She was understanding and incredibly kind, although you could tell that she once had a bit of a naughty, wild streak in her. I think Auntie saw so much of Laila in herself. If she had the choice, I am sure she would have told Laila to do what her heart desired, but Laila being her only child, Auntie was under constant pressure to show that she could and would find a suitable partner for her only daughter.

Uncle doted on Auntie and Laila. Auntie Shayla had deep regard and respect for her husband, and she also felt very much in his debt. It was a love marriage; they had met at university. It had been raining heavily the day they met. Auntie had fallen out of her rickshaw and into a puddle. Her two fat friends had insisted that the rickshaw wallah fitted them all in the rickshaw, even though he claimed it would not take the weight of all three of them. As the two enormous girls squeezed their curvaceous hips into the rickshaw seat, poor skinny little Auntie Shayla had popped upwards into the air like a cork and landed on the floor in a horrible dirty puddle. Uncle, then a young bright medical student, had seen it all ran over to rescue Auntie Shayla. They were both married within the year.

Auntie Shayla was not able to finish her law degree because Uncle had been offered an internship at a hospital in London. She had always dreamed of becoming a top barrister and saving the poor and the vulnerable. She wanted to travel to Oxford and finish her degree in England, but all concern for her education stopped once she was married. By the time they were settled in London, Auntie Shayla was already heavily pregnant with Laila. They lived in hospital accommodation, and while her husband spent hours studying in the hospital, Laila's mother was left on her own with the baby to walk the streets of London. Auntie Shayla spent hours on her own in the tiny little student bedsit and the isolation was driving her to depths of despair she had never experienced. The onset was slow, but before she knew it, she was immersed in a deep depression. Despite Auntie Shayla's lively, open nature, she had failed to make any friends, and she was lonely and miserable. She tried everything: she wrote letters to long lost friends and brothers back in the Desh, visited all the museums and galleries of London, read every book in the library she could lay her hands on, but nothing could wrench her out of the darkness that engulfed her.

One snowy winter's evening, Auntie Shayla was pushing her pram when she tripped on the pavement, cutting her nose as she fell onto the stone-cold ground. Everyone rushed by and nobody tried to help her. Humiliated, she picked herself up and checked whether Laila was OK. A car stopped by her, and a young man wound down the window. He was in a white doctor's coat, just like one her husband wore at the hospital. At first, she wondered why this man should stop and ask her to get in the car, then she recognised him. He was one of her husband's colleagues. He lived in the same corridor as them, and she had occasionally passed him in the hall. Now here he was again, offering to help her with the pram.

"Get in; it's cold. I'll drop you off at the residence."

Auntie Shayla was too exhausted and hurt to argue. He got out, cleaned and dressed the wound on Auntie's injured nose and gently placed Laila into her frozen open arms. He then folded the pram into the boot of the car. Auntie Shayla would sometimes dream and pray that Uncle would soon invest in a car so that she would not have to walk the cold streets of England; even one of those motorbikes with a small side car would do very nicely indeed. She was so cold and dejected; life had become unbearable. Auntie Shayla cupped her face in her hands and began to cry.

Over the months, Auntie's mood began to improve dramatically. She spent less time in her room getting depressed with a crying baby and spent more time in the park, enjoying the outdoors. Uncle was pleased, for a time he was worried for his wife, so he had prayed and prayed to God that her mood might change. He realised the flat was too small; it was just a room and a small kitchenette. He worked for hours at the hospital, so they might have money to move to a larger flat. He even wanted to buy a small car so that Auntie Shayla would not have to walk with the baby on the cold, icy streets of London. Uncle knew he had spent very little time with her, but if he worked hard enough and saw this tough patch through, eventually they would all reap the benefits. They were both from wealthy families in the Desh, but even with the allowance his father sent him, there never seemed to be enough money left once the fees were paid and the rent collected.

Uncle had some good news for Auntie. A friend had offered them the whole of an upstairs floor of a terraced house in north London, only a few tubes stop away from the hospital. Auntie did not seem that pleased at the news of the new accommodation, but Uncle put it down to her depressed mood. He believed many changes were on their way. Uncle had also just become a senior registrar, which meant more money and possibilities, a small car, eventually a flat, and then, who knows, even a house. His hard work paid off, and he was finally on his way up.

On Laila's father's days off, he even worked occasionally in a restaurant so that he could save more money for Auntie Shayla. The local Deshi currency did not go very far, even in those days, and Laila's father refused to ask his father for any extra money. There were sisters yet to marry and younger brothers to support through university. An old friend of Uncle's from university had found him the job in the East End restaurant. They called him Byron Bhai. Uncle had once lent this friend money to travel to England, and he had also acted as a character witness for him because his friend, once an up-and-coming journalist from the Desh, had been accused of plagiarism and sacked from his job at a top newspaper publishing company. Laila's father felt indebted to him. On one occasion at the restaurant, they had the pleasure and privilege of waiting for the entire Deshi cricket team. They were so excited, like two little village boys, and they longed to give the team their salaam and inform them how much they admired them all. As the two young waiters approached the table, one of the cricketers beckoned with his hand and shouted,

"*Eh bhettah eh digge ashor,* get me one whisky on the rocks. Quickly. I'm dying of thirst."

Uncle's friend, Byron Bhai, approached the famous cricket player and explained quite gently in his ear that whisky was, in fact, an alcoholic drink. "Whisky is alcohol, but I can bring you a soft drink, Sir."

The cricketer turned on Uncle and his friend with all his fury. He stood up, and with one almighty kick, Byron Bhai fell to the ground. Uncle crouched over his friend who lay in pain, humiliated in a heap on the floor. The cricket team were all laughing and jeering. The cricket player who had kicked Uncle's friend calmly sat down, waved his hand in the air and demanded that someone get this insolent waiter out and remove him from his sight. The famous cricketer then calmly carried on eating his food. The manager had no alternative but to sack Byron Bhai. Uncle refused to stay. If his friend went, then he would also leave. His good friend Byron Bhai went to live in Manchester, and Uncle felt sad for the loss of his dear friend and ally.

For weeks, Laila's father felt angry at how his friend had been treated. Uncle's rich friends from Manchester, a couple with a young son, had come to London for a visit and were able to offer Byron an alternative job in Manchester at their very own restaurant. Uncle knew now that Byron Bhai was in good hands. However, the arrival of these wealthy friends from Manchester brought about a painful development Uncle had not foreseen. For the first time, Uncle felt what it must be like to want to die. Dark thoughts crowded his mind and his heart ached with a pain he had never dared to feel in his life. He looked at his wife as she nursed their baby girl. "I'm falling," he cried, "I am falling." Laila's mother looked at her husband's stony face and began to cry.

I believe Laila's father must have forgiven Auntie Shayla, because they now seemed very happily married. All I know was that letters were exchanged between the English doctor and Laila's mother. I don't believe it went further than just words, but who knows? The English doctor would occasionally give Auntie Shayla lifts, and a friendship had developed between them. Uncle's rich friend's wife had seen them and told Uncle all about their friendship.

Chapter Twenty-Six

The Secret – Laila

I was in an awful situation, and I didn't know how to handle it or what to do. While Salma was visiting Kamal's seaside apartment, the weirdest thing happened to me. The problem is, if this gets out, I'll be in serious trouble. I was working at the hospital when a young Asian man walked past me in the corridor. I turned back to look at him because he just seemed familiar. But then I thought he must have caught my attention because he was Asian and tall. I don't know; there was something very Deshi about him, like from the homeland. He looked like he had just stepped out from a street in the Deshi city. I'd only caught a quick glimpse of him, but there was a look about him that was easy to remember. He was tall and unnaturally skinny.

An hour later, I saw the young Asian man hanging around outside the Accident and Emergency door, looking both a little shifty and lost. I could have called security, but I decided not to. I don't know why; maybe because the thought of the guards carting off some poor, helpless-looking Deshi boy and the possibility of them being rough with him made me feel sad inside. He could have been visiting a wife, a relative or a friend, but I just wasn't convinced. We weren't allowed to be complacent in the hospital, since we came across a whole host of weirdos on a daily basis. I decided to turn a blind eye on this occasion and walked away. As I did so, out of the corner of my eye, I thought I saw him fall to the ground. He sat there dazed for a few moments and then, with difficulty, hauled himself up on his feet again. My instinct was to approach him and help him, but as I did so, he looked straight into my eyes with a sad and painful look and then he just hurried away. I called after him, but he was gone. I didn't say anything to anyone.

The next day, I saw him again in A & E, doubled up and clutching his stomach. The receptionist seemed to be talking very loudly at him. I could just about hear the words "Address, what's your address, papers," and "passport" being mentioned. I stood and observed as he shook his head and walked hurriedly away. I saw her pull a face and mouth the words "I-L-L-E-G-A-L" to a colleague. It was then I thought, of course, he must be an illegal immigrant. That's why he was acting so dodgy yesterday. I followed him outside and watched him as he walked off into the night. He stopped for a moment and held his chest, wheezing as if he couldn't breathe. Part of me thought, *don't get involved; all suspected illegal immigrants must be treated but also reported*. I didn't want to be responsible for shopping this man to the authorities. I never admitted this to my friends, but deep down, I saw every illegal immigrant as an underdog, and I have always been keen on helping those who have nothing.

I refused to get on the anti-immigrant bandwagon and believe that people in this country would face hardship because, suddenly, there was an influx of illegal immigrants. I'm sure there were just as many Brits packing their bags and leaving the country for Spain as immigrants were trying to reside in Britain. Well, that's what Aliya told me. She was a Spanish property and homes expert. How did people's lives change if there were more immigrants in the country? My life wasn't any different; most of my friends' lives wouldn't change significantly if more immigrants were to enter Britain. We earn millions in arms deals by selling weapons to developing countries, and then we complain when these war-ravaged people seek refuge in our cosy, dreary little land.

I once knew a boy at university who couldn't bear to live in England. All he wanted to do was finish his degree and leave for a sunnier country. He said that since a child, he had always been affected by the bad weather. He had to this day never managed to settle in one place. He had lived in Spain, South America and now planned to try out the Far East. Luckily, he had his pick of countries to live in, and now he could come and go as he pleased. The world was only an oyster for a chosen few. I remember the argument I had with a nurse Kamal had dated about a year ago.

"With so many nurses from Africa and the Philippines coming to work in Britain, standards will fall, and we should only employ nurses from Europe," she argued.

"Surely it makes little difference where they are from as long, they do their job," I protested

"If we let some in, then the whole health service would be overrun by bad nurses who can't speak English properly," she replied.

"If we don't let these nurses come and work in our hospital, our whole health service would just collapse around us."

When she started criticising Asian doctors, I just lost my cool. I got so cross with her, and Kamal's girlfriend retorted by covering her ears and screaming, "I'm not listening! I'm not listening!" What she meant was, she had lost the argument and had nothing more to say. When she stormed out of the room, Kamal had stood there laughing at the whole situation and had no intention of running after her. Even though I did feel a deep sense of satisfaction at having won the argument, I did feel a little guilty, and I still encouraged Kamal to go after her. It wasn't the first time the nurse had spoken so rudely about Indian people. I had no patience with her at all. Kamal had brought her along to a meal, and she had hogged the whole conversation, telling the entire table of her wonderful life in Saudi as a nurse. Kamal's girlfriend lived the jet set life of the expats, and it was beautiful.

"You know couples can't cohabit in Saudi, so my boyfriend and I were married before we flew out. He managed a chicken slaughterhouse. The job comes with all kinds of benefits, such as a tax-free salary, free health care, cockroach-free accommodation and annual flights home. All the best single men are in Saudi and come with tax-free benefits. While I have since split with him, I am determined to go back one day and find a man who will provide me with all the same fringe benefits. Unless Kamal snaps me up first!" She laughed. Then she treated us to her experiences of 'Chop Chop' square. This is where all the people accused of crimes in Saudi had their hands or heads cut off.

The more I suggested the possibility of taking a year off to work as a volunteer doctor in South America, the more pressure there would be from my parents to sort out the romantic aspects of my life. My parents couldn't understand why on earth I would want to work in a developing country for a year. And why South America? What connection had we with that continent? The subcontinent where we came from, they understood, but South America! Where did this mad idea originate from? At first, my parents just laughed it off: "Our daughter is so sentimental. Laila has such a good heart; she wants to go to all the poorest countries and sort them out. Do you remember when Laila was a child, and she sat with an old woman on the veranda, stroking her back and feeding her rice?"

As the year passed, I brought the subject up with increased frequency. I noticed the look on their faces change from amused indifference to concerned alarm. Raj had been against the idea from the start and breaking up with him had made me realise that this was the path I wanted to take. London was beginning to feel small and oppressive: the traffic, the litter, the endless sea of people. I was bored with the place. I felt like I couldn't breathe anymore, and I just wanted to get out.

Breaking up with Raj had been painful for a moment, but once it was all over, I had felt strangely relieved. I think he had an unhealthy reliance on me. Having been brought up without a mother had affected him in every way. I think he believed I embodied an idea of the perfect Indian woman. He loved women with dark, golden skin. He would force me to sit in the sun when we snuck off on our Mediterranean holidays. Raj said I was too pale for an Asian girl and should let my skin tan. I had just come back from the Desh, and my skin was extra suntanned because I had refused to sit indoors during my visit. I thought I looked horrible from all the mosquito bite marks on my face, but he didn't seem to care. I wondered whether his father had smothered his mother somewhat because Raj tended to asphyxiate me with his overwhelming love for me. His father had locked his mother up in a concrete ivory tower, and with her long Rapunzel-like tresses, she had hanged herself. I would not allow Raj to do the same thing to me.

Raj was deep down quite a sad, lonely boy who just wanted to belong. He had attended a school with mostly Asian lads, so he naturally identified with them and not white British boys. He kept the fact that his father was ethnically British quiet from most people at school. He would even draw pictures of his mother dressed in a red saree and with her long black plait. His teachers asked where his mother was, and he just replied that she was in India. They assumed she was on some extended holiday. Raj spent a lot of time with his English Christian grandparents. They were keen on bringing him up as a good Christian boy, but he rebelled. He wanted to be like the Hindu, Muslim and Sikh boys at school. I always wondered what his mother must have looked like. He said he had a black and white picture of her when she was about 16. He said she was beautiful. I thought as much. Raj's father, however, was no pretty picture, as he was overweight, unkempt and drunk most of the time. Raj, on the other hand, was tall and athletic, with intense brown eyes, thick black lashes and soft golden skin.

I did feel guilty that I hadn't fought for our relationship. I know Raj must have been devastated. He was a truly honourable young man who would never cheat or lie in a relationship. All he wanted to do was to love and be loved by someone who would provide him with the family and stability he had long yearned for. Sadly, I failed to offer him any of these. He was angry with me because in many ways, I had given him the impression that stability and marriage were exactly what I was also looking

254

for in a relationship. He saw something of his mother in me. The similarities could only have been skin deep because in no way was my personality in any shape or form like hers. I was strong-willed, independent and would never take my own life. I had set him free, he would find the right girl and he would be happy. My parents would never have accepted him, as he was the son of a servant girl that had committed suicide and had a drunken depressive for a father. I thought it sad and even romantic.

I was determined to go to South America with or without my parents' permission. I know if they did eventually agree to let me go, it would have to be with my future husband. I just wasn't ready to make that kind of commitment yet. Oh, how happy it would make them if I married Kamal. I was always hinting to my mother what a naughty boy he was (without giving too much away), but it never seemed to register. The boys seemed to get away with more than us girls.

A couple of days ago, I saw that skinny-looking Asian boy again. This time, he was sitting on a bench outside A & E. I wasn't in my white coat, so he didn't notice me approach him. I know it was a risk, but I just instinctively knew he was harmless.

"I've seen you here quite a few times. Is there anything I can help you with?" I asked. He looked straight at me. His eyes seemed tired and confused, or were those eyes full of shame? The more I looked at him, the more I thought, *I know this person from somewhere*, but I couldn't quite place him. He didn't want to talk. He lowered his head and said nothing. "Look, I don't know if you are in trouble or need help, but I'm a doctor here.

Maybe I can help you. Do you have an ill relative at the hospital or something?"

He turned towards me, his face still full of pain. "Are you a doctor?"

"Yeah!" I nodded encouragingly.

"Ampna Deshi?"

"JEE! JEE! Ami Deshi," I replied in my awful accent. "But that's about all I could say." I pushed his arm slightly and started to laugh at myself. "But I can understand; you can speak to me in Deshi."

Already, his face was cupped in his hands and he was sobbing. I didn't know what to do. I should have known how to respond, as I dealt with pain all the time. To caress a Deshi man's back to comfort him, I don't know; it just seemed a strange or inappropriate thing to do. He reminded me of my auntie's driver Bhai in the Desh. As I watched him while he spoke to me in what sounded like well-spoken mother tongue, I noticed his face seemed thin and broken. It hid what once could have been a handsome face. His straight black hair flopped over his tired, red eyes.

He told me he thought he was ill and should see a doctor because he had started to suffer from a bleeding nose, blackouts and possibly fainting fits. He looked as if he was suffering from malnutrition. "I am living rough; I no longer have a steady job, and I am ashamed to say I'm here in Britain illegally. I planned to become a student, but that is now an impossible dream."

"You can trust me. My job isn't to shop people to the police, but it's to help them get better."

He had been hanging around the A & E because he knew he could get help. He also knew that with no papers, he could even get arrested. He had gone through such hardship this year, but he was too ashamed to tell me any details; he thought it would shock me too much.

"Going back to the Desh is not what I fear so much; it's that there is someone I know, a close friend who is in trouble, and I cannot risk being arrested and leaving England until I know of my friend's fate."

I thought the best thing to do before he told me his life story was to give him a medical. It was too risky to check him in the hospital in case he was a hardened criminal and people saw me with him. I would often sleep over at the hospital and had a room I shared with another doctor, but she was away on holiday. I took him to my car, where I grabbed my bag and packed lunch. He seemed to have all the symptoms of anaemia, but I couldn't risk having his blood checked. Could I risk taking him to my father's practice? I just wasn't sure. For now, all I could do was give him some money for food and my packed lunch. Maybe he could go to a homeless centre, but the mention of it just seemed to make him panic. He feared he could be spotted and arrested.

"Look, I know in my heart you are a good person and won't spend the money on drugs."

He looked shocked at the suggestion. "Never!" he replied.

"Meet me tomorrow in the same place, and I'll bring you food and some smarter, less conspicuous clothes." He looked grateful. "Where are you staying?" I asked him.

He just shook his head.

"I'll do what I can for you, but tomorrow you must tell me everything, otherwise I can't help you unless I know all the facts."

He nodded his head and was gone.

All the way home, I tried to think who he reminded me of and why he looked so familiar. That was the night I found Aliya's parents in the living room and sat in the dark. What a day it had been!

Chapter Twenty-Seven

Matchmaking – Salma

Neither Laila nor I had very much to say to one another; either we had run out of things to talk about, or we were both harbouring deep, dark secrets. I don't think Laila was cross with me. She was always sincere enough to talk openly with me if anything was bothering her. I felt uncomfortable about my growing friendship with Kamal and even Francisco. Was I treading all over Laila's world? I know she had asked me to be around a lot recently because she was finding it hard to get over Raj.

Laila's parents were also increasing the pressure on the marriage front. Any chance of a summer wedding was no longer a possibility, as she'd have to be engaged at least by Easter. This, however, did not stop the aunties from piling the emotional pressure on to Laila's mother: "What's wrong with your daughter? Isn't she married yet? How long has she been a qualified doctor for? She's getting old; there are younger girls with top class degrees in medicine from Oxford. Get her married, Bhabi, or soon no one will want to marry her." All these questions and remarks would drive Laila's mother up the wall. She was an intelligent, educated woman, but she still managed to fall for the pressure from the aunties. People rarely married between October and March. Laila had to be on a plane to South America by either this September or by Easter if she were to escape the matrimonial ambitions of the aunties.

I found myself in a constant state of uneasiness and confusion and kept revisiting what happened on the balcony at Kamal's coastal apartment. This was a man I disliked, so why did I spend every waking minute obsessing about that weekend? He and Francisco had dropped in while I was away in Manchester. Kamal didn't need an excuse to hang around the house, as he was besotted with Laila and intent on making my life hell. I thanked the universe he had now gone to the Desh for a few weeks, and I had time to breathe and think. I couldn't bear to face him again. Being near him freaked me out. Going home should have had a grounding effect on me, but instead, I yearned to be back in London. I felt this aching feeling of unfulfillment and longing. It was weird because I had spent the whole year secretly harbouring negative thoughts about London. I was beginning to think it would not bring my family the happiness I had once hoped for. We still needed a change of environment, but maybe London would be too big and fast for us.

The pressure of marriage had forced Laila into even considering visiting a matchmaking party. "If I'm going to have to get married, then at least let it be on my terms," she obsessed. There were various types of matchmaking events: the first type was carefully organised by the older generation and consisted of going to a party where like-minded, socially eligible doctors, lawyers, and dentists would wear appropriately coloured badges. They are organised by the more proactive aunties of the community and were based on nationality and faith. A typical chat-up line was: "So what do you do?" Why mess about with polite chit-chat when you can get straight down to the most important issue?

Knowing someone's profession tells you a lot about them. It tells you whether they failed their A Levels or not—oh, and most importantly, how much they are worth. For example, if they are a doctor and haven't bought a house, you know at some point they will, and they can. Tacky Indian music plays in the background, and a buffet of samosas, bhajis, and salad are available at a price of £15 per ticket. The second class of matchmaking party is the unchaperoned type. Young Asian professionals organise these; they arrange different nights based on different religions.

"The only alternative to those awful Deshi matchmaking dos is dressing up in your most provocative outfit and tarting about in a pub or a club where lots of Asians hang out in the desperate hope that you will catch someone's eye." Laila was quite adamant that she would die an old maid before she resorted to this last method of matchmaking. "Aliya would have no scruples in husband-hunting at that kind of matchmaking party. I am sure her day job isn't litigation and the law; it's hitting the social scene so that she can find a rich man. She's obsessed with finding the right husband and at any cost. Have you noticed we've seen very little of her lately?"

It seemed that after the episode with Aliya's parents, she had hardly been around, and when she was, I only heard her stomping around her room or throwing up in her bathroom. I think it must be the hangovers and the fast-paced partying. Poor Aliya's parents. Laila had to take them to Victoria coach station the next day because Aliya refused to see them. She stormed into the house, saw that they were there and then just stormed out again. We were just too scared to bring the subject up with her. Well, I was anyway.

I was surprised Laila had said nothing to Aliya. Laila was not normally argumentative, but when pushed, she could be very assertive and strong. Laila was really at her wits' end with Aliya because she hadn't paid any rent or bills for at least four months. Her excuse was money problems, but the shiny posh shopping bags kept piling up in her room. As Laila worked nights at the hospital, she did not always see what went on in the house. I wasn't sure whether to say anything to Laila about the shopping bags, and I didn't say anything in the end. Laila was stressed about her own business, and that's why she had said nothing about the parent's episode to Aliya. I gathered that the meeting with Aliya and Jonathan's parents had not gone too well. Even if her parents didn't agree, surely both Aliya and Jonathan would still go ahead anyway with their wedding plans. She was so independent; I don't think she cared what her parents thought.

Chapter Twenty-Eight

The Crash – Laila

When one thing starts going wrong, then everything does. First, my laptop started crashing, and then there was the business of the boy at the hospital, my parents, the marital pressure, and finally, Aliya never paid her rent. I was beginning to lose my patience with her. Things had been coming to a head for a long time. I couldn't understand how heartless and disrespectful Aliya had been about her parents. It broke my heart to see them and I had tears in my eyes when I put them on the coach to Birmingham. They were just silent and had nothing to say. They looked so lost and broken. I realised Aliya had been lying these last two years about her parents and her so-called aristocratic background. She had told us all she was from this rich landowning family in the Desh. I began to realise that this land she so frequently spoke of probably amounted to a couple of paddy fields. She managed to play on my ignorance, as I didn't know enough about my heritage. When I asked about the region her family were from, my parents told me it was highly unlikely they were from there because it was a national forest, and the Royal Bengal tiger lived there. Still, I believed her because it was easier to be gullible than to question her.

Over the last two months, all I had heard was Jonathan, Jonathan, and frankly, I was a little sick of it. I was happy for her, but Aliya was becoming sloppier, messier, and dirtier and not paying her rent, which was a bit of a problem. My parents did have money, but I still had to pay the bills and the mortgage to the bank. It wasn't as if she didn't have a highly paid job. She must have been on at least £40K, but what did she do with it all? She had her bathroom, yet she never cleaned it, which was beginning to drive me crazy. She never had any food in the fridge or her cupboards and would just east all Salma's food, though she dared not eat my mother's frozen curries. I assumed things had not gone well at the meeting between her parents and Jonathan's. After having that engagement ring shoved into my face for a whole month and even having it scratch my nose at one point, I didn't care anymore. I prayed for a short engagement because it meant she would soon be leaving. That way I wouldn't have to ask Aliya to leave or throw her out. I assumed Jonathan's parents were upper-class snobby types, so how on earth did they communicate with or even react to Aliya's parents? I can imagine it now. Aliya's illiterate parents sat on some posh handcrafted Italian sofa, sipping tea with Jonathan's posh lawyer father and society mother.

The little amount Aliya did tell me in a rare moment of honesty was that her future mother-in-law refused to talk to them and sat there stony-faced while Jonathan's father tried to make conversation about stocks, shares, and bonds. The conversation was lost on her parents who hardly understood the topic, let alone spoke a word of English. How on earth did that girl ever communicate with her parents when she was growing up? Via an interpreter? It was weird; Aliya was the perfect liar because when she did reveal the truth about her upbringing, you conveniently forgot all the other previous versions she had told you of her thoroughly fictitious life. Gosh! It must have been awkward. No wonder Aliya was mad at them. She was such a control freak. Not only was she heartless with her parents, but she was also incredibly rude to all my friends. She bullied Salma and had cliques at work which created rivalries and general bitchiness between staff at her law firm. However, one-person Aliya found it hard to be rude to was Kamal.

Kamal had soon put Aliya in her place when she had called him 'Tarty boy'—implying he was a gigolo. He had replied by saying: "At least I don't look like an East Asian whore." She was so shocked and hurt that from that day on, she was never rude to Kamal again. I would say Aliya began flirting with him. If those two ever got together! Yes, Aliya would make the perfect daughter-in-law for Auntie. However, her name-calling didn't stop there. Salma was 'Wet Girl', and I was 'Princess Laila' or 'Rich Bitch'. Aliya had a whole host of other names for people. The one that annoyed me the most was when she called Francisco 'Spanish waiter boy'.

"Kamal and some Spanish waiter boy are in the living room," Aliya had rudely commented one day. She had not even taken the trouble to say this quietly. I was furious and hushed her. She pulled a face at me, as if to say, "Oh for God's sake!" and slammed the door behind her. *That girl has got to go!* I thought.

I was still meeting the immigrant Bilal at the hospital; it had become a regular thing. Every day, I would give him some food, medicine and occasionally clothes. We would sit and talk for a little while if I wasn't too busy at the hospital. He spoke mostly of his life in the Desh. "My parents died many years ago. My father was a village school teacher. When I sold the land and the last of any remaining family wealth, all I wanted to do was study, but things went very wrong when I met Afzal, my friend, and we travelled to Saudi," he said.

When I had asked him, what had gone wrong in Saudi, Bilal just shook his head and then changed the subject. I worried at first that he might have been on drugs, but the look of shock on his face when I had suggested it told me that he wasn't. I could always tell because I dealt with addicts almost every day, and Bilal seemed too intelligent and noble. His eyes were tired, not from drug addiction but disappointment and sadness. Bilal seemed to be a man that had lost all hope, but he still came across as gentle and well mannered. I could tell he was educated because there was something knowledgeable about the way he spoke. Maybe he was a writer or a poet who had just packed his bags and run away to see the world, and now he had fallen on hard times. I hated the way we had such a black and white view of immigrants. They were viewed as faceless scroungers, political dissidents or helpless victims and lowlifes. There was nothing noble or romantic about immigrants or asylum seekers. We dehumanised them because the task of disliking them was then made easier. I decided I would help Bilal because God had given me everything, and he, on the other hand, had nothing.

My father had brothers and sisters, and while some of them were successful, others in the family were not. I had at least two wayward cousins and at least three uncles and two aunties that needed constant financial support. Knowing my father had money had made them occasionally complacent, and they relied on him heavily for basically everything—upkeep of the family home in the village, basic provisions, new fridges, building work, and even my cousins' weddings. My mother would get angry and upset every time he sent them money. My father would get equally upset with her and claim with tears in his eyes that it was his duty and his father's last dying wish. "God has blessed us with more than enough money," my father would protest.

What annoyed my mother was that she had hoped he would take early retirement, and they would spend more time together. However, my father continued to work because private consulting paid so well: the extra income came in handy for the growing demands of the family.

I still felt a little guilty about leaving poor Salma to the mercy of Kamal that weekend on the coast. However, I finally did get to meet the infamous Dr. Francisco Javier Rivera. He was very nice, a little intense, very macho Ibérico and incredibly handsome. I think there is a charm and passion in these Mediterranean men that our men have lost. I suppose what they do have in common is that they are also mummy's boys. Most of the young men that I had met in Spain had been very polite and well-behaved. They liked their big new cars, then the steady girlfriend would follow, and finally the flat and marriage. They knew exactly what they wanted, and they were pretty systematic and practical about how they went about achieving it. I suppose Spanish boys were domesticated just like Deshi boys and all of them dressed like accountants. Francisco was different; he had this way of staring through you when he spoke to you. I don't think it was a conscious thing because he was crazy about his Bosnian wife. Sonya was quiet, and Francisco was loud and alive. How did two such different people ever fall in love? Wouldn't he have wanted a wife he could spend hours and hours talking to? Sonya spoke very little English or Spanish. There was an ongoing joke that if Francisco was out and about, you could always find his wife Sonya walking two steps behind him. I didn't agree. I thought they complemented each other. Francisco liked to talk, and Sonya liked to listen.

Maybe Kamal ought to take a leaf out of his friend's book, but I could see him living the playboy life for a good few years yet until his mother throws a tantrum and forces him to marry some Dollywood princess. The girls from this country were way too beneath Auntie's standards. I remember one evening coming home and seeing some poor girl in my mother's living room being twirled around and inspected by a hoard of aunties and Kamal's mother. They wouldn't dare treat me like that. She wasn't good enough because her parents' house had been on the wrong end of town. I complained to my mother, but she said that things were as they were, and it would take a generation before attitudes would change. I don't think Kamal was ready to settle down because he still loved the freedom to play with women's hearts. Kamal did have a reputation, and everyone knew what he was like at the hospital, but women would still fall for him. They found it attractive. OK, Kamal was very handsome, but his arrogance made him unattractive to me.

Chapter Twenty-Nine

Petticoat Blouse – Salma

My mother told the funniest and weirdest stories from the Desh. One of our favourites was a quirky little anecdote. This was a folk tale by a famous writer. She called the story 'The Petticoat Blouse'. It was as if her saree had wrapped her up in a time capsule. She was sheltered from all the nastiness of modern living, and so much of society seemed to pass her by.

A teacher in a typical village in the Desh would pass by a garden on his way to school, and in the distance, he could see a young woman dancing in her petticoat and blouse. It would be seen as indecent to approach her and so he pretended to look at the floor, but out of the corner of his eye, he did manage to catch a glimpse of her. Some mornings she would be there dancing, and other times, she would not. After many weeks, he finally plucked up the courage to approach her so that they may be able to talk. He was lucky that day because just as he had hoped, there she was, the young village girl dancing in the garden, dressed in her petticoat and blouse. As he approached her, he became increasingly nervous. What would he say? Would she be insulted by his bravado and run away? He did not know. He would confront all these issues once he had spoken to the young woman. As he approached, he was surprised to see that it was no young woman, but it was just a petticoat and blouse hanging out to dry in the breeze.

Today, we were invited to the house of Francisco and his wife. While I had been in Manchester, Francisco and Kamal had visited Laila's house and invited both myself and Laila to attend a small gathering at his home. It was just an excuse to meet Laila, I was sure. I think Francisco had plans to make Kamal and Laila fall in love, or at least consider each other as potential partners. On the one hand, I thought, *yes, they are suited in many ways—job, background, both good-looking*. They were part of the young Deshi jet set or the elite. These were the boys and girls who followed certain careers, studied at the best universities, whose parents had money and provided them with their first properties. They behaved impeccably, dressed well at weddings and always talked about careers and mortgages. I was not one of these people, nor did I ever want to be one. When I observed them at weddings, I was used to feeling like the outsider looking in. Every time I thought of the possibility of Laila and Kamal finding happiness in each other's arms, I felt a strange aching tickle in my belly. Maybe I felt protective towards Laila; I know she was suffering but she would not display her true pain and feelings to anyone.

Laila was a huge hit wherever she went and blended in naturally with the guests. Francisco's ground floor flat was enormous; they were only renting it, but it was very nice. It was close to Laila's house in a very leafy street. It was a garden flat, so there was direct access to the communal gardens. There were a lot of couples and children at the house. The children, who ran in and out of the house, were oblivious to anything but their world of play. As I watched them, I remembered so clearly how I would run in and out of the patio doors on sunny days when I was a little girl. I remember my special friend, a skinny little boy with a bad cough and a bossy mum. That's all I remember. Those were the days when my mother would wear her favourite nylon lilac saree and white rhododendrons in her hair. She always wore the most beautiful smile. I often looked at the photos my father took of her before his death and wondered how such a pretty young girl of 26 managed to become so sad and lost to the world around her.

I was so glad Kamal was not here at Francisco's house, otherwise I don't think I would have come. Every time I thought of him, I would feel a blind panic, a rush of adrenaline and want to run. Why he scared me so much, I did not know. Everyone at the party was a couple, except for Laila and me. We didn't feel uncomfortable because the guests were friendly, attentive and inquisitive, so we found ourselves constantly engaged in conversation. Laila told me that with couples, you should always befriend the wife first. Then you should ask her how she and her husband met and compliment the relationship by saying: "Oh, how sweet!" or "Oh, how romantic!" Talk about your relationship a little and how happy you are with your real or fictitious boyfriend, and then you are free to go and chat with the husband. If the husband is flirty, run a mile; if he is friendly and well-behaved, compliment him on what a lovely wife he has; then you can start chatting about any topic you like.

There were four couples and their children at the party. One couple were artists; she was from Iraq, and he was Irish. The other couple were Indian doctors. The third was a pregnant Deshi social worker and her English politician husband. Finally, the fourth couple was a history lecturer and his Tunisian wife. It was such a weird and wonderful diverse mixture of guests. How did these people ever meet one another? What struck me more than anything was how comfortable they all were in each other's company. They exchanged anecdotes while munching on tandoori chicken.

Chapter Thirty

Windows - Laila

The invention of the Internet is a great thing. I had bought a computer as soon as Windows 95 came on to the market, and I was on the online and surfing by 98; it was the perfect way of keeping in touch with all my friends abroad. The downside was I was being stalked over the World Wide Web by a boy I had met through my Spanish pen-pal Pablo. I met Antonio briefly during a visit to Spain a year ago. He spoke very good, almost perfect English and had learnt most of it in Ireland. Ireland seemed to be the preferred location for Spaniards to learn their English. They descended on the city of Dublin in their droves. Maybe it was the Catholic connection. Antonio hardly knew me, but he had been extremely friendly from the day we had met. Later, my friend Pablo had joked that he thought that Antonio was madly in love with me. Soon after I returned from my trip to Spain, I was bombarded with emails and phone calls from Antonio. Once he had suggested we meet in France; I had tried to make out I was not interested, but he refused to take no for an answer. I think Antonio was fishing for an invite to London, but he annoyed me with his over-familiarity, and so I ignored him as much as I could. But he kept coming back for more. On the odd occasion, Antonio had managed to track me down on my mobile; I would talk for a few minutes and then make some excuse that I was on a break and had to go and see some patients.

A friend of mine had spent at least four years looking for a husband through ads, but now with the introduction of the Internet, replying to the matrimonial section in Deshi newspapers or magazines was becoming a thing of the past. Deshis are entrepreneurs by nature, and it wasn't long before someone had thought of a matrimonial website to fulfill the desperate search for love amongst the Deshi second generation. It was nothing that would ever interest me however, as I had a boyfriend, but lately with the pressure mounting from my mother and father, I was finding it hard to dodge all the offers. I visited my parents regularly, but lately, every time I would go and see them, the topic of introductions or marriage would be hanging about in the air. If I were to be gently coerced into an arranged marriage, maybe I should be proactive and start looking for an appropriate groom myself. I think my parents secretly would have been fine if I never married at all, as no one was good enough for me in their eyes. I was still their little girl. The pressure came mostly from their friends and other people in the community.

One night when there was nothing really on the television to watch, I had, from sheer curiosity, decided to check out one of these Deshi matrimonial websites. I ticked the checkboxes and selected Male, Aged 25 to 35. A list of names appeared sorted by age, nationality, and name. I clicked on a couple and nearly jumped out of my skin at how dodgy some of these men seemed. They all had good jobs, or so they claimed. I think it was the moustaches and 1970s hairdos that shocked me. After about 5 minutes, the website timed out and it was impossible to see details of the men without registering.

In the top left-hand corner of the web page was an option to see photos of the men. I clicked on the link, and there lay before me pictures of an array of males between the ages of 25 and 35 who had registered on the website. It was a real international bunch—Americans, Canadians,

British, and then all the usual nations of the world. You could narrow it down and check country by country. I tried putting in some obscure, random countries to see what would come out, and I was surprised to see there were even people of my faith up for marriage in Spain, Portugal, and even Eastern Europe. We did get everywhere.

Receiving such a good overview of what was out there enabled me to see that some handsome-looking males were just looking for partners, but there were also some menfolk searching for the ideal bride who fitted all their superficial criteria. Some had huge moustaches and looked square in their suits; others were completely grey and old and claimed they were only 35, while others just looked like they were members of some dodgy, shall we say, 'political' group. *Surely the good-looking ones could get women without the use of a dating site,* I thought. *Why would they go online to meet someone?* I was suspicious, I don't know why, but at the same time surprised by the type of males and females who advertised on this website. What had gone wrong in their lives that they had to find a partner like this? Maybe this was the way forward. Tarting about some bar or club meant you were limiting your possibilities to chance or fate. Perhaps fate is not always the best judge. Possibly this way you were more in control, with more chance to sit back and contemplate the pros and cons. Maybe it was a sensible, intelligent way to do things: the new dating method for the future. It was true that more and more people were finding their partners on the Internet and ending up happy, I read it in magazines all the time. I had checked out this other website called *speed8east.co.uk*; there were different nights for different religions and then one night where anyone of any religion could go. Men had to be aged 22 to 35 and women 22 to 33. *What's wrong with women aged 35?* I wondered. I suppose aged 35 meant over the hill. It was a bit mean for women in their thirties, I thought.

When I suggested the dating events to Salma, she just scrunched up her face and said she wasn't that interested in men and didn't want to go Internet dating. Aliya who had half-overheard our plans told us to our faces that we were a couple of desperate, sad women. Her attitude and rudeness made me finally decide to kick her out of the house by the end of the month. I wasn't planning to reply to any of the Internet men, but it was fun having a look at the website. I suppose Salma would probably not consider going to one of these introduction parties or speed dating larks. It was all the rage to go to a party all sticky labelled up and talk to eligible bachelors. I wasn't that interested in attending these introduction parties, but I was going as a favour to one of my friends, and it would be a giggle. It was a sad fact that younger models were fast usurping women in their late twenties and thirties. At least this way, in a mother-in-law free environment, we called the shots.

Chapter Thirty-one

Dating - Ṣalma

Aliya had been arriving home in the early hours of the morning; I think she must have been drinking and partying a lot. I heard her throwing up in the bathroom again. I didn't tell Laila because she was already angry with her for all sorts of reasons. Aliya wasn't paying her share of the bills, her room was messy, and Laila refused to let the cleaner go near her bathroom or bedroom anymore because the cleaner would spend most of her time there sifting through her makeup wipes, clothes, and other unsavoury items. I had heard things had not gone well with a meeting Aliya had arranged between both her and Jonathan's parents. According to Laila, Aliya had been lying to us about many aspects of her life, and the story of the meeting between the parents seemed to be the only honest thing she had told us in months. Everything else seemed to be one big fat façade, and we were too polite to point out the obvious and embarrass her. She responded by avoiding us as much as she could and by staying out late and only coming home in the early hours of the morning.

I hated to say no to Laila on this occasion, even though she was such a good friend to me, but I did not want to go to this Deshi matrimonial event. I managed to avoid going to the speed dating evening, but Laila had twisted my arm and begged me to accompany her to another alternative dating party.

It was the last week of August, and no supply agencies had offered me work for the beginning of September. I was worried because no work meant no money to send home or pay my mum's bills. All these issues preyed on my mind, but I couldn't let Laila down, so that afternoon I reluctantly dressed for the evening.

London is a beautiful city at night. I love to watch the city sights whisk past my eyes as you drive by in the car. It's always really busy and full of people. The streets are wide and the buildings look so majestic; many centuries merged into one great city. London was a city full of so much history and culture, as well as being the setting for many wonderful novels and tales. I loved to watch couples walk hand-in-hand and see the way London was such a mishmash of cultures and people.

The hall was an old Victorian theatre, decorated entirely in dark wood and red velvet curtains. We walked up some very majestic steps to a lobby. There were beautifully dressed women in sarees there to greet us at the door, and as we handed them the tickets, more equally elegant women showered us with flower petals.

We then walked down some steps into a huge hall where there were tables full of food at one end of the hall. It was like a wedding banquet as if someone was getting married. The room was not full, but it was filling up fast. There seemed to be more women than men. There were even girls in headscarves giggling in corners. *What a sign of the times,* I thought, *full of women, but where are the men?*

Laila was offering advice and support to her friend Leena. She was 35 and terrified she would spend the rest of her life on her own. She was an attractive tall girl but not good-looking enough for the aunties. She wasn't typically pretty, but she had a quirkiness about her that was cheerful and pleasant. She had briefly been married to a man from the Desh, but he found it difficult to settle in England and found it impossible to find employment. Through all kinds of tricks and lies, his mother and sisters had lured him back to the Desh, leaving poor Leena aged 25 and all alone. She was now 35, and after countless, pointless introductions, she had reached her mid-thirties and was still single. She was even too old to go to this introductory evening as the age limit had been set at 33.

"All I need to do is to find myself in a situation where there are lots of men, and then one of them is bound to find me attractive. I'm running on a clock here. My body's telling me tick tock, tick tock, and motherhood is passing me by," Leena explained in a desperate attempt to convince herself that tonight was the night that might change her destiny forever.

I wasn't sure whether she was trying to be funny or had gone just a tad insane because as she said it, I saw a slightly crazy, desperate look in her eyes.

"Even if I meet him tonight, I'd need at least a year to get to know him, another 6 to 8 months to set the wedding date, and then a baby takes nine months, and I would have to leave it at least a few months before I get pregnant. Oh no! I'll be 40 before I have my first child."

"No, you won't. You've got your calculations all wrong. You will get married. It always happens when you least expect it. Don't want it so much, and love will come to you. I promise," Laila whispered.

"Well, I've been waiting ten years, and nothing. I try to be me, and I am told be a little less intellectual. No man likes his wife to be cleverer than him. It emasculates them."

"Forget those men. It's because you need to put yourself out there, and you know what? Maybe expand the net, widen your horizons," Laila suggested in an attempt to calm her.

"What do you mean, a white English man?" shrieked Leena.

"Well! Better a white English man than no man at all. What do you think, Salma?"

"Yes, why not?" I replied. "If you and your parents don't mind," I added, hoping that might ease the look of sheer distress on Leena's now-sullen face. "It's not about whether the man happens to be white British, European, any other colour or ethnicity. The real question you should be asking, is he a good person, does he have a good heart, do you share similar values?" Unfortunately, Leena didn't look convinced and seemed to be on the brink of tears.

We walked straight towards the food. The evening had been quite amusing, but I didn't think I would go to another one of these marriage parties. Laila was followed around all evening by a fashionable young man who refused to take his sunglasses off. He was slim, about 5ft 8 and became obsessed with her. He tried hard to impress her while she spent all her time turning her back and trying to avoid him. He had attempted to catch a ride back in Laila's car, but she was having none of his nonsense. Poor Leena had spent most of her time hovering around on her own by the food table. Eventually, a man had approached her and spoken to her, but maybe Leena had come across as too needy or desperate because he eventually said he had to go and find a friend. Unfortunately, he didn't return. Leena was disappointed because the man had seemed nice and chatty, and she said that she was sure she had felt something. Leena wished she had asked for his phone number before he had left.

"What a sad, deluded girl," Laila had said after she had dropped Leena off. "How do you tell someone the truth without hurting them? Sometimes I wish I had an Aliya's lack of tact. She has this natural knack for telling people exactly how it is."

"I know it's hard," I replied. "Honesty is not always the best way; I think Leena would have been devastated if you'd told her the man wasn't interested" I added.

"I know, Leena's just one of these terminal cases and there's no helping her. I think I'm just going to have to be there for her when it all crashes around her. And what about you, Miss Popular? How many were running after you?"

The evening had left me feeling so sleepy. When we returned home, I fell straight onto my bed as I was exhausted. The term had started and socialising on a weekday was a luxury I could only afford while there was no work. *How would I pay Laila her rent or support my mother and sisters?* That's all I could think about. I didn't care for all this marriage and wedding rubbish. I would have to dip into my savings. In normal circumstances, she would be kind and understanding that I owed her the money, but Aliya's unreliable financial situation meant it would be unfair to burden Laila with even more problems.

I could hear Laila talking to someone downstairs. It wasn't Aliya because the voice was deep and muffled.

"Salma, are you asleep? Someone wants to say hello."

Maybe it was her dad. So as not to be rude, I walked downstairs and entered the living room. My hair was a bit of a mess, and my saree all over the place, but it would only be Laila's parents. "Hello, Auntie and Uncle!" I looked around the room, and they both began to laugh at me. "Oops, Kamal!" I exclaimed. I stood at the door, feeling a bit embarrassed and pulled my saree around me.

Kamal slumped back on the sofa and patted the seat next to him. "Come on, Salma! Tell us how your evening went. How many husbands did you find?" He was very familiar; maybe he was drunk or high on something because he was smiling and in a good mood. Laila must have read my mind because I hovered and hesitated by the sofa. She so elegantly slid from the single seater to a space next to Kamal. As I sat down, he leaned towards me. "You look nice." His face was so near to mine I couldn't help but think how dark his skin had tanned from the Deshi sun. "Not only did our little Salma look extremely exquisite tonight, but she also had lots of blokes looking at her and chat her up."

Kamal slumped back in his chair and screwed his face up into what almost seemed like a look of disapproval. "How many more of these are you going to?"

Realising something was bugging Kamal, Laila replied, "Lots, and lots, until we find ourselves a couple of men."

Suddenly he was up and by the door, ready to leave. "I think it's humiliating just tarting yourselves about like that. Only sad, hopeless idiots go to these things to find themselves equally desperate women who can't find men."

"You've got room to talk. You and Aliya would make the perfect couple!" Laila shouted as he walked down the stairs. "Haven't you just been to the Desh to tart yourself about, so you can get a wife? Some brainless Princess Dollywood!" Laila shouted, but the door had already slammed, and he was gone.

Chapter Thirty-Two

Prison - Laila

I was planning on how to tell Aliya that it was time for her to go. It wasn't working out anymore. She hadn't paid her rent for over five months. I had entered her room while she was out, something I know I shouldn't have done, but it was my house and I wanted to see the state of the room. I had also ventured to check the condition of the bathroom. It was filthy. Either I gave in and let the cleaner scrub it clean, or I confront Aliya and force her to pay the rent or get out. It seemed unfair that Bilal who I was helping had nothing, and she had everything. If I were going to let someone stay for free in my house, then it would have to be an immigrant like Bilal who needed my support.

What worried me was that he was illegal, and I could get myself into trouble. I was half-tempted to phone Raj and ask him what could happen if I hypothetically housed an illegal immigrant in my house. Could I go to prison for harbouring him? I hadn't spoken to Raj for three months, so what would his reaction be? Was he seeing anyone? We had left on such bad terms, and I don't think he would ever forgive me.

I knew one thing for certain: I would never find someone at one of these introduction parties. They bordered on crass and tasteless. I was followed all evening by a young man in a pair of sunglasses. He had a cute face, but he looked like a little boy. Unfortunately, I had promised Leena that I would accompany her to a speed dating evening. She'd already bought the ticket. Salma had already made her excuses, she said she had supply work. I was sure Salma was telling fibs, but I know facing twenty odd strangers, three minutes at a time, would be too much for her. She wouldn't be able to cope. I would have to be the sacrificial lamb for the evening then.

Salma was a good-looking young woman, but she had no self-confidence. She was one of those girls that hid behind a pair of glasses, ponytail, and no makeup. A bit of eyeliner, lipstick and loose hair just transformed her into a mini Mexican beauty. But Salma wore her beauty without any confidence. I enjoyed making Salma's face up and dressing her up in my clothes. I would then ask her to stand on a table in the living room and make her twirl around and around so that she could view herself from the mirror above the fireplace. Salma was shy and quiet in public, but in my company, she was attentive and caring. When she was timid and vulnerable, she was like my little sister. When Salma was wise and caring, I saw her as my big sister. I didn't understand why she shied away from men so much. She never made comments about men or whether she found one attractive. Maybe she was just inexperienced.

Chapter Thirty-Three

The Scholarship - Salma

Sometimes I think of my father's life, and I wonder whether he ever got a break. My parents' marriage was arranged, but they had deep regard and love for one another. My father studied English Literature and he was a great fan of the works of TS Elliot and Thomas Hardy. Work in the city was hard to come by in the late 1960s, although he was sometimes offered journalistic work in writing pieces for a local newspaper. It was just enough money to pay the rent and buy my pregnant mother food. They rented a shared room in a widow's house in the city, but it was crowded, dirty and full of cockroaches. My mother could have gone back to the village to convalesce, but my father would not be allowed to live in the widow's house without my mother's presence, so they were stuck.

My mother was heavily pregnant but underweight. She was not eating the right nutrients and diet to keep her and the baby healthy. One night when she was seven months pregnant, her belly began to ache. She was taken, bleeding heavily, to the city hospital in a rickshaw. The doctor diagnosed her with high levels of anaemia. If the baby didn't survive the night, then neither would she. My mother did survive the night, and so did the baby. My father asked around his friends and relatives for money, and at the cost of five Taka per day, my mother recovered in hospital. She was pumped with iron tablets, lentils, and rice. Within two months, the baby was born, and although my father didn't even have clothes to put on the baby's body—he took her home wrapped in newspaper—he was just glad she and my mother were alive and healthy.

My father was a good writer and he was lucky enough to have been noticed for his talent, when he won a paid scholarship to research literature for a professor at a top university in America. It would have solved all my parents' problems. My father's boat passage was paid, and my mother was now staying in the countryside with her father-in-law. My father would send her money on a regular basis to pay for milk and clothes for the baby. Just two days before he was due to catch his boat, his boss wanted to see him. He was called into the office.

"You are not the man I thought you were. I have reason to believe you are not an honest man." The boss rambled on as my father sat listening in dumb bewilderment. "I am a man of honour" and I cannot reveal my sources. What I am about to do, I do not do willingly. A man must learn from his mistakes, and only then will he truly be on the path to repentance and redemption," bellowed my father's boss.

"Please tell me what I have done," my father replied in bewilderment. "Then I can defend myself and prove my honour and worth to you," my father pleaded. "I could never go to America and start a new life, knowing in my heart that you think badly of me. You are my mentor, and I have great respect for you."

"You will not be going to America!" The final blow of humiliation came when my father boss roared mercilessly, "I have informed your sponsors of your disgrace, and I have no alternative but to ask you to leave this honourable office and not return."

My father knew exactly what had happened, and he knew deep down in his heart that there was no use pleading: his boss's mind was made up. My father knew, and God knew that he was a man of integrity. He was

286

accused of stealing his writing ideas from another undisclosed writer. The boss's son was now to travel to America in place of my father and all the doors were now closed to him. It was the rainy season, and all the streets and the city drains were overflowing with rainwater. God had spared him one last humiliation: at least the rainwater disguised his tears. As he fell into a drain and swallowed the disgusting brown water, he cried out loud, "Oh God, if this is to be my life, useless to everyone, then take me now and show mercy on my wife and child."

Two months later, my father was offered a voucher to work in England as there was a shortage of labour there. He worked in an umbrella making factory and then, through contacts and friends, he managed to find a job in a restaurant and pay my mother a monthly sum. Sadly, the baby who would have been my older sister did not live for very long. For the two months my parents had lived in abject poverty, my sister's tiny body had not been strong enough to survive. My mother had even sent her wedding ring to the town of Feni to be sold which enabled her to buy milk for the baby, but it had been too late.

I sit reading passages of Elliot and Hardy to the pupils in my classroom, and then I think back to all the suffering my father went through so that I might have a better chance in life and seize all the opportunities that were not open to him. I suppose life is a journey in which there are winners and losers. My father lost so that my sisters and I might win. You can spend your whole life running from what you don't want or don't like, but sooner or later, you must come face-to-face with those fears, and that's when the true test of your strength begins.

Chapter Thirty-Four

The Eviction – Salma

The girls' school in Hackney had asked my supply agency if I was available, so I was pleased with the prospect of regular work. I could now send money home and pay Laila her rent. The oppressive summer heat was over, and the streets of London were now dry and grey. I wanted to try to avoid Laila tonight. She was hoping I would change my mind at the last minute and accompany her and Leena to the Asian speed dating evening. I was adamant that I would not go with them, not after the last disastrous event, even if I had to fabricate a ridiculous, unbelievable lie. The truth was it had been one of those stressful days, so now I had the most painful headache and felt a little sick.

When I'd just arrived home from school, I was shocked to hear what sounded like Laila and Aliya screaming at one another upstairs. Aliya's voice was shrill and hysterical, Laila's voice deep but serious. I sat at the bottom of the stairs and tried to listen to some more of the quarrel in an attempt to find out why they were arguing with such ferocity. Someone was indulging in some serious shrieking. "You are a mean and selfish spoilt bitch," she shouted. "And everything doesn't revolve around you and your rich bitch tidy little world," she continued. It sounded like Aliya shouting at Laila.

"Look, I'm just not putting up with you anymore, and if I'm a bitch, then you are a serial liar. You say you have no money yet look at all those bloody posh shopping bags of yours and God only knows how you can live with yourself the way you treat your parents. I'd die before I treated my mother and father with such disdain and disregard," replied

Laila.

"You know nothing about my life, so don't stand there judging me, you're a self-righteous cow."

"Is that all you can do, hurl insults at me? I don't think I've used a mean word towards you, yet you've called me everything under the sun, and you expect me to show compassion towards you and let you stay here in my house after this? You know what? You're getting married anyway. Go and stay with your Jonathan: he'll sort you out."

Instead of hurling insults back at Laila, Aliya was silent, as if thinking of something to say. "There is no Jonathan. Not anymore. We've split up. I have nowhere else to go, Laila."

And then it was Laila's turn to be quiet for a moment. She replied in a low, calm, controlled voice, "Aliya, you've told so many lies I don't know what to believe anymore. So many things don't add up with you. You are just going to have to go; it's just not working out."

"OK then, I'll tell you the truth, everything, and I'll change. I have nowhere else to go," she pleaded. I had never heard Aliya seem so desperate and vulnerable.

"Listen, Aliya, I've made up my mind. You have to leave and now." Laila's voice was stern, but I could tell she too might crack at any moment and let Aliya stay.

"Look at me, can't you see I'm ill? I've just been through one of the most horrendous experiences of my life. I have no other home than here."

Laila was in no mood to hear what Aliya had to say and just walked out of the house. As Laila passed me on the stairs, she commented, "I can't stay another moment in this house while she's here. Make sure she leaves tonight. I'm sorry to dump all this on you, Salma. I'll be at the speed date thing with Leena."

I went upstairs to see Aliya in her room; she was packing her bags and crying. She looked terrible. She had no makeup on; I suppose all those tears had washed it off her face completely.

After Aliya had left, I sat in her room and wondered how such a glamorous, successful girl had managed to make such a mess of everything. The room was as chaotic as her life had become. She had only taken what she could carry, leaving clothes and makeup scattered all over the floor. Aliya was sure to be OK, and without a doubt, she would work things out with Jonathan. She did live a fast-paced life, and it was obvious that everything could come crashing down anytime. The stench of stale vomit or something similar made me almost hurl, so I left the room. I felt it was wrong for Laila to abandon Aliya when she was so obviously still unwell.

I must have dozed off for at least an hour. While I was asleep, I had dreamt about my friend Kal. He was hiding under a table, crying. His mother had found him, and she had beaten him. I put my arm around his skinny little body and sat quietly while he sobbed. A knock woke me at the front door. It was Kamal. He hadn't visited the house since that night we had all returned from the find-a-husband party. He stood at the door for a moment and looked straight at me, breathed a heavy sigh as if he were about to say something and then walked straight past me and up the stairs. He sat on the sofa, and this time, he did not reach for the remote control and ignore me. He sat facing me, which made me feel very uncomfortable.

"Can I make you a cup of tea or coffee or something?" I asked.

"Go on, then."

I left to make the tea or the coffee and then immediately returned because he had forgotten to tell me what he wanted to drink. Kamal must have realised too because as I popped my head around the door, he said that he would have a coffee. I had felt unusually nervous and a little sick while preparing his drink. Lately, I just never knew what to expect from his ever-changing personality. Laila had told me that men play hot and cold all the time and that it was often hard to predict their moods. She found this ironic because men accused women all the time of being unpredictable and emotional.

I passed Kamal the hot drink, which he immediately put to one side. As I made my way towards the door, he called me. "Salma, where are you off to? Don't go, I wanted a quick word with you."

I returned to the room and sat on the sofa opposite Kamal.

"How are work and school and the kids?"

"Fine," I replied.

"And did you get that job at the girls' school?"

"Which girls' school?"

"The one in Hackney."

"Oh, right, yes, they offered me a term or more to cover maternity leave, as someone's pregnant." I was surprised Kamal had remembered. I don't even remember telling him anything about my job prospects. I looked at him, waiting for him to come to the point. He seemed a little bothered or annoyed.

"Salma, I wanted to ask you something."

"Yes, OK, ask me anything."

But he still refused to come to the point. "I'm starving. Do you want to come out and get something to eat?" he asked.

The truth was, my appetite had been somewhat haphazard for some weeks, so within the space of an hour, I found myself sitting in a restaurant somewhere in London, eating a meal with Kamal.

Chapter Thirty-Five

Mothballs and Coconut - Laila

Years ago, during one of my childhood visits to the Desh, an uncle was engaged to be married, so the whole family had an insanely luxurious Mehndi Party to celebrate his engagement. My aunties suddenly became like little girls as they chased my uncles and their brothers-in-law around the room and rubbed their faces with turmeric powder. It looked so much fun, so I decided to join in. I relished the prospect of smearing the orange stain into my snobby cousin's face, all over her new red and chequered frilly dress.

Two particular smells always remind me of the Desh. Cupboards are sacred things to my aunties: they are always under lock and key and hide treasures such as western makeup, hair mousse, Horlicks and 20-year-old trinkets brought over from England by my uncle's fruitless business trips. If you open a closet in the Desh, there is a very particular smell of mothballs that will smack you in the nose. It keeps the clothes from smelling of damp because the weather is so humid. I also heard it's to keep the cockroaches at bay.

I remember buying a candle from one of those trendy earthy shops. I was in Seville; it was scorching and very noisy. The clamour and heat had just merged into one and I couldn't understand anything because I was only a teenager on my first school trip to Spain. I picked up this candle which was shaped like a coconut and it was supposed to smell just like a real one. I closed my eyes and held it to my nose. As I inhaled the full coconutty aroma of the candle, the mean Spanish shop assistant grabbed it out of my hands, placed it back into the basket and said, "Esto, no se hace aquí," which means, "We don't do that in my shop." As I breathed in the full fragrance of the coconut candle, I had found myself momentarily transported to another world. My aunties rub coconut oil into my hair. We sit for hours, just dressed in our orange and yellow petticoats and blouses. The ceiling fan churns away, and we gently pick headlice out of each other's hair.

Now that Aliya had gone, I had something very important to tell Salma. I wasn't sure how she would take the news. Over the last month, I had secretly been meeting Bilal, the immigrant. He was, in fact, illegal. He had come from the Desh hoping to study here. Bilal did have a job, but for some reason, he wouldn't explain why he had to leave. Now he had fallen on hard times. All he wanted to do was study, and he couldn't. He was an intelligent man, and he knew so much about classical literature. He spoke my parental mother tongue with deep warmth and passion. At first I thought he was perfect for Salma, but I knew deep down she was not ready for a relationship or an illegal husband as she had problems of her own. Then it struck me—I could finally free myself from all the pressures of those painful introductions by marrying Bilal myself. It was the perfect plan.

Marrying Bilal would allow him spousal rights and he would be able to apply for university. I would even pay his fees as a thank you for saving me and giving me my freedom, so at last there would no more carousel of arranged marriage proposals. Bilal could live in the house; no one would ever know we weren't man and wife in the biblical sense. I'd also be free to go and live in South America. Why? Because my husband

Bilal would allow me. All I had to do now was let Salma in on the secret because she would be living with us and would need to know what was going on. It was a crazy plan, I know. Maybe I'd gone a little insane, but what the heck! Life is insane. All I had to do now would be to make up some story about his family and background and convince my parents I'd found the Deshi love of my life.

Chapter Thirty-Six

The Dodgy Engagement - Salma

I was in utter shock when Laila told me about her engagement, but once I had met Bilal, he did seem to be a gentle and well-spoken man. He was skinny, and his face was a little drawn, but that's because he had not been well and was possibly suffering from malnutrition. I was surprised Laila had decided to marry him. I had always harboured hopes she and Raj would resolve their differences. No matter what Laila said about Raj being possessive, I thought he was a decent, kind person and that they made a lovely couple. I had spotted him at the beginning of the term. He had noticed me walking to the tube and gave me a lift all the way into west London in his police car. We talked for a long time and he asked a lot of questions about Laila. Of course, I was careful not to mention anything about the speed dating, but I did mention she seemed a bit stressed and that sometimes I worried about her because the hospital had her taking on lots of late shifts. Raj was so sweet and kind, but I could tell he was hurting inside. He grabbed my hand before I left the car. I think he thought that by holding on to my hand, he was somehow holding on to Laila.

I wasn't sure whether to tell Laila about my meeting with Kamal and what he had said to me at the restaurant. I know there had always been something between them, and so I didn't want to upset her. I told her as much as I could that he made me feel uncomfortable and that even though he had made some effort to be nicer to me over the last few months, I just wanted to avoid him if I could.

Kamal had taken me to a restaurant in a part of London I had not visited before. The street was lined with young, happy people, shisha bars and gourmet style coffee shops. It was a Turkish restaurant and Kamal assured me everything was halal. I wasn't sure what any of the dishes were, so he ordered for me, and it was delicious food. The only problem was that I found it difficult to eat. Kamal was weirdly quiet and now and then he would ask me the odd question about school, my sisters—and if they had been accepted into any of the London universities yet. He asked me on more than one occasion whether I liked the food or not. I knew very little about him, so I hardly asked him any questions. After a few more embarrassing minutes of silence, he began to talk to me about Francisco and Sonya.

"Francisco loved his wife from the moment he met her. He saw she was a good, kind woman, and even though his family was against them getting married, no matter what they said or tried to do to dissuade him, Francisco stood by his true feelings and married Sonya anyway." Suddenly I notice a sad look in Kamal's eyes as he related the story to me.

"I mess about with so many women and can't seem to find a Deshi woman that interests me, physically or intellectually."

I wasn't sure what to say, but when I suggested Laila as a possible physical and intellectual candidate, Kamal seemed lost in his thoughts. He ignored my suggestion and carried on talking, almost as if to himself.

"You see, Francisco's wife Sonya isn't that beautiful, but he's so damn mad about her, and that's what makes her more attractive. His love makes her. They get on, they're a team, he does everything for her, and he builds his whole life around her. I envy him, I do. I have messed around with so many women in my life that I know I can pick and choose pretty much any woman I want. I realise now that some women are not so easy to find; they come into your life maybe just once, and if you don't grab them quickly, then you will possibly lose them to someone else."

I knew where this was leading now; he'd seen Laila attend all these speed dates, and he finally realised that she was the one for him, and if Kamal didn't hurry, he would lose her. I thought it best not to tell him there was no point or use as Laila was marrying an illegal immigrant. These speed date things were not that great, because the only man that had chased her was a very annoying, arrogant guy in dark glasses. Kamal continued telling me about his quest for the right woman and that the time was drawing near. I just nodded quietly and pretended to listen, but my mind was on Laila and Raj and how sad it was that they had split up.

After Kamal's self-confessional monologue in the restaurant, there wasn't much else to say in the car. I just watched the bright lights of London pass by my eyes. I knew we were nearing home because I could feel the motion of the car slow down as it neared the drive. I was waiting for my father to gently stroke my hair and lift me in his arms to carry me to my room. I woke to find Kamal gently shaking my arm; my head was resting on his shoulder.

"I thought I'd wake you; we are home now," he whispered gently into my ear. I felt his cheek brush softly against my hair.

How strange Kamal should say that we were home when it wasn't even his home.

I felt sleepy and sluggish. I had just been dreaming about my friend Kal. In this dream, he was lying in a heap on the grass, whimpering quietly to himself. No one was around, as all the families at the party had long gone. I ran up to him and turned him on to his back and threw my arms around him. Kal was motionless but not dead. His body seemed broken and weak.

Kamal looked straight through me; I thought he was about to whisper something to me or warn me. I was embarrassed to have fallen asleep on his shoulder. He was gentle and polite about it and didn't make a fuss, so I pretended it hadn't happened.

"I think I'd better get going, then," I mumbled sleepily.

I was about to open the car door when Kamal caught my arm. "Don't leave just yet; I want to ask you something."

I looked at him in anticipation and waited for him to speak. Kamal stared at me but no words at first came out. Then he asked me, "Do you think we could go out, maybe another time?"

"Why?" I replied, a little confused.

He was in deep thought for a moment; maybe he was confused too.

"Don't you get it, Salma?"

"Get what!"

"You don't get it, do you? What do you think I've been trying to say all evening?"

I gathered my thoughts and replied, "That you don't want to be a … you want to settle down with someone like Francisco and Sonya. You are thinking of asking Laila to marry you?" I didn't know what else to say.

"I don't want Laila. Laila? It's you, Salma; it's you I want to ask out. I want you to be my girlfriend, my fiancée, my wife."

"Want me? Why? Why would you want to do that to yourself?" I replied in utter shock.

This comment seemed to cause him great amusement. He threw his head back and started to laugh. "Why? Only you, Salma, could come out with something that unique."

Suddenly, the laughter stopped. My heart was pounding, but I couldn't move.

Kamal leaned towards me and brushed his hand over my hair. "Sometimes I feel as if I've known you forever. I can't put my finger on it. I always feel this weird sense of comfort when I'm with you. I spent a long time in my head trying to figure it out and fight my feelings for you. To oust you out of my heart, but I can't. It overwhelmed me and before I realised that I was no longer me anymore." I moved my head away from his hand.

"Yes, well, the problem is solved then, because I don't want to go out with you, and I never will. I'm sorry but I want to go home now. Can I go?"

"Yes, of course, you can go. I'm not going to force you to stay here with me. I thought we were friends?"

"Friends? When have we been friends? I don't even like you."

"Oh, I didn't realise," he replied. "I hadn't realised you didn't, you never …" Kamal replied, stunned. He was struggling for the first time to verbalise his feelings. "Just give me a moment and let me explain something to you."

"No! Look, why me, Kamal? Why pick on me when you can have any woman you want in that hospital you work in? I know what kind of man you are, and that's the kind of man I would never consider in a million years. You've slept around; you've made out with women right in front of me, in a taxi. You have no morals, and I have very little, if no respect for you!"

I opened the door and walked swiftly towards the house, but I was shaking, and my legs were like jelly. I longed to reach the door. I dared not turn around to look at his face. Had Kamal shown any sign of pain, my heart would have softened for sure. I knew I had been harsh. As I turned to check whether his car was still there, I could see his head bowed, supported by both his hands. He looked sad and dejected; I had never seen him like that before. Had I caused him so much pain?

Chapter Thirty-Seven

The Beating – Salma

Laila insisted I tell her what Kamal had done or said to make me this annoyed with him. I told her he hadn't done anything in particular, it was just that he made me feel a little uncomfortable. Laila told me he wasn't that bad, he was flirty and sometimes arrogant, but it wasn't entirely his fault. Things had happened in Kamal's life that had made him behave that way.

"Just before Kamal's family moved to London, he had been ill and had been hospitalised with pneumonia. He had also been badly beaten up by his mother who had suffered some nervous breakdown due to some big family financial crisis. That's why Auntie is so materialistic and obsessed with gold bracelets and necklaces. The crisis caused Kamal's mother to lose all reason completely, and she had then taken out all her anger on her son. He ended up in the hospital, and it was then they discovered behind the bruises that he had pneumonia. As Laila explained the story of Kamal, a terrible wave of guilt began to engulf my heart.

"Kamal doesn't just cough because of the cigarettes. Most of the time, he's coughing because he's still a bit weak from pneumonia. He was in the hospital for months. Instead of his mother being prosecuted for what she had done, it was all hushed up because they had money, and my father helped find Kamal's mother private psychiatric help. She did recover, and the whole thing is now history."

How did Laila know? Well, her parents underestimated her capacity to understand their very complicated mother tongue. Laila never really spoke her parental language as a child, but that's not to say that her understanding was not short of perfect. All this time, I had imagined Kamal had been some spoilt overweight, overindulged brat as a child, when in truth, he had probably been some scrawny wretched little boy who had suffered so badly at the hands of an insane and violent mother. Suddenly it was as if someone had whacked me straight in the heart and stomach, and I could hardly breathe.

My mind turned to Kal: he was always absconding from his mother so that we could play at hide and seek together. Kal constantly appeared in my recurring dream, the one about my father and the summer garden party. It always leaves me with this enchanted elated feeling. Kal and I dashing up and down the garden, hiding in and out of silk sarees—but everything before my father died is so vague and unclear. I can't get any sense out of my mother. I ask her what happened to my Kal, but she doesn't seem to register and starts talking nonsense. I imagined he must be someone that existed only in my childhood dreams.

So, Kamal's mother was a little insane. My mother wasn't all there either, but she would never resort to violence, as she was an incredibly gentle, docile and lonely woman. My mother had never received any suitable help for her problem; now she was too far gone. The doctor had sent her to see a psychologist, but we were way too young to understand. Had she been assessed as unstable, my mother could have been taken away, and all my sisters and I put into care or sent to the Desh. There was no one else to look after us: my father's side of the family didn't care, and my mother's brothers and sisters were too poor to offer any support.

Chapter Thirty-Eight

The Mehndi - Salma

Laila finally broke the news about Bilal to her parents. She told them that all his family had been killed in a ferry crossing on the river Megna. They seemed to accept the story and agreed to let them be married. Kamal had visited the house for a couple of weeks. I couldn't stop thinking about him, and he constantly plagued my mind. I felt so guilty for the way I had treated him. Perhaps I didn't want to date or marry him, but I had no right to be so mean and unsympathetic. I constantly imagined him in the hospital as a little boy suffering from all those bruises that his mother had inflicted on him and coughing from pneumonia. All I wanted to do was comfort him. He was no longer the Kamal I had known this last year. Something had shifted inside me; now I felt sorry for him, I even wanted to be his friend, but I knew he would never want to see me again.

Laila's parents seemed unconcerned that Bilal had no family; they were just happy she finally wanted to marry someone. Laila continued her charade by explaining that Bilal was a student from the Desh, he would be studying at a university next academic year and that he was here to improve his English and take the Cambridge 1st Certificate exam that would allow him to study at an English-speaking university.

Laila wanted a quiet wedding, nothing too loud, brash or fancy, but her parents would not agree. Laila was their only daughter, and if she were to be married, they would do it once, and they would do it right. Many would be mothers-in-law were devastated and heartbroken when the news broke out. I had met Raj again when he was on patrol near my school. I tried to avoid talking about Laila, but he seemed to sense something was up. He asked me lots of questions. I was a bad liar, and when it came out that Laila was to be married, he became reticent. He no longer asked any more questions and dropped me off at the end of the road.

I had expected to see Kamal at Laila's mehndi party, but he was nowhere to be seen. His mother was present, looking very mean faced and made up with a lot of white foundation and black kohl. The party was held at Laila's parents' house. Everyone looked very orange, and everyone smeared each other in mehndi. Even Laila had henna rubbed into her pretty, perfectly made-up face. I tried my best to hide out in the shadows, but there was nowhere to escape; some tiny child spotted me and threw a lot of yellow gunge at me. Because Bilal had no family, he was left to dress in Laila's house, and the whole mehndi party would then descend to Laila's and celebrate the rest of the evening with Bilal.

A thoroughly disconcerted Bilal sat alone in Laila's house and thought of his mother—what would she be thinking of him now? Is this what she wished for him? Thinking of her brought tears to his eyes. He wanted to feel the comfort of his mother's warm, soft hand and the smell of her coconut drenched hair. What a weird world he had found himself in. He was not happy, but he was not sad either. He had been saved, and this rich girl was kind and generous. He had no physical feelings towards her, but he would honour his side of the agreement. Bilal was very grateful for Laila's generosity and wondered why such a girl would have to go to these lengths to find a husband. Laila was rich, educated and beautiful. The Bideshis and the Deshis who lived in this land of bad weather and plenty seemed so alien and strange to him. Why would they ever want to leave the

Desh for this odd way of life? He thought of Afzar—what had become of him? He had looked through the newspapers in the living room and the hospital waiting rooms to find out some clue as to his state of health, but there was no way of finding anything out.

Bilal had thought about telling Laila everything. She was a doctor, so maybe she could discover what had happened to Afzar. Laila would probably think he was a coward for having run away when the angry, racist mob of men attacked Afzar. He would have to live with the guilt for the rest of his life. Bilal had never abandoned Afzar while in Saudi and he would not abandon him now. His only fear was that Afzar was dead. Suddenly, the room was filled with a group of colourful Deshi people he did not know. The sound was familiar, but they were strangers to him. Bilal felt a lump in his throat and an ache in his heart. They threw garlands of flowers over his shoulders, the guests fed him sweet stuff, and they covered his face with saffron coloured mehndi.

Chapter Thirty-Nine

The Festival – Salma

Everything had happened so quickly in the last few weeks, so neither Laila nor I had any time to breathe or think seriously about the choices we were making in our lives. I was beginning to think that it was time to move from Laila's home or at least time to decide what to do with my family. I had thought about moving out and renting a place with my sisters and mother. When I mentioned it to Laila, she was devastated.

"Don't you dare leave me, Salma. You know this marriage is a farce, and I can't live on my own with him in this house. Bilal is a decent man who will respect me, but please don't go; we'll think of something."

We had never talked in depth about this immigrant marriage situation. I had never told Laila about my regular meetings with Raj. I thought now would be a good time to mention it. I couldn't tell her I had met him often, just that we had met on the odd occasion, and Raj had asked a few questions about her general health, etc.

"Did you mention anything about me getting married when you met with Raj?" she asked a little alarmed.

"No, of course not." I felt so guilty for lying to her and not telling her that Raj was still madly in love with her. "Are you sure you are doing the right thing with Bilal?"

Laila was quiet for a moment. "Of course, I'm not doing the sane thing. It's pretty way out there. I could go to prison and lose my licence to practice medicine because he is illegal. If Raj knew, he'd have poor Bilal handcuffed and thrown into jail or interned in a detention centre for illegal aliens on the outskirts of Dover. Bilal doesn't deserve that; he's a gentle, sweet man who has fallen on hard times. He reminds me of this man in a film I saw called "Pan Y Rosas". It's about all these poor Latin American illegal immigrants who have no workers' rights whatsoever and get paid a pittance. They slave away in these offices in New York. They are just invisible. One of the boys in the film is called Mario; all he wants to do is earn enough money to study and go to university. Mario is sacked and is sent back to Guatemala, dashing all his hopes for a better future. I cried when I saw that film. I who have been given everything while he has nothing. Bilal is Mario: he's the test sent by God, so stuff the law of the land and common sense; I must see this through. I'm on this mad, crazy roller coaster, and I can't get off anymore. Bilal's going to buy me my freedom."

Laila was so passionate and convinced that she was making the right decision. All that was left to do was to give her a huge sisterly hug and wish her the best.

To celebrate her forthcoming wedding, Laila wanted us to all go to a South American cultural festival in London. It was a huge celebration of Latin American culture, music, and history. There would be parades representing all the main countries, featuring food stalls with arepas, tamales, Argentinean beef, and dark bitter chocolate. There was a huge concert to be held by the river where all the big and little names in Latin American music would play to a live audience.

We all met by a bench near an illuminated Tower Bridge and walked through the crowds, past the OXO Tower towards the concert area. I had already been standing for a good forty minutes, listening to the crazy music and watching the colourful array of costumes and beautiful women pass by. Deep down, I hoped Kamal would turn up, but he hadn't. I wanted to apologise. Francisco and his wife had attended the mehndi party, but there had been no sign of Kamal. I must have been so unkind to him. Being such a small person, I found myself continually squashed in the crowd. I could hear the music at the concert but found it a little hard to see the artists. I watched the rest of our group, including Laila, dance away to the music. Bilal had not come; she thought it best he not be seen in public, in case he was arrested. I told Laila I was planning to go for a walk and get something to eat and would meet everyone back in this spot. She nodded and carried on dancing.

As I walked through the crowd and towards the many aromatic smelling stalls selling a wide variety of food, someone grabbed me by the arms and almost swung me around with great force.

"Hola, Senorita Salma!" It was Francisco. Sonya was just behind him and busy eating something from a paper bowl that looked like dark green fried peppers. "Are you enjoying yourself? Where is Laila? Where is the novia? I must give two Spanish kisses to the bride."

"I'll take you to her." I turned to lead them to the place where Laila and the rest of the group were dancing, but Francisco gently pushed my arm and told me to stay, he would find her all by himself.

Just as he walked away, he whispered something in my ear. "Don't be too hard on him, Salma."

I didn't quite understand what he meant but suddenly, I stood before a very meek-looking Kamal.

We both walked across London Bridge in silence. But this time, there was an understanding between us that needed no words. Kamal sensed that I wasn't angry with him anymore. There was a small clearing near the bridge wall. He guided me by the shoulders, and we stood looking over at the dark unforgiving undercurrents of the great River Thames. It was a cold autumn evening and the tide was unusually high. Christmas was not far away, and the whole of London was lit up in sparkling lights ready for the new millennium when all the clocks around the world would crash. The music was so energetic and powerful, the whole of London seemed to be dancing along. Kamal broke the ice first.

"I'm sorry if I offended or shocked you, Salma. It's just I had to say what I did. I'm just annoyed with myself for not being perhaps a little subtler or gentler with you. I was a complete arrogant ass as usual."

"No, you weren't at any fault. It's me that should apologise," I replied.

"No, Salma, you were right about me. I don't blame you for hating me. When I first met you, I wasn't very nice. I struggled with it for a long time. It wasn't your imagination; I was just shocked at myself that I found you so attractive, so lovely, so kind. Not that you aren't an attractive woman, you are. It's just my taste in women in my adult years has been so shallow in the past. Your beauty has depth and intelligence."

I listened to what he had to say but then placed my finger on his lips to hush him. Kamal gently caressed my face with the curve of his hand. I was embarrassed; I wasn't sure what to say to him, but this time, I didn't want to run away. I wanted to stay right there with him. I let him take hold of my hand and explore it gently with his. No man had ever kissed me until this moment.

Kamal and I had agreed to keep our relationship secret until after Laila's wedding, but he would talk to his parents as soon as possible. He knew his mother would take some convincing, but then again, she would freak out about anyone she hadn't chosen herself.

Chapter Forty

Laila's Wedding – Salma

Laila sat in a miniscule decorated room away from the other guests. The aunties prepared her for the celebration. They painted her face, pulled and sprayed her hair, pinned her body into a red and gold glittered saree, and so Laila emerged as every bride's dreams: as a whitened Deshi dolly bride. She asked me for a mirror to view the fruit of their artistry and then yelped in horror. I still wondered about this mismatch of a couple. Who was Bilal? He was so skinny, so lost-looking and broken. No amount of Top Man or Next fashion grooming could eradicate the 'new freshi' look about him. He was quiet and didn't talk much. I still thought of Raj and how much he loved Laila. I was currently meeting him on a regular basis; he seemed still so heartbroken with their break up that I told him bits and pieces about Laila, which he lapped up with delight. Maybe it was just a happy coincidence he always seemed to be waiting in his police car as I emerged from the tube station.

At the wedding hall, Laila spent her time giving me orders in the most diplomatic way she knew how on this oh-so-important day of her life.

"How are my parents? How many guests are here? Is that bratty family here yet?"

I suspected she meant Kamal and Co. I hadn't told her about our relationship yet. How he loved me with all his heart and soul, how he sensed from the first day he saw me something tied us together from way before we had even met. The feeling you get when you see a glimpse of your future flash before you. Kamal told me he had noticed me as soon as

I walked through the door with my nose stuck in my book, but I had just seemed to glance right past him. He had promised to respect me until our wedding night, and I agreed, as I had no prior experience with men. Kamal was gentle and patient enough to introduce me ever so tenderly to the beauty of his body and mine.

Laila had ordered me to the ladies' dressing room to find some tissue paper to wipe off some of the china white powder the aunties had smothered across her face. Not being very bothered about skin colour myself, I always wondered what the groom would think as he undressed his virgin bride only to find she was five shades darker than her arms, neck, and face. *It must be true love, then* I thought.

"Come back soon Salma, these crazy aunties are actually trying to tell me about the birds and the bees. Me! A qualified doctor who has delivered at least three babies and given contraceptive advice to at least five dozen irresponsible teens."

As I grabbed a handful of peach scented tissues from the dresser, to my surprise, a very rough-looking Aliya emerged from behind the door. She was so thin and wore a plain black dress. She had a crazy look about her and wanted to see Laila in her private room. Of course, I had no problem with that. I asked Aliya if she was OK and if there was anything she needed. She seemed war-worn and pale.

I sat in a far corner of the room as Aliya and Laila argued about their past misdemeanours, but as much as Aliya played the subjugated broken soul, Laila seemed unable to forgive her. I wanted to tell Laila that I didn't think Aliya was all that well and needed our help, but I could see

313

by the looks of fury they exchanged with one another that no amount of negotiation from me would change Laila's mind at this point. Bilal was now lodged in Aliya's room, and as far as I understood, Laila had informed me he would be lodging at the house for the foreseeable future. Aliya stormed out of the bridal suite, stumbling over some gifts as she mumbled under her breath that Laila would forever regret this.

As I wandered out of Laila's dressing room, I could see Bilal sat on the groom's gilded fancy throne looking lost and alone. He had no family to talk of and no money, as Laila's parents had paid for everything. I still couldn't understand what had attracted Laila to this sweet but misplaced foreign man. But as I, too, was now in love with a man I could once barely be in the same room with, I decided to understand without judgment. Kamal promised me he would formally introduce me to his mother today. I still had worries and reservations after my meeting with his mother months ago at his sister's birthday party, but I hoped whatever her issue was, she would be happy and relieved her son had fallen in love and wanted to be married to a Deshi girl.

The guests were arriving dressed in their multi-coloured suits and sarees. They made their way to the seats at the brightly coloured circular tables. Rimi's crazy pink thematic designs had come in handy, as she and her friends had hand decorated the tables with pink and white balloons and tiny pastel boxes of sweets and sugared almonds which had been carefully placed on each plate for the guests. It was a quick and cheap wedding, but Laila had insisted this was precisely what she had wanted. "Simple," she said, "I want it simple."

I looked around for Kamal, but he was nowhere to be seen, and then just as I had finished scanning the room, I spied a group of people I had not expected to see at the wedding—my mum and two sisters. They were led into the hall by Laila's father. I felt elated. What were they doing here? Where were they staying? What a happy coincidence. Now I could introduce them to Kamal and his parents.

I could see Laila was emerging from her room as a very whitened but beautiful bride, but just then, my youngest sister threw her arms around my neck while sister number two guided my mother towards me. My mother was lost, but she was still very affectionate and showered me with kisses all over my face. I felt this crazy butterfly fluttering in my stomach. I was so delighted at the thought of my two happy worlds meeting at last. Just then Kamal entered the wedding hall, and as he weaved his way through crazy kids playing tag and waiters with spicy starters, I waved over to him to come and meet my mum. I would only introduce him as a friend at this point. My mother wouldn't understand the concept of a boyfriend or even a fiancé, so I felt a gentle introduction would suffice.

Kamal looked my way but seemed nervous and distracted; he seemed to be looking out for someone. I guessed it must be his mother. I knew she had a reputation for being hard work, and my first experience with her wasn't exactly the best. I ran over to Kamal and grabbed him by the hand, but he pulled away, so I gently grabbed him by his shirt sleeve. I could feel the slight resistance in his arm as I guided him over to my mother and sister.

"Ama this is my friend Kamal. Ama, meet Kamal."

I looked for some recognition in her eyes, but I was not expecting her reaction.

"Kal chuto Kal." My mother began to caress his cheeks gently with her fingertips.

Kamal was visibly confused, but to my surprise, he didn't flinch or stop her. His face seemed lost in some faraway place. He seemed to almost melt at her touch.

Before I had time to process this bizarre event before me, Kamal's mother bulldozed her way into this strange reunion like a jealous she-lion protecting her prized cub. She dragged my mother away from Kamal, grabbed her by the neck and began insulting my mother in front of the whole wedding party. "You wife of a thief and liar!" she screamed. "How dare you come back into my life and curse me? How dare you!"

My mum was too weak and let herself be thrown about like a broken, well-worn Deshi rag doll, while my sisters did all they could to protect her from Kamal's deranged mother. However, Kamal was in too much of a daze to react. He held his hand to his cheek as if awakening from a long sleep. He kept stepping back as if to take a wider view of the chaos.

At this point, I waded in and finally surgically detached Kamal's mother from my poor beaten mother. I looked at Kamal and beckoned frantically for him to intervene. "Kamal! Tell your mother we are getting married. She can't do this. What is wrong with her?"

At this point, the fury that I could sense in Kamal's mother's face was at its very peak, but Kamal did nothing. He continued to look on like a lost little boy.

"Married? Married into this family of thieves? Never! Over my dead body!" Kamal's mother bellowed.

I looked into Kamal's eyes for some support, but he stood impassively as if he no longer recognised me.

His mother interjected. "How can my son marry you when he is already engaged to a Minister's daughter? Not a thief's daughter, but a Minister, a high-ranking Minister!" she repeated arrogantly.

I immediately felt the pain and hurt shoot into my throat and rock my head about twenty times until I felt dizzy. There was no response from Kamal.

"Is this true?" I demanded. "Is this true?" The tears of defiance and anger welled up in my eyes. I knew immediately my world was imploding and crumbling before me.

Kamal just took a step towards me as if to grab me in his arms. He whispered my name, but no sound came out. I couldn't let him touch me and so, enraged with agonising pain and fury, I pushed him towards his mother and witnessed with a sense of satisfaction and revulsion as the heartless son fell on top of his mother. I stood there for a moment, along with a crowd of confused onlookers. Defiantly, I silently fought back the tears as mother and son both lay broken and shamed in a heap of saree silk and white muslin. A thoroughly humiliated Kamal picked himself and his mother up from the floor. Kamal's father, who rarely appeared anywhere in public, brushed both son and wife down with his hands in full view of all the traumatised onlookers. Even Laila and her parents began to wade through the throng of shocked guests and collateral damage.

"Enough is enough!" wailed Kamal's father. "Leave this family alone. They have suffered enough, and I been witness to your lies all these years. My wife, in fact both of us, are flourishing off the stolen money of others. And we have done for many years. So enough now."

It hit me hard before I had time to process this news. Everything made sense now: My father's downfall. The scrawny little boy Kal I used to play with as a child. I looked at the now grown up Kal with eyes of joy at having finally found my friend again. However, my happiness soon turned into pain at this public humiliation that the adult Kamal had bestowed upon me. I ran out of the wedding hall, my heart shattered into a million pieces, the ache in my throat choking me, and my eyes streaming uncontrollably with tears.

As I left the wedding party, hordes of police officers stormed the wedding hall to the horror of the bridal party. Had we been that loud and unruly? The police made their way towards an already startled, equally lost Bilal.

"Bilal Chowdhury, we are arresting you for the attempted murder of Afzal Khan. You have the right to remain silent, but anything you say …"

As I stood outside the wedding hall and wiped my face of humiliation, I could spy Raj as he sat in a police car, visibly ashamed at the immoral crime he had just committed.

Chapter Forty-One

The End – Laila's Letter

Today I received a letter from Laila. She apologises for not writing to me over the last few months. She says she loves it out there in Peru, and soon she will be moving on to Central America to work in Guatemala and then El Salvador. Laila says that there is a lot of poverty but not quite on the scale of India and the Desh, and just like Asia, there are wealthy people as well as poor. Laila's Spanish is almost fluent now, although at first, she struggled. All the old ladies call her 'Mi Hija', which means my daughter. Now Laila's year is coming to an end, she feels sad and would like to extend her stay, so she can explore all of the treasures South America has to offer. Laila loved Buenos Aires and Peru; she'd even visited the Andes Mountains and can't believe how amazing they are—the highest and most well-known are the Machu Picchu range. They rise towards you, as if from nowhere and everything looks so vibrant—the colour of ancient green. Most of all, Laila will miss all the wonderful friends she has made among the aid workers and volunteer doctors from across the World. What makes Laila giggle is that the locals can't believe she is Deshi from the Indian subcontinent and think she is from their hometown, that is, until Laila starts speaking in her London Spanish. The old ladies can't understand why Laila speaks English with a 'Guiri' (white man's) accent. I suppose it's like us hearing an Indian with a strong Glaswegian pronunciation, although I'm sure it's not that rare. Laila had even searched for Eduardo and his family but when she arrived in their village they were no longer there. His family had packed up all their belongings and headed north for the border.

Laila's parents went out to visit and forced her to stay with them in their 5-star lodgings in Lima. When Laila told them that she was thinking of going next to help out in the Gaza Strip, they nearly flipped and told her to come home as soon as possible. But seriously, Laila says they are overall very supportive. Bilal has just finished his foundation university year and did brilliantly in his exams. Laila's parents decided to sponsor him officially, and there was the talk of her parents adopting him so that he could have their full protection. He's like the son they never had. Laila loves the fact that all the attention is not focused on her anymore. "Thank the universe and our legal system for that speedy annulment." Even Raj moved on eventually. He married a colleague and was promoted to temporary inspector on the fast track promotion scheme. Deep in his heart I don't think he ever stopped loving Laila

Although Bilal barely remembers his face, he believes the Bideshi doctor who spoke so fondly of his wife and daughter and had encouraged him to travel and study so many years ago in Dhaka may even have been Laila's father. When Afzar recovered, he finally returned to the Desh, and Laila's dad sourced him a job in a factory. Now Afzar never wants to come back to England again.

Laila tells me not to worry about our living accommodation; we will all squeeze into the house, and she may even convert the attic into a proper room. She has asked my sisters, my mother and I to live in the house rent-free so that I can save more for our own new house, but she doesn't know that I have put some money aside for her. Laila's already been too kind to us. She also mentioned that she might even sell the place to me, as she wants to downsize and buy a flat when she returns.

One of my sisters is now at university and the other is just finishing her A Levels and applying for a place at Oxford. My mother has made a huge recovery in just a year, although she can still behave a little spaced out sometimes. She attends a local college and has made a lot of friends with many Deshi women. They sew, arrange flowers and even take yoga classes. My mother seems to live more in the present now rather than the past, especially when she talks about my father. She seems to accept now that my father is gone. As horrible as that incident was at the wedding, it seemed to have jolted something in her memory. Some of my mother's old friends visit her, and she is invited to weddings and social gatherings, but she normally only goes with Laila's mother, who looks after her and makes sure none of the aunties say silly things to her that may upset her.

No one knows what happened to Aliya; she just seemed to disappear. She took all her clothes but left her room in a horrible mess. After she had gone, we received credit card bills in her name. We didn't have the heart to burden her poor parents, so we sent them to Aliya's ex-fiancé. Laila visited the law firm and made an appointment to talk to Jonathan. She told him the whole situation, how Aliya had disappeared and about her poverty-stricken parents. Laila was surprised at how polite and sorry he was for the whole situation; he even admitted he wished he had handled things differently, because he had truly loved her. Jonathan offered to pay all her bills. He told us that his mother and Aliya had arranged a lunch to discuss the wedding, but in fact, his mother had no intention of talking about the nuptials at all but was there to warn her to stay away from Jonathan. Aliya had told Jonathan's mother something that shocked her—that Aliya was, in fact, pregnant. His mother reacted badly and accused her of lying and then slapped her across the face in front of everyone during high tea at the Dorchester. Jonathan's mother then proceeded to complain about her to the staff at the restaurant, and Aliya was thrown out.

I remember now the night before Laila and Aliya had engaged in that huge row, Aliya had come home looking very subdued and ill. She wore no makeup and was just dressed in a pair of jeans and a sweatshirt. I had never seen her looking so plain in my life, and she was unusually passive. Her face just looked tired, grey and dishevelled. Aliya's eyes seemed confused; she kept blinking and just looking aimlessly around the room. I know she hadn't eaten properly for weeks because she was constantly throwing up. She said she was hungry but was too tired to prepare anything. I offered to make her a sandwich.

"I could do with a massive plate of chips, you know? A really big dish of deep-fried potatoes." Aliya sounded bizarre when she said this as if she had gone a little bit insane. She hated chips, or anything fried, for that matter. She called it the food of the plebs. I remember her mumbling senselessly to herself. "I'm just so tired; I think I'm just going to go to bed and sleep for a long time."

"What have you been up to today? Have you been anywhere interesting?" I asked.

"Today?" she replied. She paused a moment and then answered, "Nowhere you'd ever want to end up, Salma, believe me, nowhere you'll ever end up."

It wasn't until now that it dawned on me. Maybe Aliya had done the unthinkable that day. Perhaps she had terminated her pregnancy. This meant that not one of us had been there for her when she had needed us, and Laila had told Aliya to pack her bags and had thrown her out the next day. I could never tell anyone this: it would make both Jonathan and Laila feel wretched.

It was strange how different Aliya's life seemed to us all compared to those two runaway girls, Rozi and Dolly, who had stayed with us two years ago. With all their lies and living beyond their means, Aliya was not so very different from them after all. All three would constantly be on the run from the messes they had made of their lives.

Soon after the whole business about a year ago, Francisco had made a considerable effort to keep in touch with me and see how I was getting on. He never mentioned Kamal because he knew the situation was a sensitive subject. No one ever mentioned Kamal's name in front of me until today, when I read Laila's letter. I knew he had gone back to the Desh with his disgraced family and I presumed that he had married the Minister's daughter. His sister Rimi had just finished her A Levels in an international school in the city, and she and her father were now coming back to England, as Rimi would be starting university in the autumn term. *I bet she'll be studying medicine*, I thought. Kamal's mother had decided to stay in the Desh indefinitely. People were polite enough not to talk about what had happened; well, not to her face anyway. I presume she felt she could not face living in London at the risk of bumping into any of my family, especially my mother. We had lived in the shadows for long enough, and now it was our turn to lead a normal life. My family was not going anywhere. I'm sure she was living a life of luxury in the Desh with servants, marble staircases and gold-plated telephones. The house they had lived in was now sold, and Kamal's father and Rimi were to live in a much smaller, but comfortable home on the outskirts of South London.

Kamal's father had always hated that huge house. Kamal had spent very little time with his family in the Desh and had passed most of his time working as a volunteer doctor at clinics for the poor in the slums, much to his mother's dismay. Laila said it had made her laugh because he had always teased her and called her naïve for wanting to do the same thing. I didn't know what to think. Was Kamal trying to redeem his past behaviour and prove to people he wasn't a wayward rogue anymore? Who knows? While it was a shock to hear that the events of a year ago had changed his family's lives and mine, I just wished him luck. I didn't feel angry anymore.

This evening I was invited to Francisco's house. He and his wife were having a small party with a gathering of a few friends, and they were keen for me to attend. I liked their home; it was cosy and warm and always filled with the aroma of spiced apple, incense sticks, and eastern wood. The living room looked like a Moroccan tea house. There was a low wooden table in the centre of the room and wall-to-wall comfy Middle Eastern sofas. Francisco answered the door and seemed delighted to see me. He welcomed me into his home with a strong hug and two customary Spanish kisses on each cheek and then hurried off into the kitchen. I was surprised he hadn't led me into the living room and introduced me to the other guests. I just assumed he was busy. As I took my coat off and reached up to hang it on their already overloaded coat rack, someone tapped me on my shoulder.

"Hello, Salma," whispered a soft male voice. I turned around, and to my surprise, it was Kamal. He realised how shocked I was by the expression on my face. He gazed down at me. "Please don't run away; I was wondering if we could chat for a while or something." His voice sounded different; it was quieter, and he seemed almost nervous. Kamal's skin was darker from the Deshi sun, and he also seemed a lot thinner, but his eyes were still bright, and his hair had grown longer as it fell in a side parting across his face. He looked more like a driver Bhai than the well-fed, toned, arrogant, playboy doctor I had known last year. I almost felt sorry for him.

We were called into the dining room to begin the feast of Middle Eastern delights. The guests gathered around the food. I sat on the opposite side of the table to Kamal, so there was no possibility of him talking to me. I threw a stern look at Francisco. He knew exactly what I was thinking.

Why did you set me up like this? I thought. Francisco shrugged his shoulders apologetically and carried on talking to his guests. I knew Kamal was constantly looking over in my direction, and so I did my utmost to avoid any eye contact. However, throughout the entire meal, I dreaded the prospect of conversing with him and opening any old wounds now buried and forgotten. I wasn't angry anymore; I knew Kamal was repentant and had made moves to change his lifestyle, but I did feel a sense of stubborn pride. I had little to say to him and I couldn't engage in small talk after all that had happened. I had kept myself engaged in conversation with as many of the guests as possible, which was a ploy to avoid speaking to

Kamal.

It was 11 p.m. when I thanked Francisco and his wife for a lovely evening and said I must go. Francisco told me not to be a stranger and that I was welcome in his house anytime. He joked about not being able to guarantee any surprises, but he could see by the look on my face I had not taken his comments as a joke. His wife Sonya kissed me goodbye and told me she had told him not to interfere.

"There's no harm done, he means well," I replied. I knew they were good people and would never do anything to hurt me purposefully.

As I walked down the road towards my car, Kamal came running up behind me. He was exhausted and out of breath. "Salma, can I talk to you for one minute? Just listen to me, and then I'll never bother you again."

I was silent, so he carried on.

There was a slightly crazy desperate look about him; his eyes appeared almost moist, and I noticed to my surprise that his whole body seemed to be gently trembling. "Look, all I'm asking of you is that we can be friends again."

I sighed and looked away. But Kamal was insistent.

"I've changed. I can't help what my family did to yours, and I am truly sorry. Not a day's gone by without me feeling guilty for what happened, and not a moment has gone by that you haven't been in my thoughts, but I knew it was pointless writing to you. I think maybe now is the right time to see whether things can be fixed between us." The silence lingered as Kamal stood in hopeful anticipation. I needed time to think. I

326

wasn't sure I wanted to see him again. I felt healed and reborn and I had survived without him for over a year. My family was happy, and I was in a safe place at last.

"I am sorry Kamal, I am not sure I need you in my life anymore. I have changed. I am not the same person you left broken hearted a year ago."

"But Salma, my darling sweetest Salma, don't you remember me? I am your little Kal. I am me again. I found myself. I am now the man I was supposed to be before I forgot who I was. I loved you when I was a boy and I love you now Salma. Without you, I am still lost."

My heart ached to hear my Kal pleading me for forgiveness. I wanted to hold him in my arms, stroke his thick black hair, calm his pain and whisper in his ear that since a little girl I had loved him too. As much as I tried to reconcile my Kal with the man who now stood before me, all I could see was the Kamal who had been too weak to fight for me.

"Well, you're not to blame for what happened to my family twenty odd years ago, but you were responsible for your behaviour towards me last summer," I replied obstinately.

"Look, all I'm asking for is that we start off with friendship. That's how we started over twenty years ago. If we begin with even just that, then we can take it from there. I will never let you down again."

Faced with such desperation, I found it difficult to be unkind and aloof with him. "And all you are asking for is friendship?"

"Whatever you want Salma," he replied.

"I don't think I can face your family; well, not your mother anyway."

"My mother is in the Desh; she won't come back to England now."

It was such a risk; I wasn't sure whether to take that leap of faith and trust him. Kamal did seem different. The arrogance and cool manner had gone, and in its place was a man pleading to be forgiven for something he probably wasn't even guilty of committing. During the first few months when he had returned to the Desh, I had felt a tremendous amount of pain. It was the kind of hurt that is both unbearable and yet at the same time comforting. For so many years, I had learned to be strong in the face of so much tragedy in my family. I held back my tears and took the place of carer for both my mother and my sisters; now this time, it was my chance to mourn. It only lasted a few months. Time and the right amount of hate can heal all.

I was contemplating his words and then sighed. Kamal grabbed my hands and held them gently in his. I let it happen. It felt safe, and I felt that I was finally home.

Before me, all I can see is my Kal. The summer of 1980 is coming to an end, and a scrawny boy and sun-brushed rag doll of a girl sprint their way through undulating waves of yellow, crimson and cinnamon saree silk. The sky is burning saffron spice as the sun gently descends beyond the horizon. Salma and Kal hide under a table oblivious to the chatter and gossip around them. Kal places a ruby and emerald necklace around Salma's tiny sparrow-like neck and kisses her gently on her blushing face.

The End

Black Diamond Silk

It has been too long
Black diamond wrapped across my body
I see your smile from across the room
I am no longer me
My heart and soul are as a young girl again
You ask for my hand
My stiletto heel crushes jewels of sapphire on a wave of ebony
silk
Deep into the stone floor
I cannot walk
I trip and falter
Nor can I speak
I mumble and giggle to myself
I am a girl again
And you are gone

ABOUT THE AUTHOR

Sabera Ahsan grew up in the UK in the 1970s. She studied Spanish, politics and screen writing at university and trained as a primary school teacher. After leaving policing and the civil service after 12 years as an equality, crime and Prevent policy officer, Sabera now dedicates her time to writing, blogging, campaigning and running online magazines for women.

CONTACT

https://www.facebook.com/azaharabooks

http://azaharabooks.com/mothballs-and-coconut

http://twitter.com/azaharabooks or @azaharabooks
Email: info@azaharabooks.

Printed in Great Britain
by Amazon